The Sinclair Betrayal

**A Jayne Sinclair
Genealogical Mystery**

M. J. Lee

About M. J. Lee

Martin Lee is the author of two different series of historical crime novels; The *Jayne Sinclair Genealogical Mysteries* and the *Inspector Danilov* series set in 1930s Shanghai. *The Sinclair Betrayal* is the fourth book featuring genealogical investigator, Jayne Sinclair.

He also writes a contemporary crime series set in Manchester featuring Detective Inspector Thomas Ridpath.

ALSO BY M. J. LEE

Jayne Sinclair Series
The Irish Inheritance
The Somme Legacy
The American Candidate
The Vanished Child
The Silent Christmas

Inspector Danilov Series
Death in Shanghai
City of Shadows
The Murder Game
Killing Time

DI Thomas Ridpath Series
Where the Truth Lies
Where the Dead Fall

Historical Fiction
Samuel Pepys and the Stolen Diary
The Fall

We are such stuff as dreams are made on,
and our little life is rounded with a sleep."

William Shakespeare

Contents

Chapter One 11
Chapter Two 16
Chapter Three..20
Chapter Four..24
Chapter Five 32
Chapter Six 37
Chapter Seven..41
Chapter Eight..46
Chapter Nine..51
Chapter Ten 57
Chapter Eleven 61
Chapter Twelve..66
Chapter Thirteen 69
Chapter Fourteen 76
Chapter Fifteen..87
Chapter Sixteen 91
Chapter Seventeen 97
Chapter Eighteen 100
Chapter Nineteen 104
Chapter Twenty 108
Chapter Twenty-One..111
Chapter Twenty-Two..115
Chapter Twenty-Three 120

Chapter Twenty-Four 124
Chapter Twenty-Five 127
Chapter Twenty-Six 131
Chapter Twenty-Seven 134
Chapter Twenty-Eight 138
Chapter Twenty-Nine 140
Chapter Thirty 142
Chapter Thirty-One 149
Chapter Thirty-Two 154
Chapter Thirty-Three 157
Chapter Thirty-Four 161
Chapter Thirty-FIve 167
Chapter Thirty-Six 170
Chapter Thirty-Seven 175
Chapter Thirty-Eight 181
Chapter Thirty-Nine 184
Chapter Forty 188
Chapter Forty-One 193
Chapter Forty-Two 197
Chapter Forty-Three 201
Chapter Forty-Four 206
Chapter Forty-Five 209
Chapter Forty-Six 216
Chapter Forty-Seven 218
Chapter Forty-Eight 222
Chapter Forty-Nine 225

Chapter Fifty	229
Chapter Fifty-One	232
Chapter Fifty-Two	239
Chapter Fifty-Three	245
Chapter Fifty-Four	249
Chapter Fifty-Five	253
Chapter Fifty-Six	257
Chapter Fifty-Seven	263
Chapter Fifty-Eight	267
Chapter Fifty-Nine	270
Chapter Sixty	274
Chapter Sixty-One	279
Chapter Sixty-Two	283
Chapter Sixty-Three	287
Chapter Sixty-Four	291
Chapter Sixty-Five	295
Chapter Sixty-Six	297
Chapter Sixty-Seven	304
Chapter Sixty-Eight	307
Chapter Sixty-Nine	312
Chapter Seventy	317
Chapter Seventy-One	323
Chapter Seventy-Two	326
Chapter Seventy-Three	329
Chapter Seventy-Four	334
Chapter Seventy-Five	336

Chapter Seventy-Six 340
Chapter Seventy-Seven 344
Chapter Seventy-Eight 347
Chapter Seventy-Nine 353
Historical Note 357

Chapter One

Sunday, July 11, 1943
Harrington USAAF base, Northamptonshire

'Are you the Joes we're droppin' tonight?'

The airman was dressed in dirty grey overalls with a baseball cap pushed back off his forehead. Monique thought he was young, no more than eighteen.

'We are. Four of us.' Philippe Lemaitre pointed to each one of the agents sitting on the bench in the Nissen hut that served as the airfield ops room. 'Nanny, Elviron, Wallace and myself, Boris.'

'You Brits think up the cutest code names.'

'I'm French,' said Monique.

The airman ignored her. 'Any more of you guys?'

'That's all of us,' answered Philippe.

'You got your gear?'

Their bags were lying at their feet. Next to Philippe was the suitcase containing the radio.

Each one had checked the other's kit. The contents of each bag had been searched and anything that might betray their British identity was removed; bus ticket, cigarettes, receipts, bills, and letters. New papers with their French names and identities were given a final check and francs inserted into their wallets.

They were as French as the SOE could make them with all the resources at its disposal.

'Okey-dokey, if you wanna come with me, we'll kit you out with the best American silk. But I need to take this,' the airman said, picking up the case with the radio inside. 'It's too heavy to jump with. I'll get the guys to pack it in one of the containers.'

'How long will it take to Reims?' asked Monique.

The young airman shrugged his shoulders. 'Beats me. Should be about two and a half hours but it depends on the weather. Why? You got somewhere you gotta be?'

She shook her head. She liked the casual tone of this man. For some reason, it made her feel calmer even though her heart was beating like the wings of a startled swan.

They all stood up and followed him to a table in the far corner.

'Any of youse jumped before?'

'All of us have completed the parachute training course at Ringway.' Once again, Philippe answered. He had appointed himself the spokesperson for the group.

The airman laughed. 'I asked if any of you have jumped before. You know, a real jump.'

There was a moment of silence before Elviron answered. 'This is our first time.'

'Right, listen up. Here are your chutes. Fasten them properly and check each other. I'll make a final check myself. We don't want none of you to hit the dirt at six hundred miles an hour. It might put a ladder in your stockings.' He stared at Monique's legs. 'We'll be flying at two thousand feet across the Channel, dropping to eight hundred feet as we approach Amiens. There are two lights; red and green. Red is your thirty-second warning, green is go. Don't hesitate over the hole. If you do, I will push you out. Clear? Your dropping time is a little over ten seconds, so not long after you leave us you'll be standing on French soil.'

They nodded their heads.

'Right, get moving.' He checked his watch. 'We're leaving at 02.00 hours. That's in thirty minutes for those of you who can't tell the time. The other aircraft have left already, we're the last.'

'Have you flown this route before?' asked Philippe.

'Me? No, but Charlie has.'

'Charlie?'

'Captain C. Thomas Charles the Third. He's the commander of this Carpetbagger squadron. So you guys must be pretty important if you got him flyin' you.'

'Has the equipment been loaded?'

'The guys are just doing it. The containers will be dropped from the bomb bay and the nodules through the Joe Hole on the second pass. Two of you drop on the first pass, two more on the third. Okay?'

'Won't that give the Germans time to spot us?'

'It might, but you've got too much equipment and the hole ain't that big.' The airman shrugged his shoulders. 'We done three drops before and the French team know what they are doing.'

Philippe nodded.

The airman checked his watch. 'Twenty-eight minutes, you better get movin'.'

They struggled into their jump suits and strapped on the parachutes, checking each other as they had been taught on their training course.

After they had finished, the airman went over their harnesses one more time with a rough professionalism, tightening straps and adjusting the position of the chutes.

'Right, this way.'

They walked, or rather, waddled, on to the airfield, the reserve parachutes hanging between their legs, making it difficult to proceed.

A single B24 Liberator was parked in front of them, its four engines making a thunderous roar as the pilot warmed them up. The aircraft was painted a deep, dark, matt black, which blended into the night, with one single American star on the port side but no lights.

Turbulence from the engines tugged at Monique's jump suit. She smelt the air. It was heavy with the sweet, sickly aroma of aviation fuel.

'This is Doris. She makes a hell of a racket but she'll get you there, and us back, as sure as Daniel Boone was from Kentucky.'

Monique took one last look behind her. Someone had already switched off the lights in the ops room. Immediately behind it stood an ash tree, its branches still without any leaves, bare and stark in the pale glow of the moon. Would she ever see England again? Would she ever see her son?

Philippe nudged her in the back. They both climbed aboard and sat next to each other on a wooden bench aligned against the metal side of the plane, Elviron and Wallace sitting opposite them. Both were English and had grown up in France. She was the opposite; a Frenchwoman who lived and worked in England. Monique knew them both vaguely from the tradecraft course in Arisaig, but they were not part of her group. On arrival, they would separate, with Philippe and her staying in Reims and Yvonne and Ron heading east to the Vosges.

Nobody spoke.

The airman climbed aboard, closing the door behind him. He handed them flasks of coffee and sandwiches wrapped in greaseproof paper.

'For the trip,' he shouted over the sound of the engines. 'Courtesy of Uncle Sam. Only baloney, I'm afraid, but she'll do.'

As he spoke, the pitch of the engines increased to a sharp whine. The airman crossed himself three times, lifting his eyes to the heavens and mumbling a short prayer.

The plane lumbered down the runway, shuddering as the wheels hit uneven lumps of grass. The noise increased as the pilot coaxed more power from the engines. For a second, Monique's heart skipped a beat as the plane lurched forward.

She thought of John, her darling John, dead for nearly two years now. His face flashed through her mind, smiling that knowing grin of his. It was as if he were a guardian angel looking down on her.

The plane wobbled once more before floating upwards, losing contact with the rude earth that desperately tried to hold it down. Monique felt the sudden release of tension as they rose into the night sky and headed across the Channel to her beloved France.

Would she ever see England again?

Chapter Two

Monday, December 25, 2017 – Christmas Day
Macclesfield General Hospital, Cheshire

After leaving Christie's and the Roberts family, Jayne drove down the A523 to Macclesfield. She pressed the accelerator with her foot and felt the BMW surge forward.

The wide road was empty. On Christmas morning, most families were spending time together, swapping presents, eating chocolate and nuts, preparing turkey or simply enjoying the special joy that is Christmas morning.

This year, she wasn't able to do any of those things. Instead, she was driving to see her stepfather, Robert, who was seriously ill with pneumonia in Macclesfield General.

As she drove, memories of Robert and their life together kept coming back to her.

The time they had gone to Blackpool and she had so wanted to ride the Big Dipper but her mother had said no, until Robert stepped forward to accompany her even though he was scared of heights. As she hollered and whooped, he'd spent the whole ride with his eyes closed and his hand tightly gripping hers.

Or the time she had come home from school with her uniform ripped and torn after a fight with a boy who tried to bully her.

Robert had taken her out to buy a new uniform before her mother saw the damage to the old one.

Or the time when they had sat and listened to Candle in the Wind over and over again on the day of Princess Diana's funeral, both of them with tears in their eyes while her mother looked on in bemusement.

She realised she had shared so many wonderful times with her stepfather. A man who was more of a parent to her than her mother had ever been.

She parked the car and hurried up to his ward. Vera, her new stepmother, was waiting beside his bed, a book open and her knitting in the bag by her side.

Robert was still sleeping in his bed, but the oxygen mask no longer covered his mouth.

'How is he?' Jayne whispered.

'Fine. I think he's getting better. The doctor said he didn't need oxygen any more. The colour has returned to his cheeks and his hand isn't so clammy.'

Jayne heaved a sigh of relief. If Vera thought he was improving, it was a good sign.

'How are you?' Vera whispered again.

'Not bad, a little tired but I can manage.'

'How was the case?'

'Good. All worked out in the end. In fact, the result was better than good.'

She had found the missing ancestor, Tom Roberts, and the meaning of the three objects he had left behind in the box in the attic. The football and the label were going to be donated to a museum, as they were valuable artefacts from the Christmas truce of 1914.

Jayne approached Robert's bed. 'He still looks a little pale,' she whispered.

'Why are you two whispering?' Robert's voice was weak. 'I can hear everything, you know. Not deaf yet.'

Jayne and her stepmother looked at each other. It was Vera who spoke first.

'How long have you been awake?'

'Quite a while. Time for me to get up.' He tried to lift his shoulders from the bed.

Vera was up in a flash, pressing his body gently back down. 'You stay right where you are, Robert Cartwright,' she ordered. 'You're not going anywhere.'

His eyes were open now and Jayne was stunned by the brightness of the blue irises.

'You gave us a scare, Robert,' she said.

'I know. Sorry, lass. What day is it?'

'Christmas Day.'

'I could murder a turkey leg.'

'I'll see what the hospital has to eat,' said Vera. 'You must be starving.' She rushed out to the nurses' station.

'I've been so worried, Robert.'

'I can imagine, lass.'

'Vera has been brilliant, staying here with you.'

'She's one in a million, my new wife. I'm so lucky to have found her.'

Jayne glanced towards the door.

'I hope you realise why I've been nagging you for so long to look into your own past, Jayne, your own family history. I'm not going to be with you much longer, you know.'

'Shhh, Robert, don't talk like that.'

But she knew what he said was true. He wasn't going to be here for ever. But whether it was two days or ten years, she vowed to enjoy every second of every minute with him.

'You know he was my best friend.'

'Who?'

'Your real father. He wasn't a happy man and he wore his heart on his sleeve...'

'Shhh, Dad,' Jayne interrupted. 'Save your strength, we'll talk about it later.'

'No, we'll talk about it now,' Robert said forcefully. 'You see, I think he's still alive.'

Chapter Three

Monday, December 25, 2017 – Christmas Day
Macclesfield General Hospital, Cheshire

'What? What did you say, Robert?'

The old man closed his eyes and took a deep breath.

In the rest of the ward, the three other patients slept quietly except for one who was watching television, chuckling along at a comedy sketch, earphones clamped to his head.

Then Robert Cartwright began to speak again, the words struggling to leave his lips. 'I said I think your father is still alive. I'm sorry, I'll make it clearer, my mind isn't working as well as it used to: I know your father is still alive.'

A noise like a train leaving a tunnel rushed through Jayne Sinclair's head. 'My father… alive? That can't be. He died when I was seven… My mother told me he died just a few years after he left us.'

'You have to understand she thought she was doing what was best for you, Jayne.'

Jayne shook her head, trying to understand. 'So… so he didn't die?'

Robert shook his head, his white hair brushing against the fabric of the NHS pillow case.

'But my mother said he died in a car accident.'

'That's what she told you.'

'But I remember the day of the funeral. She went to the church service and the burial, and you stayed to look after me. It was before you two were married.'

The old man lying in the hospital bed had been a wonderful father to Jayne as she was growing up, even though they had no biological connection. He was the one rock she could always rely on as her mother's behaviour became increasingly erratic.

Always supportive, always understanding, always there for her.

'I remember the day well too, Jayne. We went to the shops and you insisted we bought a pineapple. I'd never had a fresh one before, only ever eating pineapple chunks out of a tin. We made a right mess of hacking it to pieces.'

'It tasted so good, though. Even now, the smell of fresh pineapple always takes me back to that day.'

Robert turned his head towards the monitor beeping softly beside his bed. 'She didn't go to a funeral, Jayne, she went to see him,' he said softly.

'But I remember her leaving, dressed in black. She even wore black gloves.'

'She thought they were the right clothes to wear to go to a prison.'

'A prison?'

He took another deep breath. 'Your father didn't die, Jayne. He was sent to prison for a long time. That's why your mother thought it best that you didn't know.'

'She lied to me?'

'I tried to make her tell you the truth but she wouldn't listen. She insisted she knew what was best for her daughter. I wasn't your father, and as I wasn't married to your mother at that time. I had no real say.'

'She was never very good at listening.'

He chuckled again. 'She had many good points, your mother, but listening wasn't one of them.'

Jayne reached out and touched his hand. 'You put up with a lot from her.'

'I loved your mother, Jayne, and I love you. It was only after I met Vera that I realised love didn't have to be so… so exhausting.'

'Says the man in the hospital bed suffering from pneumonia.'

He laughed again. 'Not Vera's fault, just my own stupidity. Should look after myself better. But let's not change the subject, Jayne, I was telling you about your father. If I don't do it now, I don't think I ever will.'

She grasped his hand tighter. 'You're the only father I ever had, Robert. I don't think I could have survived my teens without you. So many arguments with my mother; about clothes, boyfriends, eating, about everything really. And when I joined the police…'

Jayne had joined the Greater Manchester Police as a cadet, quickly making her way through the ranks to Detective Sergeant, on the cusp of being promoted to Inspector.

She had spent nearly half her life working there, and had loved every second of it until one incident destroyed everything; the shooting of her partner, DS Dave Gilmour.

After that, she couldn't face the work any more. Too much guilt, too much sorrow. It was all too much. Six months after his death, she resigned from the force.

It had taken a while, but with Robert's encouragement, she had finally found something she loved doing; being a genealogical investigator. The tougher and more difficult the investigation, the better she enjoyed it.

Robert reached out and patted the back of her hand. 'Thank you, Jayne, but you must know the truth. I won't be around much longer…'

'Shhh, don't talk like that.'

'But it's true, Jayne. When you get to my age, the reality of death is staring you in the face. It's not something that's far away in the distant future.' He laughed to himself. 'God's last joke on us. We know we are all going to die, we just don't know when.' He coughed; a harsh, wracking sound.

'Quiet, Robert, you must take it easy.'

'No, I have to tell you now, you have to know…' He began coughing again, as though trying to bring up something stuck in his throat.

Jayne jumped up from her chair and held his shoulders as the bout of coughing racked his body. She felt his bones through the fabric of his pyjamas. He was so thin and sickly these days, so different from the robust, healthy man she had always known.

As if reading her thoughts, he wiped his mouth and began speaking again. 'I'm getting old, Jayne. I have to tell you now before it's too late.'

'Don't talk like that. You'll soon be better and out of here, running around with Vera.'

'I must tell you. I received this before I was taken ill.' He struggled to take his wallet from the bedside table. Jayne stood up and passed it to him.

He lay there for a moment, holding the old wallet against his chest, rheumy eyes staring into the distance. And then, as if waking from a dream, he turned his head towards her.

'In 1980, when you were seven years old, your father was sent to prison. He's still there now.'

'But that was thirty-eight years ago, Robert. How can somebody be kept inside for thirty-eight years?'

'Your father shot a man in cold blood.'

Chapter Four

Monday, December 25, 2017 – Christmas Day
Macclesfield General Hospital, Cheshire

'Murder? He killed someone? What? Who?' A million questions raced around Jayne's brain.

'He knocked on an old man's door one day in September. It was your father's birthday – the third of September, 1978 – and he shot the old man dead.'

'But why? Why would he do that?'

Robert shrugged his shoulders. 'He wouldn't say. I read some of the case in the papers. But he pleaded guilty so it was all over very quickly. He was sentenced to thirty years in prison.'

'Hold on. There must have been a motive, a reason. The police would have kept asking why he did it. Remember, I was a detective. You have to find out not only what happened but why it happened too. And you said he was sentenced to thirty years. With remission, he should have been out after twenty.'

'Apparently, when he was in Strangeways he attacked and wounded another prisoner with a knife.'

'I don't understand. Is he violent? A psychopath? Schizophrenic? Of course, I asked Mother about him. She always said he was a gentle man – quiet, unassuming, slow to anger.'

'I can't answer these questions, Jayne. But you could ask him yourself…'

'What?'

Robert opened his wallet and pulled out a single sheet of notepaper that had been folded in four. 'I received this the day before I collapsed with the pneumonia. I was going to tell you about it next time you came to the Home. Vera said I had to tell you.'

'Vera knows?'

'She insisted I told you. She said I couldn't keep it secret any more.'

Jayne opened the letter, slowly, tentatively. Her heart was beating in her chest as if it were ready to explode. All sounds in the hospital ward ceased. It was as if time had stopped. She read the address at the top.

HMP Belmarsh, Thamesmead, London.

'This is the first and only communication I have received from him since he went to prison all those years ago,' said Robert.

Jayne looked up from the letter. 'How did he know your address?'

Robert shrugged his shoulders again. 'I don't know. He was a clever and resourceful man, your father. I guess he found it online, not so difficult these days.'

Jayne stared down at the letter. The first line was stark on the white Basildon Bond notepaper.

Dear Robert,

The words swam out of view. Jayne wiped her eyes. This was her father's handwriting; rounded letters, leaning to the right, the 't' crossed extravagantly. A solid, slightly old-fashioned hand.

She placed the letter down on the bed and wiped her eyes again.

'You need to read it, lass.'

'It's addressed to you.'

'But the message is for you. Read it.'

Jayne nodded silently, picking up the letter and started to read once more.

Dear Robert,

It's been such a long time since we met. An age and half a lifetime ago. I am sorry that our friendship lapsed. Unfortunately, it was one of the things Marjorie said to me when she visited me in jail before my trial. She insisted that Jayne would never visit me, nor would there be more visits from herself from that day forward.

I agreed as long as she promised to send me pictures every year. It was always the best thing for Jayne, if not the easiest agreement for me.

But I made my choice when I shot David Strachan. There was no going back afterwards. I understood it then and I understand it now.

Marjorie also kept her side of the bargain. Every year, at Christmas, she would send me a picture of Jayne and let me know how she was getting on…

Jayne thought for a moment, her eyes darting upwards to the right as she searched for long-forgotten memories. 'So that's why I used to take those photographs every year in December. She always made me pose in front of the same place just before Christmas each year. Said it was for her family album. I used to hate doing it, but Mother insisted. Did you know she was sending them to…?'

Jayne let the end of the sentence trail away. She didn't know what to call the man who had written the letter. 'Father' seemed so wrong, and anyway, Robert was her father.

Always had been. Always would be.

Robert shook his head. 'No, I didn't. I just thought it was one of your mother's traditions; always take a picture in December for Christmas. And his name is Martin. Martin Sinclair.'

There it was, the name of her father. Martin Sinclair. Jayne began to read the letter again.

I used to love looking at those pictures, even when she became a goth when she was fourteen. They were the one thing that kept me going all those years in here. And when I first received the picture of her as a police cadet, well, I can tell you, I nearly fell off my chair. But I guess it was inevitable that Marjorie would push her to join the police, given what I had done.

'But that's wrong. Mother hated me joining the police. I remember she wanted me to go to university and study.'

Robert remained silent.

Jayne stopped talking and continued to read.

Of course, I received no more pictures when she turned 18. Inevitable, I suppose. Did Marjorie ever show her the birthday cards I sent? I suppose not, otherwise she would have replied.

Jayne looked up at Robert. 'Birthday cards?'

Robert shrugged his shoulders.

Her mother even kept secrets from him, it seemed. She continued to read the letter out loud.

I followed her career as best I could. The internet has made it easier recently to keep abreast of people, what they are doing and even what they are eating!

Thankfully, Jayne has not become one of those food obsessives (you can imagine what pictures of food do to a man who has eaten nothing but prison fare for the last 38 years!). I have followed her career as a genealogical detective with interest. I'm sure that was your influence, Robert, and given what I have to ask her to do, it is a useful profession to practise.

But enough of this. You must be wondering why I am finally writing to you after all these years.

I have cancer. The doctors in the prison are all very positive and talking about chemo and radiation treatment, but I have refused their advice.

I won't be taking any drugs or having any treatment. I intend to die as quickly and as painlessly as possible.

But before I do, I would like to see Jayne. I want to ask her to do something for me.

Can you please show her this letter?

I would like her to come to see me. That's all I ask. If she doesn't want to meet I will understand. After all, I've never been a father to her. If she does, she needs to know my birthdate — September 3, 1939 — and my place of birth, London, before the prison authorities will allow her to see me.

You were a good and faithful friend before I went into prison, so I ask that you do this one last thing for me.

Please show her this letter. I want to meet her before I die. Thank you.

Best regards from an old friend,

Martin

Jayne let the letter fall slowly to the bedcover. 'He wants to see me, Robert?' she said in a quiet, child-like voice.

'I think he does, lass.'

A strange weakness washed over Jayne's body. Normally, she was the strong one. The one who knew what to do, how to solve the problem, the one that people relied on.

In this case, she felt lost. 'What shall I do?' was her only question.

Robert took her hand. 'It's a decision you have to make, lass, not one I can make for you.'

'What did Vera say?' Jayne trusted the judgement and common-sense of her stepmother. A woman who didn't call a spade a sharp-edged object for digging into the earth.

'Vera thought you should go to see him, lass. It's the only chance you have to meet your real father. He hasn't got long to live.'

'You are my real father, not him,' Jayne said more forcefully than she intended.

'Your biological father, then. This is the only chance to meet your biological father.' Robert suddenly started coughing, his chest heaving as he fought for breath.

Instantly, Jayne was by his side, helping him sit up. 'Are you okay?'

'Fine, lass,' he said after a while. 'Something caught in my throat. It's your decision, but…'

She lowered him back down on to the bed, glancing down at the letter lying on the coverlet. 'What do you think? Please tell me the truth.'

Robert took a deep breath. 'I think… You specialise in family history, Jayne. This is your one chance to discover the truth about your own family. If I were you, I would go. You only have to see him once and you needn't see him again. But it means you can start looking into your own history. He's your only living relative.'

'I don't know, Robert…'

Vera appeared at the door, accompanied by a nurse. She was carrying a cup of tea and a plate of biscuits. 'This is all they had, I'm afraid, but Dolores has arranged for lunch to be delivered early, Robert.'

The nurse bustled into the room. 'Is everything okay, Mr Cartwright? Feeling better?' She adjusted the pillow, fluffing it up and placing it back to support Robert's head. 'You shouldn't tire yourself. You've just recovered from pneumonia. Rest and sleep is what you need.' She turned to Jayne. 'I would let him sleep now if I were you.'

Jayne stood up. 'You're right, nurse. I've tired him out too much.'

Vera put the tea and biscuits on Robert's bedside table. 'I'll stay with him, you go home. It's Christmas Day, after all. You told her, Robert?'

Her father nodded.

Vera touched Jayne's shoulder. 'It's a lot to take in. You should go home and have a good sleep, think it over.'

'But you've been here all night…'

'Don't worry about me. I'll stay with him for a bit longer and then head home myself.'

Jayne realised she was exhausted. A combination of working on the Roberts' investigation, and now this explosive news, had left her feeling like an empty, tired shell.

'If you don't mind…'

'Away home with you, Jayne Sinclair. Get a good night's sleep and think it over,' said her stepmother.

'Go on, lass, I'm feeling much better today and it is Christmas. Go home.' Robert smiled at her from his bed.

'Robert, we forgot Jayne's present,' said Vera suddenly. 'It's still at the Home…'

'I don't need any presents this year.' Jayne glanced across at her stepfather. 'I've already received the best Christmas present ever.'

'Your father should rest now, Miss Sinclair,' interrupted the nurse.

'Okay, I'm going. Please look after him, Vera, you don't know how much he means to me.'

'I know, dear. Don't worry, he'll be fine from now on.'

Jayne put on her coat and wrapped a scarf around her neck. 'I'll come back tomorrow to see you, Robert.'

'Okay, lass, but think about it, will you? Think about seeing your father.'

'I will.'

He reached down to the end of the bed and passed her the letter. 'Take this with you.'

Jayne folded it up and placed it in her pocket.

'You know that whatever you decide, I'll always love you, don't you, lass?'

She bent over and kissed the top of the old man's head, holding him close, smelling that strange hospital aroma clinging to his skin and hair. 'I know, Robert. And I'll always love Vera and you, whatever happens.'.

Chapter Five

Monday, December 25, 2017 – Christmas Day
Didsbury, Manchester

As soon as she opened the door of her home, Mr Smith rushed out to greet her, mewing softly and rubbing his body against her legs as she took off her coat.

She picked him up and nuzzled his soft black fur against her face. For once, he didn't struggle in her arms but seemed to accept she needed comfort at this time. 'You understand, don't you, you big softie,' she whispered in his ear.

At her words, he twisted his body and leapt from her arms, landing agilely on his feet before striding over proudly to his bowl, tail erect in the air.

'Is that all I am to you? A bowl of chopped liver with chicken gravy?'

He miaowed loudly in reply.

'Okay, okay, it's coming.' She followed him into the kitchen, opening the fridge door. Inside, it was full of the food she had intended to cook for Vera, Robert and a few close friends; turkey, ham, Christmas pudding, rum butter and mince pies, plus a special selection of champagne, wine and chocolates.

Of course, there was also Mr Smith's gourmet meals. She reached in and selected one of his favourite pouches of cat food. 'Succulent chunks of liver smothered in a rich chicken gravy,' she read aloud. 'I could almost eat it myself.'

She snipped the top off the pouch and poured the contents into the waiting bowl, Mr Smith's eyes watchful and his body tense.

As soon as she finished, he pounced, attacking the food as if he hadn't eaten for the last seven years.

Normally, she would now switch on the laptop and check her emails. There were usually some enquiries that needed answering regarding her current investigations, or updates to provide for clients. But it was Christmas Day and she decided that, after her news, she deserved one day away from the computer.

She sat down heavily on the stool in the kitchen and watched the cat devour his food. Her mind returned to the conversation with Robert.

Her father was still alive.

Her father was still alive.

She shook her head. Perhaps she should have a glass of wine and some chocolate. It was Christmas Day, after all.

She went back to the fridge. Inside was a bottle of Cheval Blanc 2005, which she had bought as a special Christmas treat, alongside a block of rare Chuao chocolate. But, for one of the few times in her life, she suddenly lost her appetite. Even the thought of a good bottle of wine and some succulent chocolate no longer appealed.

She closed the fridge door and rested her forehead against its cold plastic exterior. She felt strangely sad and despondent.

It wasn't the usual sadness she often felt when a job finished; that emptiness left behind by solving a puzzle not knowing where or when the next challenge would come. Nor was it the sadness of being all alone on Christmas Day with just a cat for company. Nor was it missing anybody, even though it would have been wonderful to have cooked Christmas dinner for Robert and Vera.

It was the sadness of knowing her whole world had been turned upside down.

Her father was still alive.

Since the age of seven she believed he had died in a car accident. The details from her mother were convincing; he had been driving alone on a dark, stormy night. He went around a bend too fast, skidded on the wet surface and his car had slammed into a tree. He had been killed instantly.

As she turned over her mother's story in her mind, it all seemed so pat, so film-like: like the sad end of Marc Bolan. The sort of story one would tell a seven-year-old to help them understand what had happened.

But it was all lies.

Her father was still alive.

She took the letter out of her pocket and read the words again.

But before I do, I would like to see Jayne. I want to ask her to do something for me.

There it was in black and white. After all these years, he wanted to see her. All these years she had believed him dead, he had been alive.

And now, out of the blue, he had written to Robert, asking her to go to see him.

Well, he could bugger off. How dare he abandon her, a seven-year-old child with nothing in the world? How dare he approach her now, when she was happy and content, loving her job and her life?

Mr Smith had finished his food and began lapping his water. Soon he would want to go out and take his nightly stroll through the neighbourhood. She strode over to the patio doors and opened them wide. Outside, the night was dark and the air sharply scented of frost. Two doors down on the left, there was the sound of a party at one of her neighbours' houses.

For the first time since she and Paul had split up, she felt lonely. Perhaps it was the Christmas effect; the one day of the year when people were supposed to be with friends and family.

They were still separated and not yet divorced, but it was only a matter of time. He had found somebody else in Brussels, where he worked.

In a strange way, she was happy for him. They had split up long ago but they hadn't realised it, staying together out of habit and fear of the unknown.

When he had finally been offered the job in Brussels, she realised she couldn't leave Robert or her job as a genealogical investigator. She just didn't love her husband enough to make that sort of sacrifice for him any more.

Quite simply, her job and her stepfather meant far more to her than her husband did. One day, they would make the divorce official, but there was no rush. Not at the moment.

It was Christmas Day and here she was on her own with a cat for company. Her breath fogged the night air as she spoke to Mr Smith. 'Well, off you go, I can't stay here freezing all night.'

The cat just sat in the middle of the kitchen floor, unmoving.

'Hurry up,' she encouraged him, 'get a move on, Mr Smith.'

But he just sat there, staring at her.

'Not going out tonight? Okay.' She closed the patio doors, shutting out the noise of the party and the world outside.

'I'm off to bed, then.' She walked over to the light switch and turned off the light. Mr Smith followed her to the door.

'Are you coming with me? You never come with me.'

A plaintive miaow was his only response.

She picked him up and carried him upstairs to the bedroom. For the first time, he was going to spend the night on her bed. Perhaps he realised she needed company.

Later, snuggling in bed with the cat curled up at her feet, the words from the letter came back to her.

But before I do, I would like to see Jayne. I want to ask her to do something for me.

As the cat snored quietly at her feet and her eyelids began to droop, two questions ran round and round inside her brain.

Should she go and see him?

What did he want her to do?

They were questions that were to dominate her dreams that Christmas night.

Chapter Six

Tuesday, May 17, 1938
St James' Park, London

On fine days, Monique Massat often took George out from Ashley Court. He would sit in the stroller watching the world go by with the wide-open eyes of a three-year-old just discovering what life had to offer.

If the spring sun was too bright she would pull up the black hood, which immediately started a deafening howl of anguish as if he were being tortured. People stared at her accusingly.

Once an old police constable had sidled up to her, saying, 'Is your charge not well, miss?'

She had to spend the next five minutes explaining in her halting English that he wanted to see the world, not be enclosed in the three walls of the hood of the stroller.

Finally, the constable wandered off, muttering about 'bloody foreigners'.

She would have much preferred George to sit with the hood always open, but Madame had insisted. 'Monique, please ensure George does not get too much sun. My husband and I were out in India, you know, and we are aware of the perils of sun on a baby's skin, particularly one as delicate as George.'

She didn't think George delicate at all. In fact, for her he was a happy, healthy baby who took joy in running around naked after his bath and watching the world go by.

Just like her, really. She had always spent time outdoors, growing up on the family's smallholding just outside Orléans. But her parents had both died when she was in her early teens and the aunt she went to live with made it very clear that Monique should leave as soon as she was old enough. Luckily, she heard of a job with a family in England, looking after a young baby. She was just eighteen years old when she stepped off the ferry at Dover and was whisked into the centre of London.

George was her new charge and she quickly fell in love with his round, rosy cheeks and his happy, contented smile.

From the Dodds' home in Ashley Court she often walked down to the Thames at Vauxhall Bridge. She loved the breeze as it blew down the river, shoving away the smells and tastes of the air of the city. George loved watching the boats as they chugged past: the long, low cargo barges filled with goods going who knows where.

Or they spent afternoons at Vincent Road, watching the cricket players. She had no understanding of the rules of the game - in fact, they seemed to make them up as they went along - but she loved the colours; the vivid green of the grass, the bright white of the uniforms and the slash of red that was the ball. And the sounds that echoed off the surrounding buildings; the thwack of wooden bat on leather ball and the shouts of the players, all counterpointed by the song of the birds in the trees.

If she closed her eyes, she could imagine she was back in France, and instead of boys playing cricket, she could hear the sound of the old men playing pétanque in front of the café in the centre of her village, of wine-soaked arguments instead of shrill shouts of 'howzat'.

She still missed her home in France, despite having lived in London for the last two years. The family she worked for were not too bad.

She never saw the master – he was either working late at the ministry or working even later in his club. And Madame, well, she enjoyed a life of leisure, spending more time and money at Harrods than she did with George. She did love her son, but she wasn't very good at showing it. A peculiarly English character trait.

But in many ways, Monique was glad that Madame was so uninvolved with the young boy, because it gave her the freedom to do what she wanted, when she wanted. As a nanny, and a French one at that, the other servants ignored her, not interfering in her care of George at all.

Some days she felt lonely, but then she looked across at George's smiling face – his curly blond hair sticking up like one of the Indians in the Mohican film she had just watched, and his one tooth white against his pink mouth – and she started to smile too.

Life was good.

Today the sun was shining, the air was fresh and she decided to walk to St James' Park. Not one of their usual places for an afternoon stroll, but George enjoyed feeding the ducks along the lake.

She wrapped him up well in his new red coat from Harrods, placing him in the cane stroller and fastening the cover using the press studs. His eyes were wide open and blue. He knew he was going out today. Out of the stuffy flat for another adventure.

She fastened her black gabardine coat around her waist and put on the hat Madame had given her to wear.

'Princess Alexandra's nannies wear these cloches. I do think they look so elegant, don't you?'

She didn't agree, but wore it nonetheless. She had to have something to cover her head, didn't she?

Pushing the stroller into the elevator, she closed the doors herself and was whisked down from the second floor to the lobby.

Out on Morpeth Terrace, the weather was a little warmer than she thought but she wouldn't take George's coat off yet. The tower of Westminster Cathedral opposite rose up into the blue sky, its red and white bricks still showing through the dirt and grime of the city. This was her church. Every other Sunday, on her day off, when George was being looked after by one of the other servants, she went to mass, delighting in the heavy Byzantine mosaics inside. A little piece of the south of France in the middle of London.

She strode past it today, though, pushing the heavy pram. Left along Palace Street, right down Wilfred Street, a quick dash across the road, her hand held up to force the taxis and buses to stop, or at least slow down.

And she was there, St James' Park.

Now to find somewhere quiet with a touch of shade, for George to feed the ducks and so she could read her book. An hour of peace, away from the flat and away from the world.

Chapter Seven

Tuesday, May 17, 1938
St James' Park, London

A scream from George.

She woke with a start, the book falling from her lap on to the grass beneath her seat.

Where was he?

Another scream to her right, louder this time, close to the water.

She blinked her eyes. Where was he?

A man in the grey uniform of the Royal Air Force was running down to the waterside.

She stood up and stared, running towards the lake too, shouting, 'George! George!' as loud as she could.

People turned to stare at the mad Frenchwoman.

A flash of white wings, the hissing of a bird, people staring towards the lake.

Where was George?

Then the man in grey uniform, swooping down and lifting something small high into the air.

George, still clutching his slice of bread.

She ran up to the officer. 'Thank you, thank you. He must have run away.'

He hugged George to his chest. The young boy was smiling, totally unworried by the aggressive swan. 'He's a brave young chap, but you need to be careful of the birds here, especially those with their young.'

He looked across at the swan, now paddling serenely away, her three cygnets trailing after her.

'I fell asleep… I…'

'It happens, don't worry. And no harm done, hey, little man?'

George reached out to touch the man's peaked cap. The man took it off and placed it on George's head, where it sat askew.

'Thank you ever so much. Madame would have been angry with me if…'

'He's not your child then?'

Monique smiled shyly. 'I'm his nanny, looking after him.'

The officer tilted his head. 'Do I hear a French accent? *Etes-vous francaise?*'

'Mais oui, bien sur. Vous parlez bien, monsieur.'

'Non, pas du tout. J'ai vecu a Paris pendant deux ans.'

'Vraiment, vous parlez bien. Comme d'habitude les anglais ne parle que leur langue maternelle.'

'I know,' he said, switching back to English, 'it is one of the least attractive attributes of my country. You know, we have a belief that foreigners all know how to speak English, but they only use it when we are not looking.'

Monique laughed and was joined by George, still wearing the pilot officer's hat. 'We say exactly the same in French.'

'My name is John Sinclair, Flight Lieutenant John Sinclair. *Enchanté,* mademoiselle.' He put out his hand, moving George over to his left arm.

She shook it. 'Monique Massat, pleased to meet you. But let me take him off you now, he must be getting heavy.'

'This little chap? He's light as a feather.'

She looked behind her. The pram was still parked next to the bench with her book lying on the grass.

42

'I must be going back now. Madame will be waiting for us.' She held out her arms and George moved into them without a murmur.

'He's very well behaved for such a young chap.'

She tugged George's nose. 'He's a dear, aren't you, George?'

John Sinclair touched George on the back of the hand. 'Would he like an ice cream? There's a tea garden over there. Perhaps you would like to have something to eat? You must be famished.'

Monique looked back towards the pram. 'We must be going, Madame, she—'

'We won't be long and I'll escort you back.'

Monique thought about it. He was a very nice man, older than her, but with a charm and a joy in his green eyes she hadn't seen in many Englishmen. She shook her head. 'I'm sorry, I can't. Madame…'

'Not to worry, perhaps another time.'

'George, we have to go now. You must give the officer back his hat.' She went to reach for the RAF hat. George immediately grasped his hands on top of his head, letting out an almighty scream as if all the banshees from hell had been released at the same time.

'George, you must give the officer back his hat.'

The screaming increased and became louder, if that was possible.

Monique placed George down on the ground and began to talk to him. 'George, this is not yours, it is the Mr Sinclair's.' The screaming subsided, becoming a series of whimpers. 'Would you like it if somebody stole your hat?'

George shook his head, eyes red with tears and mouth trembling.

'Would you take something that wasn't yours?'

More snuffles and another shake of the head.

'We should give the officer back his hat.' Monique went to reach for it and the screaming began again, even louder. A foghorn of a noise. All the other visitors to the park stared at the woman who was torturing this young boy.

John Sinclair came to her rescue. 'Give it to me on Saturday. Why don't you and George have afternoon tea with me then, in Hyde Park? There's a wonderful café there and George can have his ice cream.'

'But won't you need your hat?'

'I have another.' He knelt down in front of George. 'You can play with my peaked cap for three days, and then you can give it back to me on Saturday. How does that sound?'

As George nodded his head, the hat slipped off and he stooped quickly to pick it up.

'Is it a deal?' asked John Sinclair as he stood up and looked at Monique.

'I don't know…'

'You can come on Saturday with George?'

'I suppose so, but the weather…'

'It's going to be fine according to my reports. We're in for a bit of a heatwave for the next week or so.'

'How do you know?'

He tapped the wings on his jacket. 'RAF, remember? We get to know these sort of things well in advance.'

'I'll ask Madame.'

'I'm sure she'll say yes. Shall we agree on three p.m.? They do a lovely afternoon tea…'

Monique slowly nodded, staring back towards the stroller beside the bench.

When she turned back, the officer was already walking away, waving and saying, 'See you on Saturday.'

She waved back and so did George. The young boy continued to wave as John Sinclair walked down Birdcage Walk and out of sight.

'I suppose we're going to tea on Saturday, George,' she said, a smile playing at the edge of her lips.

Chapter Eight

Saturday, May 21, 1938
Hyde Park, London

The café was in the middle of Hyde Park, next to a brick pavilion. Each table was sheltered from the sun by an assortment of large umbrellas. Tail-coated waiters danced between the tables and there was a buzz of conversation.

John Sinclair was already sitting at a table when Monique arrived, pushing George in his stroller. He stood up immediately and helped her sit down at the table whilst the waiters created room for George's cane pushchair.

For a moment, they sat down awkwardly opposite each other at the table.

'I'm so glad—'

'We walked here—'

They both spoke at the same time. He indicated that she should speak first.

'George has something for you.'

Reluctantly, George reached into the pannier attached to the chair and brought out the RAF cap, handing it over to John.

'Thank you, George, my commanding officer will be very pleased you have returned this. And now, a little something for you…' He brought a smaller, child's version of the cap from behind his back.

George's face lit up. The cap was placed at a jaunty angle on his round head as a place was found for him at a table.

'And now, let's have some sandwiches and cake.'

Without ordering, a three-tiered selection of food was set up on the table, followed by milk for George and a pot of tea for the two adults. 'I hope you don't mind, I took the liberty of ordering.'

'This is the English afternoon tea, yes.' Monique picked up a small square of sandwich on white bread.

'Cucumber, I think. Horrid stuff but very traditional. You might prefer the potted salmon. Equally horrid but at least it has some taste.'

George immediately reached for the cream cakes on the bottom tier. Monique slapped his hand away and then placed a single cake on the plate in front of him. 'Madame will not approve, but I suppose this is a special occasion.'

'Is it?' asked Martin.

'Mais oui, it is not often that I have afternoon tea with an officer in uniform.'

He looked down at the blue-grey of his dress jacket. 'Yes, very sorry. I should have worn civvies but I was at the Air Ministry this morning in Berkeley Square... Too much to do,' he added as an afterthought.

'Will there be war?'

His face lost its smile. 'I don't know, one never does. Germany has marched into Austria and is now making noises about the Sudetenland. It's difficult.' He shrugged his shoulders.

'I hope there is no war. My father fought at Verdun in 1916. He never spoke about it but used to wake up in the middle of the night screaming and covered in sweat. The nightmares haunted him right to the end.'

'He passed away?'

She nodded. 'And my mother too, in 1930. I'm all alone now, tout seule.'

'I'm sorry to hear that. No brothers or sisters?'

'I was the only one at our farm near Orléans. And you?'

'One brother, I'm afraid.'

'Why are you afraid?'

'Well, he's a bit of scoundrel, always has been, expelled from school and all that. Went off to make his fortune in Canada and haven't heard from him for years. There's an Uncle called Dan, another oddball, the family seems to specialise in them. But at least he's married to a lovely woman called Betsy.' He leant closer and stage-whispered, 'She's wonderful, tends to mother me, but I quite like it if truth be known.'

'And your parents?'

'Killed in a car crash in 1932.'

'We're both orphans then.'

He poured them both a cup of tea, adding milk later.

'To afternoon tea. One of the better British institutions.' They clinked cups, joined by George with his glass of milk.

'Oh, George,' Monique exclaimed, grabbing a wet cloth from the pannier. His mouth was covered in strawberry jam, cream and a huge grin.

After she had wiped it off and George had selected another scone, they sat in silence for a few moments.

'Do you like living in England?' John asked.

She thought for a while. 'Yes, I think so. The English are very strange sometimes…'

'What do you mean?'

'Well, the parents have little to do with their children. Mr Dodds hasn't seen George for three days now, and Madame, well, she will allow him to say good morning and kiss her goodnight. In between, she lives her own life.'

'Yes, very English of a certain class. Children are meant to be occasionally seen and not very often heard.'

'And why do you send your children away to prison when they are five years old?'

He laughed. 'Boarding school is not prison. Although, come to think of it, the one I went to was probably worse than a prison.'

'George will leave in two years' time, poor boy.' She ruffled his hair and was rewarded with a huge, cream-covered smile. 'I do not understand. Children are there to be loved and cherished, not sent away. Were you sent away too?'

'At five, it's supposed to be character building.'

'Poor boys…' She ruffled George's hair again.

They spent the next two hours talking about everything and nothing, until Monique noticed the time on John's wristwatch. 'I must be going. We'll be late for George's supper.'

They both looked across at the young boy. Half-chewed sandwiches, bits of cake, dollops of cream and bitten scones lay on his plate.

'I have a feeling he's not that hungry,' said John.

They both laughed. 'We should be going back anyway.' She stood up and busied about George, wiping his mouth and removing splodges of strawberry jam from his shirt.

'Let me walk you home, at least.'

'No, you shouldn't. It's out of your way.'

She lifted George gently out of his seat and placed him in his pushchair, where he immediately yawned twice, took hold of his rabbit and curled up to sleep.

John took the hat off the table and put it carefully over his legs. 'At least let me see you again.'

She stared at him for a moment, before smiling. 'That would be nice, yes.'

Then she began to push George away to their home.

'When?' shouted John.

'When what?'

'When can I see you again?'

'On my day off. A week on Sunday. I must go now.'

'Here, a week on Sunday at eleven a.m. D'accord?'

'Later, at noon. I have mass in the morning.'

'Noon, then.'

'D'accord.'

She hurried away, the wheels of the pushchair bouncing over the grass and George snoring gently, holding tightly on to his rabbit.

She didn't hear John's whispered words as she walked away.

'You'll do, Monique Massat, you'll do.'

Chapter Nine

Saturday, November 26, 1938
Kensington Registry Office, London

They were married in the elegant rooms of Kensington Registry Office on a cold, blustery Saturday six months later.

George was in attendance, wearing his best sailor's uniform and his RAF peaked cap. Mr and Mrs Dodds both came, Madame complaining loudly that they were losing the best nanny they ever had and she would never be able to find another. While Mr Dodds kept glancing at the fob watch hanging from a chain on his waistcoat.

There were no relatives from France in attendance, while the only people that came from the Sinclair family were John's Aunt Betsy and Uncle Dan.

His auntie was a large, florid woman wearing the biggest hat Monique had ever seen. Her husband, on the other hand, was quiet and taciturn, blending into the background behind his wife's exuberant personality.

'Now, you come here and give me a big hug, John Sinclair,' she announced on her arrival at the Registry Office.

John and his uniform were immediately swallowed up in an immense bear hug. He managed to emit a grateful, 'Thanks for coming, Aunt Betsy.'

'Wouldn't have missed it for the world – my favourite nephew getting married, and to a French girl, too. Who would have thought it?'

Monique held out her hand.

'Will you give over with that? Aren't we relatives now, too?' And she too was swallowed up by the arms of Aunt Betsy.

The best man was one of John's RAF colleagues at the Ministry, David Strachan. Four other officers attended, each in their best blue-grey uniforms. They formed a guard of honour with their raised swords as the now-married couple exited the wooden doors of Kensington Registry Office. The bride wore a simple white dress and matching silk veil bought from Madame Desmarchais in Covent Garden, while John Sinclair was resplendent in his best dress uniform, complete with ceremonial sword.

The ring which John placed on her finger had been chosen by both of them from Hancock's on Bond Street. The matching old gold bands were incised on the inside with the initials J and M surrounded by a heart.

As the pictures were being taken and confetti being liberally thrown over their heads, he leant forward and whispered in her ear: 'You've made me the happiest man alive.'

She smiled back at him, staring up into his eyes as the photographer called for one more shot to be taken with the newly weds.

Afterwards, they retired to 'The French' in Soho, where Victor Berlement and his son, Gaston, welcomed them with open arms and buffalo-horned moustaches.

'A wedding, it should be gay but not too gay,' pronounced Victor as he led them upstairs to the Dining Room. 'Loving but not too loving – this is a marriage, after all. But more than anything, it should be for fun, friends and feasting.'

A feast certainly awaited them; oysters to start, pâté de campagne, French onion soup, sole meunière, coq au vin and a sticky toffee pudding drowning in hot custard. The latter was a special request from John, which Victor, after some grumbling, finally agreed to serve. The wines matched each course; a champagne from Frezier in Monthelon, a chilled Sancerre, followed by Pinot Noir, and Claret, finally ending with a special bottle of Château d'Yquem 1929 as the wedding cake was cut.

George tried on all the officers' peaked caps, while even Mr Dodds stopped looking at his watch after the second glass of champagne.

Betsy, on the other hand, took two glasses, downing both as if they were going out of fashion. Her husband sat quietly in the corner, never saying a word.

The Best Man's speech was delivered by David Strachan, alternating in both French and English. David spoke French with a strong Midi accent, having grown up in Aix-la-Provence with his French mother. 'My lords, ladies, brother officers and George...'

The child looked up for a moment as his name was called, before continuing to play with the caps. 'It is an honour to be asked to speak at the wedding of John and Monique. It doesn't happen very often, and let's hope for both their sakes that it is the only time I have to do it. I've known John since we were at school together. He was always insufferably good at what he did; a first in Latin, school blue in rugby and cricket, and when we both went to Cranwell he, of course, came top of his class whilst I continued my excellent tradition of unparalleled mediocrity.'

He paused for a moment as laughter shook the room. 'Even in love, it seems John will upstage me.

How he managed to win the hand of the beautiful Monique with ears like those amazes me. In Cranwell, they were known as "his wings", and we often wondered whether his success as a pilot was a function of their ability to give him extra lift.'

The officers clapped as the waiters served the Château d'Yquem with a reverence that was peculiarly French.

'Monique, on the other hand, lights up every room she graces, and even with the dark clouds now gathering over Europe, she brings a brilliance to any day and any occasion.'

'Hear, hear!' The officers banged the tables.

'And her ears? Well, they are French, that's all I am permitted to say in mixed company.'

Laughter around the table.

'Now, a few words just for the both of you. I hope you always remember that love isn't perfect. It isn't a fairy tale or a story book, and it often doesn't come easy. But you two seem to be the exception.'

More 'hear, hears' from the officers.

'Love is like flying. It's overcoming obstacles, facing challenges, holding on and never letting go. It is soaring high into a blue, blue sky and reaching for the stars… together. Love is a short word, easy to spell and difficult to define. It's being as one, loving each other, and realising that every minute of every hour of every day, the flight is worth it, because you both did it… together.'

He paused for a moment. 'Ladies, gentlemen, brother officers and George, I ask you to raise your glasses and drink to the good health and lifelong happiness of our loving, and lovely, couple: Monique and John. May they always reach for the stars.'

Everybody stood up and joined in the toast. 'To Monique and John.' Even George forgot his peaked caps for a second and raised his glass of milk skywards.

And then, after a lot more wine, more conversation and extra helpings of sticky toffee pudding, people gradually began to depart. First the officers went back to their base at Tangmere. Aunt Betsy and her silent husband were next.

'Now, you are to come to stay with us in Hereford,' she said. 'We have a big old house with plenty of rooms and even more apple trees. John loves his cider, he does.' She pulled her nephew's cheek as if he were a three-year-old.

'I'd love to,' said Monique, 'but I think we have to get settled in London first.'

'And bring young George with you. There's plenty of space for him to run around, and the air is a sight cleaner than here in London.'

'We will come and stay, I promise.' Monique held out her hand, only to be wrapped up in a final bear hug.

The last to leave were the Dodds, he to his office and Madame to lie down. 'I have such a headache. It's the champagne, you know, I love the bubbles but they give me the most awful migraines.'

Monique's friends from church, and David Strachan, stayed to wish the happy couple 'Bon Voyage' as they poured themselves into a taxi for the short trip to Victoria station. Here, they would catch the train to Brighton to spend the first night of their new marriage in the luxurious embrace of each other, and the Grand Hotel.

Once more, as the taxi pulled away from The French with Victor Berlement, his staff and the remaining guests waving goodbye, John reached over to hold Monique, whispering in her ear, 'I wish this moment would last for ever.'

'Moi aussi,' she whispered back, holding him close.

But a strange sense of unquiet filled her soul. This should have been the happiest day of her life, yet somehow, she was filled with fear. What was wrong with her?

Chapter Ten

Tuesday, December 26, 2017 – Boxing Day
Didsbury, Manchester

The next morning's dawn revealed a beautifully clear, eggshell-blue sky with just a few lazy clouds slowly meandering from west to east. Boxing Day at its beautiful best.

When Jayne awoke the sun was streaming through the curtains, Mr Smith was stretching himself on her bed and she felt a thousand times better than she did the night before.

Somehow, as often happens, she had reached a decision during her sleep. Her subconscious had decided a course of action for her.

She was going to see her father. Whatever he had done in the past, whatever hurt she felt from his abandonment of her as a young girl, was over. Robert and Vera were right. This was the one chance to find out about her family and to lay to rest the demons that had been haunting her for so long. Questions she had answered for her clients but had avoided asking about herself.

Who was she?
Where did she come from?
What was her family history?

She leapt out of bed, startling the cat. 'Come on, , no more lazing around, we have work to do.'

Downstairs in the kitchen, she fed the perpetually hungry Mr Smith. While the computer booted up, she put a Ristretto pod in her Nespresso machine, smelling the delicious aroma of freshly brewed coffee as it filled the kitchen. She always preferred the taste of a freshly ground espresso served from some ancient machine in a lively Roman café, but as she was living in a sleepy suburb of Manchester, she had to make do with Nespresso.

Before she started work, she opened the patio doors. It was one of those winter mornings when the world was fresh and beautiful; the sky was a bright cerulean blue, a dusting of frost rimed the square foot of grass she laughingly called a lawn, a red-breasted robin was hopping from branch to branch in search of food, and the air had a wonderful tang of winter.

Mr Smith joined her for a second, twitched his whiskers and then ran for his favourite place to sleep post-breakfast; beneath the sunlit window in the hall.

A shiver went through her body and she closed the patio doors. Perhaps she would go for a long walk this afternoon to clear the cobwebs from her mind and then visit Robert afterwards.

Meanwhile, work called. Time to research her family. And the best place to start was with herself.

As the computer was clicking and whirring itself awake, she thought for a moment. Do you really want to do this, Jayne? You could be opening a Pandora's box, which would be impossible to close.

She sat in front of the computer screen for a good five minutes before finally opening the FreeBMD website and typing her own name and birth year in the search box.

How strange this is, she thought. At least now you know how your clients feel when they commission you to do research: the wonderful excitement of discovering something new combined with the awful fear that the discovery might not be what you want to hear.

She pressed 'search' and waited for the results. They came back almost immediately.

Quarter	Name	Mother's Name	Reg Dist	Vol	Page
1973 Jun	Jayne Sinclair	Harrison	Barton	8e	456

Herself. A babe in arms.

Even though she had checked so many other birth records, seeing her own on the screen sent a shockwave through her.

Here she was, here she would always be.

Written down in some ledger so long ago. When, perhaps, her mother and father had loved each other.

For the first time in a long time, Jayne felt tears forming in her eyes.

So long ago, yet so near.

For a second, she thought about turning off the computer, abandoning the search, forgetting all about the research into her own family history.

Then the professional in her kicked in. She had to find out the complete truth. After all, wasn't that what her job was about; finding the secrets hidden in the past? The secrets that couldn't be revealed in any other way except by diligent and painstaking research?

She couldn't postpone it any longer, not now.

Deciding to concentrate on her father's line first, she entered the search parameters for the birth date her father had given in his letter. She remembered it clearly because it was the day war broke out in 1939.

She would save her mother's genealogical history and that of the Harrison family for the future.

As the records were arranged quarterly, she entered the correct year and his surname.

Birth. Sinclair. 1939.

Her right index finger hesitated for a second over the return key.
She took a deep breath and hit 'enter'.

Chapter Eleven

Tuesday, December 26, 2017 – Boxing Day
Didsbury, Manchester

The machined whirred for a second before displaying the result.

138 matches.

'I didn't know there were that many Sinclairs out there. Time to narrow it down,' she said out loud. The cat interrupted licking his paws for a second to stare at her. Then returning to the far more useful and enjoyable task of staying clean.

Jayne added her father's Christian name.

```
Quarter      Name            Mother's Name  Reg Dist    Vol/Page No.

1939 Mar    Sinclair Martin   Blackman       Portsmouth   3a 418
1939 Mar    Sinclair Martin   Moss           Sunderland   1c 100
1939 Mar    Sinclair Martin   Stocker        Bolton       3a 237

1939 Jun    Sinclair Martin   Burgess        Bethnal      3a 1214
1939 Jun    Sinclair Martin   Michel         Manchester   3a 923

1939 Sep    Sinclair Martin   Fryer          Edmonton     3a 444
1939 Sep    Sinclair Martin   Baker          Brighton     3b 326
1939 Sep    Sinclair Martin   Treadle        Plymouth     3b 234
1939 Sep    Sinclair Martin   Kerfoot        Chester      3a 237

1939 Dec    Sinclair Martin   Brian          Bradford     3a 121
1939 Dec    Sinclair Martin   Massat         Kensington   2a 928
1939 Dec    Sinclair Martin   MacLeish       Hull         3a 444
```

The letter stated her father had been born in London. Was that correct? If it was, he was the eleventh name on the list. There were only two other Martin Sinclairs born in that last quarter of 1939 – one in Bradford and the other in Hull. She was pretty certain this was him. Martin wasn't a very common Christian name, and the surname was spelt correctly.

Then she stopped. For a second she stared at the results before realising she now had her grandmother's surname. If he was the second name in that quarter, registered in Kensington, then her grandmother had the surname of Massat.

Was that French? Was her grandmother French? Or was it something else? Spanish or Italian, perhaps. Whatever it was, it wasn't common, which would help her considerably.

With the excitement building up in her, she went back to FreeBMD, selected marriages instead of births, and added wider time parameters of 1930 to 1939. They could have been married earlier, but she reckoned that, like many children in the 1930s, her father would have been born fairly early in the marriage.

Finally, she typed the surname 'Massat' into the correct box.

She crossed her fingers and pressed 'enter'.

One result came back.

Quarter	Surname	First Name	Spouse	Reg Dist	Vol/Page No.
1938 Dec	Sinclair	John	Massat	Kensington	3a 1066

'Yes,' she shouted.

One result and it was the correct one. A Massat had married a John Sinclair in the period from October to December 1938, with the marriage being registered at Kensington Registry Office: the same area where her father's birth was registered later on. One more piece of proof that she was on the right track.

The winter, not the most romantic time for a wedding. Did they love each other or was it a marriage of convenience? And judging by the dates, she must have become pregnant quite quickly.

Jayne immediately went to the General Register Office website and ordered certificates for her father's birth and her grandparents' wedding, paying £23.40 each for the priority service. She didn't know when the Register Office went back to work after the Christmas break, but at least the certificates would arrive quickly.

For a second, she considered continuing her search by looking for the great-grandparents. But without their Christian names, it would be like searching for a needle in a haystack. She thought about checking up on her grandfather's birth, but Sinclair and John were both common family names from the period, and without knowing exactly how old he was when he got married, she could be searching from 1880 to 1920 and still not be certain to find him.

Was it time for a cup of tea?

10.35 a.m.

Definitely. An early elevenses with a couple of squares of good energy from chocolate would be perfect.

The block of Chuao from Venezuela was still in the fridge, so she took it out to warm up slightly before making her tea. Nothing fancy for her this time, just a couple of PG Tips bags in the pot and some very hot water. It wasn't one of those subtle times of the day at all.

As she sat, nibbling her chocolate and drinking her tea, an idea came to her. She knew her grandparents were living in London in 1938. Had they remained there or moved away?

She logged on to Ancestry.com and went to the 1939 England and Wales Register. This was a census of the population that was initially taken with the onset of war, to help the government produce National Identity Cards. It was later used as an aid in the issue of ration books, and from 1948 as the basis for the National Health Service Register. It was the only available governmental resource for the period, as the 1931 Census was destroyed in the Second World War and no census was carried out in 1941 due to the ongoing conflict. The enumerators had collected the data on September 29, 1939, so her father should have been registered.

She typed in the surname 'John Sinclair' and narrowed the field to London. It was a long shot, as evacuations from the city started a couple of days before war was declared in September 1939 and continued through the month. She pressed 'search' and waited.

87 results.

She scanned the names, but it was no use. There was no other occupant of the same address with the name Massat. It wasn't surprising, her grandmother had probably adopted John's surname after their marriage. Even if she hadn't, the 100 year rule applied to this register. If the people were born after 1918, their names would be blacked out, unless the government were officially notified by a relative that they had passed away.

She removed the London search filter.

7246 results.

That meant there were over 7000 households with at least one Sinclair living under their roof. It would be an impossible task to search all of them.

She scratched her head, looking at Mr Smith as he scratched his own.

There was nothing to do until the birth and wedding certificates arrived with more information. She drained her tea and had one more square of chocolate.

And then it hit her. There was one thing she could do right now. Something she had avoided doing since her mother had died six years ago.

It was time to look in the suitcase on top of the wardrobe. What secrets were hidden within?

Chapter Twelve

Friday, December 09, 1938
Flat 2, Albany St, London

The first six months of marriage were adorable. Mrs Dodds had been amazing and found them a lovely two-bedroom flat in Albany Street, just around the corner from Regent's Park.

'I'm afraid it's not much,' Mrs Dodds said as she opened the door. 'It's my cousin's. He only uses it as a pied-à-terre when he comes back from India.'

They both walked inside and fell in love immediately. The ceilings were high, the space light and airy, it was close to the tube and it was going to be their first house. Together.

'It's perfect,' cried Monique, turning around to give Mrs Dodds a big hug.

'If you like it, I'm sure he won't mind you staying here for a while. He won't be back on leave for two years. You'll have to be careful of his things, though.' She stared at a gilded, metal statue of Shiva on a mahogany side table. 'Clarence is awfully particular about his things.'

'Do not worry, Mrs Dodds, we'll look after everything for him, won't we, John?'

John simply smiled, glad to see his wife so happy.

'Well, that's agreed. Part of the contract is for you to continue taking George out twice a week, on Tuesdays and Thursdays. The new girl wants those afternoons off to go to college. What she's going to do with an education I shall never hope to discover.'

'I'll look forward to taking care of George, he's such a wonderful child.'

'He's a boy. I can't be dealing with boys myself, messy creatures. He'll be off to school next year, so it won't be for long. When do you want to move in?'

'Tomorrow,' they both said at the same time.

'Right-oh, I'll tell the concierge.'

They moved in the following day and immediately settled into the routine of a newly married couple. John went off each morning to his job at the Air Ministry in Berkeley Square, while Monique read the papers, went on long walks in the park, or simply listened to the radio. In the evenings, they went to see shows at the Palladium, plays at any of the theatres in Drury Lane, and ate in a Lyons or, for a special occasion, at Wiltons.

They also bought a portable HMV gramophone in the deepest, deepest blue. When they didn't go out, Monique enjoyed nothing more than listening to the operas of Mozart or Verdi, sung by Caruso or Gigli. John, on the other hand, preferred the more modern recordings of Django Reinhardt.

Occasionally, Monique attempted to cook, but her oeufs en cocotte looked like pebbles one might find on a beach, whilst her coq au vin definitely had more of the taste of wine than chicken.

'I'll just drink my dinner tonight,' said John, smiling as Monique pouted.

'When my mother made this dish, it was so good. For me, it is too bad.'

Twice a week, she went back to Morpeth Terrace to take George out to the park or to the cinema. He had recently fallen in love with the afternoon matinees at the Gaumont, loving the antics of George Formby.

Then life changed one night in February 1939. It was just one month into the New Year and John had been working late most evenings at the Ministry.

Outside, the wind was howling and sleet swept over the park, angled across the street, beating against their window. John arrived home, closing the door as quickly as he could behind him before the wind blew in.

Monique sat in a darkened room, lit only by the soft orange glow of the fire.

John threw off his coat and rushed over to kneel in front of her.

She was crying.

'What is it, Monie? What's wrong?'

She wiped her eyes, smearing her make-up. 'I have news,' she whispered.

'What? What can be so bad?'

'I'm pregnant.'

John laughed. 'Is that it? That's wonderful! We are going to be parents?'

She nodded. 'I thought you'd be upset. Our lives will change, and the world is so unhappy at the moment.'

'Upset? I'm so happy. We should go out and celebrate, drink champagne at The French.'

'You're really happy?'

He took her hands and wrapped them in his immense grip, looked into her eyes and said, 'It's what I've always wanted, my own family with you.'

She put her arms round his neck and kissed him deeply, finally saying, 'Let's not go out tonight. Let's just stay at home, the two of us.'

Chapter Thirteen

Sunday, September 03, 1939
Flat 2, Albany St, London

She was sitting at home listening to Mr Chamberlain on the radio when the first contraction came.

It was 11.15 on a Sunday morning and bright sunlight was shining through the sash windows of her apartment. She hadn't seen much of John over the last few days. Even with the impending birth of their child, he had been forced to spend more and more time at the Air Ministry, even at the weekends.

She would always remember the words coming from the radio's speaker as if they were engraved on her heart.

'I am speaking to you from the Cabinet Room of Ten Downing Street. This morning the British Ambassador in Berlin handed the German Government a final note stating that, unless we heard from them by eleven o'clock that they were prepared at once to withdraw their troops from Poland, a state of war would exist between us. I have to tell you now that no such undertaking has been received, and that consequently this country is at war with Germany.'

She clasped her stomach and sat down at the kitchen table, taking deep breaths. The next contraction came as he was finishing the speech.

'The government have made plans under which it will be possible to carry on the work of the nation in the days of stress and strain that may be ahead. But these plans need your help. You may be taking your part in the fighting services or as a volunteer in one of the branches of Civil Defence. If so, you will report for duty in accordance with the instructions you have received. You may be engaged in work essential to the prosecution of war for the maintenance of the life of the people - in factories, in transport, in public utility concerns, or in the supply of other necessaries of life. If so, it is of vital importance that you should carry on with your jobs.'

She got up and waddled to the armchair in the sitting room where John usually sat to read his paper. A searing pain shot through her stomach as she fell into the chair.

Chamberlain was still speaking.

'Now, may God bless you all. May He defend the right. It is the evil things that we shall be fighting against - brute force, bad faith, injustice, oppression and persecution - and against them I am certain that the right will prevail.'

Martial music replaced the normal light tunes of the Jack Hylton Band. She sat back in the armchair and closed her eyes. The pains had subsided now and she no longer needed to gasp for breath.

Twenty minutes later, another stab of pain shot through her body.

She clumsily hauled herself up out of the chair. 'What I need is tea,' she said out loud, 'a nice hot cuppa.' Despite her French upbringing, she had succumbed to the British belief in the universal healing qualities of warm, milky tea. Even worse, she now preferred it to coffee.

She waddled back to the kitchen and filled the kettle when it felt as if her stomach was suddenly clamped in a vice. Her legs shook and a pool of liquid appeared at her feet.

Outside, the first air-raid warning wailed across Regent's Park.

'Not now. Time to get moving,' she said out loud. She wished John was here to help her, but he wasn't. She hobbled to the telephone, stopping for a moment as another contraction clamped her stomach.

Luckily they had prepared for such a situation; her bag with a clean nightie and her toiletries was packed and waiting. A telephone had been put in the flat six months ago on the orders of the Air Ministry, in case John was ever needed urgently. She had hated the big, black Bakelite monster at first, but today she recognised it as a friend in her hour of need.

She searched for the midwife's number. 'Where the hell is it?' She scrambled through the papers next to the phone before eventually finding the right one. She dialled the number, waiting impatiently as the rotary dial wound its way slowly back.

The phone on the other end rang and rang.

No answer.

Panicked, she scrambled through the papers once more, looking for the hospital's number. Another stab of pain convulsed her body. What was she supposed to do now? Time the contractions, that was it. She checked the clock on the mantelpiece as another contraction tightened across her stomach like a boa constrictor.

Only 90 seconds had passed between the pains.

'Too quick. It shouldn't be that quick. What should I do?'

She bent over the table. Should she go downstairs to Arthur Green, their neighbour? But he would already be at work. Should she ring John at the Ministry? Where was the number? The papers were all over the floor and she couldn't bend down to search through them again.

Another contraction gripped her.

She breathed in and out slowly.

Call 999, that was it. That's what John said to do if there was ever trouble.

She picked up the receiver and heard the dial tone. Slowly, she dialled the number. A male operator answered immediately.

'Nine-nine-nine, what service do you require?'

A nice voice. A calm voice.

'Hospital. I'm having a baby.'

'Then you will need the ambulance service, madam. Just a moment, I'm putting you through now.

A few seconds of silence.

'Ambulance service. What's the nature of your emergency?'

A female voice this time, the vowels clear and cutting.

'I'm having a baby,' Monique gasped, not recognising the sound of her own voice.

'What is the timing of your contractions, madam?'

'One minute.'

'Oh, your little one is in a hurry. What is your address?'

'Flat Two, number ten, Albany Street.'

'I'm dispatching an ambulance as we speak. They should be there in five minutes to take you to Elizabeth Garrett Anderson. Do you know what to do?'

Monique found herself nodding to the phone before saying, 'Sit down and take deep breaths. Keep timing the contractions.'

'Exactly, madam.'

'But it hurts,' Monique gasped again.

'It will soon be over, Mrs…?'

'Mrs Sinclair.'

'It will soon be over, Mrs Sinclair. I've had three myself and each one was different. The second came in less than an hour. It sounds like yours is in a hurry too. Now please sit down. Remember to breathe evenly and deeply.'

'Please don't go,' Monique begged.

'I'm not going anywhere, Mrs Sinclair, but please sit down.'

Monique did as she was told.

'Good, that's better, isn't it? Now breathe deeply,' the operator said.

Monique took three deep breaths.

'Good, that's better, isn't it? Now, do I detect an accent?'

'I'm French, but my husband is English.'

'Our allies.'

Another contraction stabbed into Monique's stomach. A scream of pain erupted from her mouth.

'Remember to breathe deeply, it will help.'

Monique gritted her teeth and did as she was told. In the distance, she could hear the ringing of a bell. 'I think the ambulance is coming.'

'Should be there any second, the hospital is very close.'

The ringing became louder and louder, before stopping completely to be followed by the beat of feet on her stairs.

'I think they are here.'

'Good, I told you they would be quick.'

There was a loud banging on the door.

Monique took a deep breath and put down the phone. She stood up and immediately bent over as another pain shot through her body.

More banging on the door.

'Coming,' she whispered, hobbling to the door and slowly opening it.

A tall, thin man dressed in blue was standing outside.

'I think I'm having a baby…' was all she managed to say before the world went black and she fell into his arms.

* * *

Of course, John missed everything.

By the time he arrived at Ward 10 of Elizabeth Garrett Anderson Hospital that evening, their son Martin had already been born and was nestling in Monique's arms.

'He looks so small,' said John.

A wrinkled red face was peeking out from the hospital cover.

John used his index finger to pull the cover down and away from the baby's mouth. 'And angry. See the way he's frowning even as he sleeps?'

Monique glanced down at her baby. John was right, a large crease ran across his forehead.

'He's just dreaming,' she said.

'I know now is not the time to tell you, but they are sending me to a squadron. I'm to report to Digby the day after tomorrow to start training reservists before we send them to France.'

Monique vaguely remembered Chamberlain speaking on the radio before she passed out, his words punctuated by the pain of her contractions. 'Is it war?' she said.

'It's real this time. We're being mobilised. There are going to be more evacuations from London.'

A wave of tiredness washed over Monique.

She pushed her head back into the pillow and closed her eyes. 'What sort of world have we brought him into?' were her final words as the comfort of sleep drowned her tired body.

Chapter Fourteen

Tuesday, December 26, 2017 – Boxing Day
Didsbury, Manchester

Jayne Sinclair reached up to the small brown suitcase that she had put on top of the wardrobe in the spare room so many years ago. She pulled it down and blew off a thin film of dust that had settled on top.

On the cover was an old label with her mother's name and address written on it in bold letters. The black ink had faded to a dark brown now, but the strength of her character in the writing was still evident, her mother's presence there despite all the years since she had died.

It was more of a vanity case than a full-sized suitcase. Jayne always remembered her mother packing it if they went for short trips in the car. 'You can never be too prepared,' she announced as she carefully folded their spare clothes and underwear even though they were only driving to Blackpool to see the illuminations.

Jayne took a deep breath. What would be inside? Would she be disappointed?

Her fingers hovered over the once-silver latches. She hesitated for a moment, her heart beating faster, before pressing the lock and hearing the latches of the vanity case spring open with a loud click.

Here goes, she thought.

She lifted the lid.

Inside was a small metal tin, the kind that used to contain biscuits in the past. Next to it was a bundle of photographs of a young Jayne growing up. Had her mother done this on purpose? It was almost a document of her development, the phases of her life clearly seen in the changing clothes and hairstyles of her youth.

The innocence of her primary-school years, a succession of uniforms, sweet smiles, staring at the camera against a backdrop she remembered of the wallpaper in the living room of their home. Why had she forgotten these photos?

After the pictures of her primary-school years, there were photos from the eighties. She flicked through them all, realising in the many changes of style, a desperate search for her own identity in her teen years. She remembered these photos, her mother insisting she take them, Jayne desperate to get out from the house and away from this woman. The easy compliance of her youth had long vanished in a haze of spots, pimples and hormones.

And then a picture of her as a police cadet, her smile stating how proud she was to wear the uniform, and a defiance in Jayne's eyes.

Finally, the last shot: Jayne as a probationary constable. She remembered coming home from work that day, still in her uniform, and her mother insisting she stood there for the photograph. She was tired and exhausted after a hard shift when she had arrested some idiot for assault and battery, twisting his arm up his back and forcing his head into a brick wall. For some reason, she had enjoyed the feeling of preventing him from hitting another woman, enjoying being the instrument of revenge.

But this photograph was the last straw. She had moved out of her mother's home the next day, sharing a flat with another probationary WPC. She had said goodbye to Robert, giving him her new address, but had deliberately not given it to her mother.

There were no more photos after that, as if by moving out Jayne had finally escaped from the documentary of her life. Finally found freedom from the confines of her mother. Or was it simply that her mother lost interest in photographing her? The child had become a girl who had grown into a woman.

And sitting there in the spare bedroom, staring at these photos, Jayne wondered if she had been wrong all along. Had she seized the moment and escaped the baleful influence of her mother, as she always thought? Or had her mother released her into the wild, as one would an injured bird one had nursed back to health?

Had her mother been far cleverer, far more astute, than Jayne ever knew?

Jayne considered the possibility, weighing up the evidence in her mind.

Perhaps. But she would never know the truth and it really didn't matter. She was who she was. A delicious cocktail of DNA and millions of experiences that had created her personality, made her the person she was.

She placed the bundle of photos in their envelope on the bed. The metal tin, with its image of some foreign castle in front of a lake, was waiting for her. She lifted it up and opened the lid.

Inside, lying on top of the documents, was a single sheet of paper folded in two and bearing the words 'For Jayne' in her mother's handwriting.

She opened the letter. It was dated 10 June 2010, just one week before her mother died.

Dear Jayne,

If you are reading this little letter, it means you have finally decided to take a look at the memories I have kept all these years. You have probably decided to research your family.

I encouraged an interest in history, and in particular family history, in you, but I always cautioned Robert not to push you to look into your own family background until you were ready.

It seems the day has arrived.

This box contains a few memories - clues to who you are and where you came from. Unfortunately, there is not much, I'm afraid. Stuff gets lost, mislaid or simply vanishes or is thrown out in any one of our many moves. Besides, Robert was always better at keeping things than I was.

I've placed what I have in the metal biscuit box. There is a separate brown envelope for the Harrisons, my parents. Robert did a little research on them for me. More skeletons in the cupboard, I'm afraid.

I don't know which side you are researching, but I suspect it is improbably your father's. I guess you have already discovered the truth about him. I apologise for not telling you, but it seemed to be the best way at the time. I hope you can forgive me my white lies. It was for your own good – and mine, of course, I will not deny that. He had abandoned us and so, for me and for us, the best idea was to forget him.

I should never have married him in the first place. There was a morass of madness there, a great well of loneliness, but perhaps that was what attracted me in the first place.

After all, what is more attractive than a love you can never have? Goodbye, Jayne. If you are reading this, then I will have certainly died by now. I did love you very much, but I was never very good at showing it.

Your mother, Marjorie

Jayne put down the letter, a film of tears clouding her vision. The voice of her mother had returned to her as she read, speaking to her in that way she always did; slowly, enunciating every word, like a teacher educating a particularly stupid pupil.

But the words in the letter had a softer tone than usual. A tone of regret rather than anger.

Had Jayne misjudged her mother?

She reached into the box and pulled out the first document. It was her birth certificate. The last time she had seen this was when she'd applied for her first passport. There had been a school trip to Switzerland when she was fifteen, and on it she had met Johann, her first love, the son of her skiing instructor. Of course, nothing happened between them other than holding hands and snogging in the snow-heavy shadow of a chalet. But it was the beginning of her rebellion against the strict confines of her mother's rules.

She remembered coming home from the school trip, running up to the bathroom, closing the door and crying a flood of tears. Tears of unhappiness at returning home. Robert knew and understood, of course. Her mother remained oblivious.

Jayne stared at her own birth certificate.

CERTIFIED COPY OF AN ENTRY

BIRTH

```
Registration Distict:   Barton
Administrative Area :   Metropolitan Borough
                        of Trafford
Date/Place of Birth :   April 13, 1973.
                        Stretford Memorial
                        Hospital
```

```
Name and Surname   : Jayne Monique
                     Sinclair
Sex                : Female
Father's name      : Martin Sinclair
Place of Birth     : London
Occupation         : Businessman
Mother's name      : Marjorie Harrison
Place of Birth     : Manchester
Occupation         : Student
Usual Address      : 23 Tone Avenue, Sale
Informant          : Mother
```

Her father's occupation was given as 'businessman'. But what did he actually do? She realised she knew so little about him.

She reached for the second piece of paper. It was her parents' marriage certificate.

CERTIFIED COPY OF AN ENTRY OF MARRIAGE

Registration District: Manchester

Marriage Solemnised at Manchester Registry Office, Town Hall, Manchester.

```
Date    Name/Surname        Age   Prof.     Father's name    Prof.

Oct 6   Martin Sinclair     33    Business  John Sinclair    RAF Pilot
1972    Marjorie Harrison   22    Student   Sean Harrison    Teacher
```

So, they were married in Manchester Registry Office on October 6, 1972. Her father's occupation was again given as 'businessman'. So vague. But her mother was listed as a student.

What had she been studying?

Her mother never mentioned anything about being a student. She had worked her whole life in the same insurance office in the centre of Manchester, travelling in each day on the same bus at the same time.

And then Jayne noticed the date.

If they were married in October 1972 and Jayne was born in April 1973, it must have been a shotgun wedding. Jayne's mother was already pregnant with her when she walked up the aisle of the registry office. Did Martin want to get married, or did he feel obliged to because Marjorie was pregnant?

Her question was answered by the next sheet of paper in the box. It was folded in two, and inside was a photograph of a couple in front of the doors of a Registry Office.

Her mother and father.

The black-and-white shot wasn't posed at all, but taken in the moment. Her mother had her head thrown back laughing. She was wearing a short white dress and carrying a bouquet of flowers. The man next to her had his arm around her shoulders. His white suit was immaculately tailored, with huge lapels. The black shirt beneath the suit had a long pointed collar that reached out over the lapels like crow's wings. The man's hair was dark and long, well over his collar, and his thick sideburns extended down to the angle of his chin.

This was her father. It was the first picture of him she had ever seen.

Jayne felt a strange feeling of nausea wash over her. How could she have been so blind as to ignore the fact that he existed? Why had she believed her mother's stories? Or had her anger at him for leaving the family when she was young been so strong, she had avoided dealing with the issue?

Now here she was, staring at his face.

A happy face, looking into the eyes of the woman beside him. A woman he obviously loved. What had happened between them?

Jayne looked in the tin, just two bundles remained.

She picked up the first. A small, hand-made parcel created from pink crepe paper wrapped with a pink raffia tie. She undid the bow and unfolded the paper. Inside was a single gold band.

Was this her mother's wedding ring?

The gold looked brand new as if it had never been worn. She carefully picked up the band. It glinted in the light from the window and, as she tilted it, she could see inscribed on the inside the initials J and M inside a heart.

Was this her mother's initial but then who was the J? Her father's name was Martin and she couldn't ever remember her mother mentioning a different name. On the marriage certificate he was called Martin Sinclair, no middle name or initial.

Frowning, Jayne placed the ring back in the pink crepe paper, wrapping it up loosely. She took out the last bundle in the tin. Again, it was wrapped in a single sheet of writing paper. She opened it up to find a bundle of yellowing cards.

The first one was shop-bought and had on the cover a simple verse:

On this very special date
Happiness comes to those who wait,
Now you are four,
You can open the door.

The illustration had a child opening a door to reveal a stack of balloons and presents. Inside was a short message.

To Jayne, may you enjoy a wonderful fourth birthday.
April 13, 1977.

Martin

Not 'Dad', or 'Father' – just Martin, as if he were her uncle or something. A relative, remote but friendly.
Not a father.
Definitely not *her* father.
All these years thinking he was dead, believing the story told by her mother. All these years he had been sending her a birthday card every year. All these years, she never knew he existed.
Did he know that she had been told he was dead?
Obviously not, if he had been sending her a birthday card every year. Why had her mother hidden them all from her? Why had she told her he was dead?
All through her primary years her mother had thrown birthday parties for Jayne and her school friends, but she had never given her a card from her father.
She reached for the next one the pile. This was for her fifth birthday and inside was another short message.

To Jayne on her fifth birthday,
I hope you have a wonderful day.
April 13, 1978.

Martin

And then it struck her. The cards started to arrive after her mother had married her step-father Robert. Had her biological father been coming to her birthdays before then?

She struggled to remember, but nothing came. Did he start sending her cards because he wasn't allowed to come to see her in person? Was that what had happened?

She quickly scanned the next two cards. Each one was shop-bought and signed on the inside with his name and a message.

He had remembered her birthday. Every year, he had remembered.

The next card looked different. It was hand-drawn and coloured with a huge number 8 in the centre which had been obviously cut from coloured paper and pasted onto the card.

The message inside was far more personal than the others.

Sorry, I can't buy you a card for your 8th Birthday so I've made one instead. I hope you like it and have a great day.

April 13 1981.

Martin

There were more handmade cards after that, each one different and each one celebrating the year of her birthday. Inside, there was always a handwritten personal message for her.

The last card in the pile was marked for her 18th birthday. Inside it simply said:

To my daughter Jayne, who is now a woman.

April 13, 1991.

Martin

There were no more cards.

Jayne's eyes filled with tears as she let the last card slowly tumble back into the suitcase.

Chapter Fifteen

Tuesday, December 26, 2017 – Boxing Day
Didsbury, Manchester

Jayne didn't know how long she stayed upstairs, sitting on the bed. The sun was already begging to drift down below the houses at the rear when she roused herself. Carefully, she packed away all the documents left by her mother into the suitcase and placed it back where it belonged on top of the wardrobe.

The envelope containing the details of her mother's side of the family, the Harrisons, lay untouched beside her. That could wait until later. Something had made her mother the way she was and, at the moment, Jayne was loath to discover what it was. She decided she couldn't face more family secrets right now; she had more than enough to handle as it was.

As she made her way slowly downstairs, Mr Smith pounced. She bent down to rub his ears. 'I know, I know, you're hungry and you want to go out. Which is it to be first?'

Understanding her words, he slinked over to his bowl and smelt it as if to say, 'It's empty, woman.'

'Okay, okay.' She opened the fridge door, pulling out one of his gourmet pouches. After the cat had been fed, she made herself a cup of warm milky tea.

'Looks like you can't put it off any more, you're going to have to do it, Jayne,' she said out loud.

Mr Smith looked up for a moment, thinking she was talking to him. When he realised she wasn't, he lapped some water, stretched his back legs and ambled over to the patio doors.

'I get the message. But it's cold outside, are you sure you want to go out?'

He looked at her, then back at the glass door.

'Okay, don't blame me if you freeze to death.' Jayne opened the door and a blast of cold air whistled into the house. 'Off you go then.'

In a repetition of the previous evening, Mr Smith stood for a moment at the open door, his whiskers twitching, then he turned and raced back to his favourite place on the window ledge in the hall.

'Scaredy cat,' she shouted after him.

Then, realising how ridiculous she sounded talking to a cat, she sat down in front of her computer and booted it up.

While it whirred and buzzed, she checked the address of her father's prison, HMP Belmarsh near London.

She had been to prisons before to interview witnesses or suspects, but generally they had been in the north; the aptly named Strangeways in Manchester, Wakefield in Yorkshire and Thorn Cross near Warrington. According to its website, Belmarsh was a high-security prison, with strict visiting rules. Why was her father being kept in a high-security prison after all these years? Surely he should have been in an open prison, at least?

She clicked the online booking system for visitors. She began to complete the form, realising that although she had his name and birth date, she didn't have the details of his prison number.

Luckily, the government website gave her an out; in case of a problem, she was to ring the prison directly and speak to someone from the Prison Advice and Care Trust, the charity who ran the visitor services.

She rang the number, hoping somebody would be there even though it was Boxing Day. The phone was answered on the third ring by a calm, mature male voice.

'HMP Belmarsh, Ronald speaking, how can I help?'

For a moment, Jayne was silent, unable to think of what to say.

'Ronald speaking, how can I help?' the man repeated.

'I'd like to visit my father but I don't know his prison number.' She stumbled over the words 'my father'.

'No problem. What's his name and date of birth?'

'Martin Sinclair, and his date of birth is September third, 1939.'

'The day war was declared,' said the man on the other end of the phone.

'Yes, I suppose it is. Not a great day for anybody to be born.' Jayne immediately regretted her words.

The man on the other end of the phone carried on speaking. 'Okay, he's in House Block One, which means the earliest you can visit is tomorrow between two-fifteen and four-fifteen in the afternoon. As you are his daughter, I can book a time for you. Do you have any proof of your relationship?'

Jayne thought for a moment. 'My birth certificate lists his name. Will that do?'

'Perfect. Please bring it with you and remember to bring one other form of ID with a photo, such as a passport or a driving licence, plus a utility bill to prove your address.'

'Security is so strict?'

'This is a high-security prison, I'm afraid. If he were anywhere else it would be easier, but Belmarsh prides itself on the protection it offers staff, prisoners and visitors. So, unfortunately, you will also be photographed and fingerprinted. This information will make subsequent visits easier. There's also an extensive list of rules and regulations covering prison visits.' The man's voice had become monotonous now. He had obviously used these words many times in the past. 'I've booked you in for two-thirty, I hope that's okay? You'll receive confirmation once the inmate has approved the visit.'

'So my father will know I'm coming?'

'Of course, he has to agree first. Some prisoners do not want to see members of their family. Anything else?'

'I don't think so.'

'It's all on the website, and please do check the rules and regulations. We wouldn't want you to be turned away by the prison staff.'

Jayne switched off her mobile.

She had done it.

She was finally going to see her father. A man she had not seen since he walked out on the family in 1977, just before she was four years old.

A shiver went down her spine.

'Pull yourself together, Jayne,' she said out loud.

Chapter Sixteen

Tuesday, December 26, 2017 – Boxing Day
Macclesfield General Hospital, Cheshire

It was already dark when Jayne reached the hospital. Robert was sitting up in bed, a rosy glow on his cheeks and a broad smile on his face.

'They say I can leave tomorrow, lass.'

'So quick? I thought they'd keep you in longer for observation.'

'I think they need the bed,' said Vera, holding his hand, 'and with the Matron at the Home being a trained nurse, the doctor thinks Robert is well enough to go back there as long as he spends a week or so taking it easy.' She glanced across at him, obviously making sure he understood.

'Don't worry, Vera, all I want to do is sleep and do the crossword.'

'That's great news, Robert.'

'And you, lass, what have you decided to do?'

Jayne took a deep breath. 'I'm going to see my… Martin Sinclair tomorrow.' Again she hesitated before saying the words 'my father'.

'So quick?' said Vera.

Jayne nodded.

Robert clapped his hands. 'That's my girl. Once she makes a decision, nothing holds her back.'

'You're not upset?'

'Of course not, lass, I think it's the right thing to do. You need to find out the truth about your own family, you can't ignore it any more.' He held out his hand and Vera placed a folder in it. 'I asked Vera to go online last night and print out some newspaper reports on his case. They don't say much, but at least it's a start.'

He handed the file to her. Jayne opened it and began reading. The first printout was dated May 4, 1979.

The headline on the front page loudly proclaimed, Maggie's made it, with a subheading below: Now for No 10… it's wonderful.

Jayne looked up. 'The election of 1979? What's it got to do with the election?'

'Not that, lass, the sidebar…'

Jayne read out the headline of a small article at the side. 'Civil servant shot dead on doorstep. Man held.' She turned over the printout and found another beneath it, with the continuation of the story on page seven.

MAN CHARGED WITH MURDER

Martin Sinclair of Withington, Manchester, was last night charged with the murder of David Strachan, aged 66, a retired civil servant living at 25 Peacock Street, Lymm.

At 4 o'clock on the eve of the election of May 3, Mr Strachan opened his door to find Sinclair standing outside with an old ex-German Army Luger. Sinclair fired three shots into the retired civil servant before calmly sitting down on the doorstep next to the dead body of his victim.

Armed police were called to the scene, but Sinclair put up no resistance as he was arrested, and was taken to Warrington Police Station where he was later charged with murder.

'This was a heinous crime, committed in broad daylight with no apparent motive or reason,' said Detective Chief Inspector Harold Morris of the Cheshire Constabulary.

'This is just another example of the breakdown in law and order over the past years as the Labour government has struggled to contain the crimewave. It has become one of the major issues at the election.'

'This was my father?' asked Jayne.

Robert nodded.

'But why? Why did he kill this man in cold blood?'

'I don't know, lass. He never said. Read the report of the trial.'

Jayne picked up the next printout. This time it was from page 13 of the Daily Telegraph, dated January 11, 1980.

SINCLAIR PLEADS GUILTY

At Manchester Crown Court yesterday, Martin Sinclair of 12 Creole Street, Withington, pled guilty to the murder of David Strachan, aged 66, a retired civil servant. When asked why he committed the crime, Mr Sinclair refused to answer, simply stating boldly, 'No comment.'

Detective Chief Inspector Harold Morris was called to the witness stand. He gave a stunning and brief timeline of the events. Sinclair drove to Mr Strachan's house in the leafy, exclusive village of Lymm and parked outside. After sitting in his car for fifteen minutes, he walked up Mr Strachan's drive and knocked on the door. As soon as Mr Strachan answered it, Sinclair produced an old German Luger and shot him three times; twice to the body and once to the head. Mr Strachan died instantly. Sinclair then placed the gun on the floor and calmly waited for the police.

DCI Morris said, 'We have investigated this crime thoroughly. There seems no known motive and Sinclair refuses to tell us why he committed the murder. Mr Strachan used to work in the Civil Service and had retired to Lymm after a long career. There seems no connection between the two men and nothing that warranted such a deadly attack.'

Mr Charles Roper, acting on behalf of Sinclair said, 'I am at a loss to explain to your Lordship why my client committed this crime. He refuses to tell me and has simply decided to plead guilty.'

Mr Justice Arnold, presiding over the court, has accepted the plea of guilty and will pronounce sentence later.

Jayne turned over the last printout, this time from The Times.

MAN SENTENCED TO 30 YEARS

Yesterday, Judge Arnold sentenced Martin Sinclair to 30 years in jail for the cold-blooded killing of a retired civil servant, Mr David Strachan. Before sentencing the offender, the Judge was scathing in his language. 'This is one of the worst crimes I have encountered in the twenty-five years I have sat on the bench. A retired man, a good man, church-going and with an exemplary record of service to his country, was murdered on the doorstep of his own home. The offender, Martin Sinclair, has offered no reason or motive for his action. Indeed, his one answer, repeated ad infinitum since his arrest, has been "No comment". In addition, he has shown no remorse or contrition for his actions, nor has the psychiatrist found any evidence of mental instability. This killing bears all the hallmarks of one of the heinous acts of the IRA or the Baader Meinhof gang, yet the police can find no links to any terrorist organisations. Nonetheless, I feel it incumbent on me to sentence Martin Sinclair to thirty years in prison to be served without any possibility of parole.'

The prisoner was taken down to the cells without saying a word. He will spend his sentence in the confines of Wakefield Maximum Security Prison.

'The new government of Mrs Thatcher faces a dire law-and-order challenge left behind by the wasteful socialism of Mr Callaghan,' the judge summarised. 'Such heinous crimes must continue to be punished with all the severity the law possesses. The sentencing of Martin Sinclair is a good start. Let all other criminals who decide to kill with impunity suffer a similar punishment.'

Jayne put the printout back with the others and closed the folder. 'My father was a murderer?'

'Looks that way, lass.'

'And you knew about this but didn't tell me, Robert?'

Her stepfather looked away. 'Your mother insisted. I wanted to tell you, but—'

'You didn't have time in the last thirty-seven years…'

'That's not fair, Jayne,' protested Vera, 'Robert was forbidden from telling you. You keep your clients' secrets, don't you?'

'This wasn't a client, Vera, this was my father.'

A silence hung between the three of them like a shroud before Robert spoke again. 'I'm sorry, lass, I should have told you before now. It wasn't fair…'

Jayne held up the folder. 'According to the reports, it seems like an open-and-shut case. He was even waiting on the doorstep for the police to arrive. In all my years in the force, I never met anyone who ever did that. The first reaction in a serious attack or murder is to flee the scene, get away from the body as fast as you can. This doesn't feel right, Robert. The trial – it was too easy, too simple. There was no motive, but there's always a motive. And why didn't my father say anything? Why did he keep quiet?'

'You could ask him tomorrow when you see him,' said Robert.

Jayne nodded. 'Martin Sinclair didn't have many friends at the end of his trial, did he? No wonder his sentence was so harsh. I'm sure DCI Morris was happy with the result.'

'No, not many friends,' said Robert. 'Not even me, his best friend. I abandoned him too.'

Jayne stood up and bent over her stepfather's bed to hug him tightly. 'Let me find out the truth. I know it's out there, somewhere.'

Chapter Seventeen

Tuesday, September 12, 1939
Flat 2, Albany St, London

The early days of the war passed in a blur for Monique. Her first attempts to feed Martin, as they had named the baby, were not successful. It took the midwife forcefully squeezing her nipples and massaging her breasts to finally produce milk. The pain was immense but soon Martin was suckling away happily.

They left the hospital in one of the free hours John had from work.

Monique immediately noticed London had changed in the few days she had spent on the maternity ward. Barrage balloons had gone up in Regent's Park: great, ponderous lumps of cream silk floating high in the sky, tethered to the ground by a steel cable. At their base, anti-aircraft guns had appeared, surrounded by a defensive wall of sandbags.

The shops had changed too. Each one had its own covering of sandbags, with masking tape crisscrossing the large glass windows.

'I've already done the same to ours, and I've hung blackout curtains.'

'Blackout curtains?' said Monique, carrying Martin into the taxi that would take them home.

'So the enemy bombers can't see any light.'

'We are going to be bombed by the Germans?'

He put his arm around her shoulders. 'I'm sure it won't come to that but we need to be prepared. The Dodds family have already left for the country, taking George with them.'

'Wasn't he due to start boarding school this week?'

'His education has been postponed, so George is very happy. It's happened to a lot of children. Many have been evacuated out of London and the other big cities to the countryside.' He paused for a moment. 'I see quite a lot of Alf Dodds, he's co-ordinating supply for the new Ministry.'

'I'm sure he'll enjoy spending even more time at work.'

As she looked out of the taxi, she noticed the people on the street had changed too. There was more purpose, more energy to their walk, as if the declaration of war had given a new meaning to life. Each of them carried a small white box for their gas mask. A few of the more elegant women had even accessorised the box, adding a ribbon or darkening the white canvas.

Perhaps Monique was imagining it, but the colour seemed to have leached out of London.

People's clothes were drabber. Gone were the bright reds, oranges and yellows of last year, already replaced by blacks and greys and browns. The colours of war.

This could have been her imagination, but she saw it in the way the women were dressed. Gone was the frivolity of the thirties; a new seriousness had arrived along with the outbreak of war.

They arrived home and she saw their windows were indeed criss-crossed with masking tape. 'It feels like a prison with white bars,' said Monique, 'it's all so depressing.'

She went to bed as soon as she got in and stayed there for the next two days.

*　*　*

'When do you have to go back to work?' she asked John as they lay in bed early that morning.

'Tomorrow.'

'In Lincolnshire?'

'Yes. They've moved me from training to a wing in 73 Squadron, I'm flying again.'

She saw he was happy, like a child who had just discovered a new toy and couldn't stop playing with it.

'The Hurricane is a great plane. I've got an awful lot to do with my reservists to bring them up to scratch, but they are all keen.'

'There won't be any fighting, will there?'

'I don't think so,' he said softly.

But the news on the radio wasn't good. The Poles were retreating in the face of Hitler's overwhelming strength, and France – France was slowly mobilising her army to man the Maginot Line.

John rose from the bed, smoothed down his uniform trousers and reached for his grey RAF jacket hanging on the back of a chair.

'Do you have to go?' she said softly.

He sat down and kissed her forehead. 'I must. They are expecting me at the Ministry, some problem Churchill has stirred up.'

As he finished speaking, Martin let out a loud wail. She manoeuvred him on to her right breast and he clamped his tiny lips around her nipple.

When she looked up John had already gone.

Chapter Eighteen

Wednesday, December 27, 2017
HMP Belmarsh, Thamesmead, London

The taxi from the station dropped her off in a car park in front of the main entrance of the modern prison, its name proudly displayed on a board next to the road. Above her the imposing yellow brick walls towered over the road, solid and threatening.

That morning, she had caught one of the early trains from Manchester Piccadilly, arriving in London Euston nearly three hours later. A transfer to another train, via the underground, had taken her out into the vast eastern suburbs of the city to HMP Belmarsh.

Before leaving, she had checked everything. Two forms of ID, two different utility bills with her name and Manchester address, and her birth certificate were placed in a plastic folder. She re-checked the long list of regulations. Most of them seemed to be subjective restrictions rather than anything to do with security.

No see through or revealing clothing
Skirts, dresses and shorts must not be any higher than just above the knee
No low-cut tops or short tops that reveal the stomach
No vests to be worn on their own that reveal underwear or undergarments of any kind.

No clothing bearing slogans that can be deemed racist, insulting or derogatory

No uniforms (except children in school uniform and police officers on a legal visit)

No watches

No cufflinks

Jewellery must be kept to a minimum (use a ten-pence piece as a guide for earrings)

No chains that resemble key chains

No ponchos

No baseball caps

No damaged clothing

No sunglasses

No fluorescent tops

Only one pair of trousers to be worn at any one time

No diaries

She had dressed as conservatively as possible without wearing a kebaya. Finally, she had fed, watered and released Mr Smith to roam for the time she was away. She would be back later that evening to feed the monster again. One day, that cat would eat her out of house and home.

Then she had taken a deep breath, calmed her nerves and stepped out of the house, closing the door behind her with a loud bang.

Now here she was, stood in front of the prison. Inside, her father, a man she had not seen for forty years, was waiting.

Off to the left a large sign indicated the entrance for visitors. A queue was already forming, composed mainly of women with a few young children in tow. The queue shuffled forward remorselessly until Jayne reached its head.

'Name?' asked the officious officer.

'Jayne Sinclair.'

'Not your name. The name of the prisoner?'

'Martin Sinclair.'

The man peered down at his clipboard, following the names with his pen. 'Here he is. ID and details of address?'

She gave him the utility bills, her driving licence and passport. He checked these against the details she had completed online. When he finished, he asked her, 'First time?'

Jayne nodded.

'Off to the left for fingerprinting and photo.'

Jayne felt like a giant impersonal cog in an enormous machine. She was processed with as much warmth as a pork sausage. Finally, she reached the security checkpoint, surrounded by CCTV cameras in a carpeted reception area. She removed her shoes and belt and put all her belongings through an X-ray machine. She walked through a metal detector and was given a body search – the lining of her jeans, the soles of her feet and inside her mouth were all checked.

'As an ex-copper, you're just getting a light check,' said the tattooed female prison guard.

'How do you know I'm an ex-police officer?'

'You don't think we check people out?'

'I'd hate to see what you do to the inmates.'

At the end of the reception area she saw a red iron gate. She strode up to it and stood outside. Above her head, a camera zoomed in to stare directly at her face. Some unknown guard hidden in a control centre far away was studying her face and comparing it with security footage taken when she entered the prison.

Finally, she was shown into a room with a single desk, separated in two by a solid wooden board running across the centre. In one corner, a sullen, bored prison officer stood with his hands behind his back. In the other, a coffee machine was covered with out-of-order signs, leaving just milk, tea and orange juice as the only available drinks.

She sat down at the table and waited. Despite herself, she found her leg was jiggling nervously and her palms were clammy.

A noise outside made her jump. The sound of a door being unlocked. Two men entering, one wearing metalled boots, the other shuffling along.

The prison guard in the room took the keys from his belt and stood in front of the door.

'Prisoner CJ7604 to see a visitor,' said a voice.

The prison guard unlocked the door and pulled it open.

Jayne slowly raised her eyes.

Chapter Nineteen

Wednesday, December 27, 2017
HMP Belmarsh, Thamesmead, London

An old man stood in the doorway. Head bowed over; clad in prison grey; sallow, pasty complexion; grey hair combed over to cover the top of his head. In her mind, she tried to compare him with the picture she had seen of his wedding day. The two men looked completely different.

And then he lifted his head and she saw his eyes. Emerald green with flashes of gold. Strange eyes. The eyes of a fanatic.

Jayne looked away.

His voice when it spoke was strong and firm, unlike the body. 'Hello, Jayne. Long time, no see.'

The tone was flippant, ironic. Was he making fun of her?

He shuffled into the room, feet encased in old-man's slippers. The guard locked the door after he had entered and then stood with his arms behind his back, guarding it.

The old man – her father – shuffled across the room, pulled out the chair in front of her and sat down at the table, placing a pack of cigarettes and a box of matches in front of him.

After a few moments he spoke again. 'Well, this is a surprise, I didn't think you'd come.'

There it was again, that mocking tone. Was he making fun of her or was that simply the way he spoke? Was this how he survived in prison? Hard, unflinching, as stern as a concrete wall. This man was her father but she felt nothing.

No warmth. No love. No empathy. No anger.

Just emptiness.

She turned to stare at him. In the harsh light from the ceiling bulb, his complexion looked even paler, even more sallow than she had first thought. The face was deeply creased and lined with that dull tone of the heavy smoker. The chin was strong and square, much like her own. The hair, so black and long in the wedding photo, was now a dull grey, cut short to the head with visibly scabby bald patches.

It was the eyes, though, that stood out; still sharp and penetrating despite his years.

'Am I what you expected to see? I don't suppose Marjorie showed you any pictures of me. Not much chance of taking holiday snapshots when you're stuck in prison.'

Jayne shook her head. The words when they left her mouth sounded false, unlike her. 'No, she never showed me any photos. I found one yesterday, though. Your wedding picture.'

He smiled for a second. 'A great day, probably the best of my life.' A long pause before he said in a quieter voice: 'You didn't answer any of my cards.'

'I thought you were dead.' Jayne breathed in. 'She told me you were dead, a car accident.'

His face remained impassive. 'Marjorie was good at inventing stories even when she was a student at Manchester University.'

Jayne frowned. 'Manchester Uni?'

For the first time she saw animation in the face of the man sitting opposite her.

'She was a student of psychology. She was always good at assessing people, was Marjorie. Even better at manipulating them…'

Jayne stared at him, unable to speak. Her mum was a psychology student? But she spent her life working in that dreary insurance office. Why?

'You saw my letter?' he asked.

She nodded, dragged from her thoughts. 'Robert showed it to me.'

'Ah, Robert, my best friend who married my wife.'

'You weren't married, remember? You were divorced after you walked out on both of us when I was three.' Her speech was angrier, more accusatory than she intended.

'I don't suppose your mother told you why I walked out?'

Jayne shook her head. She had never discussed it with her mother.

'I had something to do, Jayne, something to finish. Your mother never understood—'

'But you had a wife and child to look after. You walked out, leaving us with nothing.' Forty years of pent-up anger racked Jayne's body. She found herself grasping the edge of the chair tightly as if holding herself back from leaping across the table and striking this man, this stranger. Her father.

'I tried to explain to her, to make her understand, but your mother wouldn't listen. She was never very good at listening, Marjorie.'

From her own experience, Jayne knew that this much was true. She thought for a moment before speaking in a softer voice. 'But what could have been more important than looking after a small girl of three years old?' Jayne recognised as soon as she finished the question that it wasn't the adult woman speaking now. It wasn't the former police officer with a reputation for handling the most difficult and complex family history cases. It wasn't the mature, sensible, confident woman.

It was the three-year-old girl who didn't understand why her father was no longer there to hold her and hug her.

The man in front of her brushed a grey hair from his eyes. 'I had to find out the truth, Jayne.'

'What truth? What could have been more important than your family?'

He looked down at his feet before lifting his head and staring at her with those bright green eyes. 'I had to find out who betrayed my mother.'

Chapter Twenty

Friday, November 10, 1939
Flat 2, Albany St, London

It was a bitterly cold day in November when John came back to the flat one evening. He had come down from Lincolnshire to the Air Ministry for a day of briefings. Monique didn't see much of him these days, except at weekends. Most of the time he was on the east coast, working with his squadron.

But she was busy, never had she been so busy. There never seemed enough hours in the day to get everything done. Martin was a voracious eater; either she was feeding him, preparing to feed him or washing his nappies. It went in one end and came out the other with a surprising, and smelly, regularity.

In between, she tried to get some rest but always found it particularly hard. Inevitably, her mind drifted to John. What was he doing? Was he eating? Would he be safe?

There were reports of aircraft crashes in the newspapers but these always seemed to be glossed over with schoolboy bravado. 'Prangs', 'knocks' and 'little bits of bother' lessened the impact of what she knew were serious events.

He came home earlier than usual that evening. For once, Martin had finished eating and was quietly napping, his mouth still attached to her breast.

'We're off to France,' John announced casually.

'What?'

'Joining the rest of the squadron, we're off to France. Billeted with some Blenheims in Rouvre.'

Her heart gave a momentary jump. He was going to the front line. This emotion was followed by a slight twinge of jealousy; he would be back in France and she would still be here without him. She was finding it difficult enough managing alone. But at least he came back most weekends. When he moved to France that would be impossible.

'You'll be careful?' she asked both as a question and as a warning.

'Don't worry, it's as quiet as London on a Sunday morning over there. We're just to escort the Blenheims on their reconnaissance flights. All very boring, I'm afraid. Far more dangerous crossing the A1 on a Wednesday in February.'

She knew he was lying, but now was not the time to challenge him. 'When are you going?'

'A week from today.'

Her heart jumped again. 'So we can spend your last week together?'

He shook his head. 'Sorry, old girl, need to go back to the airfield. Moving a squadron with all its kit is a major task. I can't let the erks handle it alone.'

She noticed his language had changed in the last couple of months. Becoming more military and clipped, just like the moustache he now sported on his upper lip.

'I'll see you before you leave?'

'Of course, and France is only a hop across the Channel. I should think I'll be home quite often.' He sat down next to her, putting his arm around her shoulders. 'Don't worry, it's a really boring posting. And Mr Jerry is stuck in front of the Maginot Line.

The French will just sit in their blockhouses and blast him to pieces if he dares to come forward.'

She laughed falsely; she could hear it in the sound. 'At least you'll be able to drink some decent wine.'

'And eat well. If nothing else, your countrymen know how to eat.'

She was silent for a moment, looking down at Martin. Not a care in the world nor a crease on his forehead.

John leant forward and kissed her on lips. 'Don't worry, I'll be home soon.'

An image of flames searing a closed cockpit flashed through her mind. She knew then she would never see him again.

Chapter Twenty-One

Wednesday, December 27, 2017
HMP Belmarsh, Thamesmead, London

'Betrayed your mother? Is that why you killed that man. David Strachan, wasn't that his name? Why didn't you tell the police? At least it would have given you a motive, and perhaps the judge would have accepted it as extenuating circumstances, lessening your sentence.'

He blinked once. 'I couldn't tell them.'

'Why not? Why couldn't you say anything?'

The old man stared down at a stain on the table. 'Because I killed the wrong man.'

Jayne shook her head. What was he saying? 'I don't understand.'

He looked up at her again, green eyes flashing with anger. 'Nobody ever understood. Somebody betrayed my mother and she was murdered.'

Jayne was struggling to understand what he had just said to her when he spoke again, enunciating every word as if it were a mantra he had been chanting every day of his life.

'I killed the wrong man. He didn't betray my mother.'

'How do you know?'

'Because he told me before he died.'

'But the newspaper report said he died instantly.'

Her father shook his head. 'He didn't. He died in my arms. His last words were "it wasn't me".'

'He could have lied.'

Again, the flash of anger in his eyes. 'He didn't.'

'How do you know?'

'As he lay dying, he told me about his wartime diary. I found it in his study. It was obvious he had nothing to do with my mother's death. In fact, he went out of his way to find out who betrayed her.'

Jayne's head was swimming. 'Let me get this right. You killed David Strachan, but he wasn't the man who betrayed your mother?'

The old man nodded his head slowly.

'But why were you killing people in the first place? For God's sake, you had a wife and child to look after.'

'You don't understand—'

'I understand you shot an innocent man in cold blood for no reason.'

As she was speaking, the death of her partner, Dave Gilmour, flashed back to her. A routine house call in Moss Side, Dave knocking on the door as she stood at the side. Without any warning, two shotgun blasts through the wooden door. Dave falling, falling, blood drenching his chest, his eyes staring at her helplessly, watching him die as another shotgun blast tore a gaping hole in the door.

The old man reached for his cigarettes, lighting one and blowing a circle of smoke up to the ceiling. 'That's why I need your help, Jayne.'

'You need my help.' Jayne's voice rose. 'After what you did, you have the gall to ask for my help. And one other thing, why are you still in a high-security prison? You were only sentenced to thirty years.'

He ignored her question, quietly saying, 'I'm dying, Jayne.' He held up the burning cigarette, blue smoke curling upwards. 'Lung cancer. Years of these, I suppose. But what else is there to do in prison besides smoke? The doctors have given me three months, six at the tops.'

'So?' Jayne said cruelly.

'So, I want to know the truth before I die.'

Jayne frowned. 'What truth?'

'Who betrayed my mother.'

'And you think I'll help you?'

'I think so.'

Jayne laughed. 'You don't know me.'

'Oh, but I do, Jayne. I've followed your career closely. The John Hughes Case, Lord Trent, the missing marriage and the vanished child – even the American candidate and his heritage. I know about them all. You have proved to be a persistent and clever investigator, Jayne.'

'How? How do you know all this?'

'It's amazing what one can find on the internet, Jayne, even in prison. Your work is well documented by your clients.'

'Why should I help you?'

The man smiled. 'Because I'm your father.'

'You never were.'

He smiled again. 'Because you're the only person who can find out the truth.'

'Why should I care? You mean nothing to me.'

The man stopped smiling. He leant closer to the table. 'Because I am the only person who can tell you about your family. When I die, you will never know the truth. Could you live with that, Jayne?'

He sat back and casually smoked his cigarette.

Could she live with that? Could she live with never knowing about her past? Who she was and where she came from?

'What do you want me to do?' she said quietly.

'It's a simple job. I want you to find the bastard who betrayed my mother and had her murdered.'

The guard stepped forward and announced. 'Time's up. Visiting time is over.'

Jayne took out her notebook. 'You'll have to tell me what happened. Give me something to start with.'

The old man stood up, shaking his head. 'You'll have to work it out for yourself. I went wrong somewhere and ended up killing the wrong man. You need to investigate yourself, don't make my mistake.'

'But I need somewhere to start…'

He reached into his pocket and produced a packet of letters wrapped in a purple ribbon. 'Here, these will help you. It's all I have left of her.'

He began to shuffle towards the door. 'Don't make the mistake I made, Jayne. Check your research.'

The guard unlocked the door leading back to the cells.

Her father stopped for a second and turned back towards her. 'Come back when you have an answer, Jayne. But don't take too long…'

'But I need more…'

He began to walk through the door back to his cell, halting for a second time and turning back as if he had just remembered something. 'You asked me why I'm still here after so many years…'

She nodded her head.

He held up the pack of cigarettes. 'Ten years ago, I stabbed another prisoner over a packet of Marlboro.'

And then he was gone.

Chapter Twenty-Two

Wednesday, December 27, 2017
Virgin Train from London to Manchester.

The journey back to Manchester was a nightmare for Jayne. As the lights of the English countryside sped past outside her window, she experienced a flood of emotions.

How dare he come into her life after so long? How could he ask her to work for him? Why now? What good would it do her? Where would all this lead? And stabbing another prisoner over a pack of cigarettes... Was he mad? Deranged? Or had prison changed him so much he no longer had any humanity?

A few times she found herself close to tears as she played back the meeting in her mind. The four grey walls, the prison guard and his shiny shoes, the grey hair of her father. His emerald-green eyes sparkling with anger.

How could she have a father who was a murderer? She had been a copper for most of her life. She had upheld the rule of law, sacrificed everything – including her marriage – to do what was right. And now, she discovered she had a father who'd killed a man in cold blood.

Was the universe playing a dirty trick on her? Was God smiling down at her now, saying, 'You got too arrogant, Jayne Sinclair, you were too proud. Time to take you down a notch or three.' And could her father be trusted? Was everything he said just a pack of lies?

She stared out of the window at the dark night of an English spring.

Occasionally, the train travelled through brightly lit towns. At other times the countryside was dark, with just a few distant yellow lights betraying the presence of other human beings. At one point, all the lights vanished completely, leaving just the blackest of black nights.

Luckily, there were few other passengers on this late train back to Manchester, just an old couple and a young man sitting a few seats away from her.

Jayne let herself cry silently, seeing her face reflecting in the window. A face she had seen so many times in her forty-five years on this earth. But a face that felt somehow different from before. She had now met her real father, knew who he was, had sat across a table from him.

The problem was, he wasn't a very nice man.

What was she going to do?

Investigate the past for him, or simply walk away, pretending he didn't exist? After all, she had managed fairly well without him. True, she had made some mistakes, but she hadn't done a bad job with her life; she'd been a good copper and was a better genealogical investigator. It gave her real pleasure to help people, to see the happiness on their faces when she finally revealed the truth to them.

Then it struck her.

'You can't put the genie back in the bottle, Jayne.' She said it out loud, too loud. The young man reading a book three seats away looked up and stared at her quizzically.

She turned her head to look out at the dark night.

She had met her father and knew who he was. If she was going to understand where she came from, she would have to investigate his story.

It wasn't about him, but about her. After all, the woman who had been killed was her grandmother. Shouldn't Jayne discover what happened to her own grandmother?

She pulled out the bundle of letters he had given her. They were written in thin, cheap stationery with a RAF monogram on the top left. The outsides of the envelopes had a grubbiness that came from being handled too much.

The envelope on top had an address written in a sloping hand:

Monique Sinclair
Flat 2,
Albany St,
London

This was her grandmother. After her marriage she must have taken her husband's name. Jayne carefully undid the purple ribbon and slipped the first letter out of the envelope.

20 November 1939

Darling Heart,

Well, I'm in your country now and stationed just south of (CENSORED).

We've settled in nicely in the aerodrome, setting up a joint officers' mess with the chaps from the Blenheim Squadron. We've commissioned the local Café de la Paix to provide the food. I'd forgotten how well, and how often, your countrymen eat and drink.

Did I mention the wine? Being so close to Champagne, we have bottles in profusion plus some rather excellent Beaune. Frankly, the only thing missing is decent whisky. That we have to fly in with the replacements from England. At least one of them is tasked to bring in a crate when he comes.

And how are you, darling heart? Still being kept awake by young Martin? I know it's difficult without me being there to be with you, but hang on for a little while longer, I'm sure to get some leave for Christmas.

Is he growing big and strong? I'm sure he is.

Here, everything is very quiet. We fly the occasional sortie, usually escorting the (CENSORED) on their reconnaissance missions.

Two days ago, I saw my first German fighter. He was up above in the clouds. But we have instructions not to attack unless we are fired upon first. Even though we are at war, we don't want to provoke the Jerries.

Strange sort of war, if you ask me, but ours not to do, etc.

The chaps are a decent bunch on the whole, mostly reservists but a few full-timers like myself. Our saving grace is the erks who at least know what they are doing. They had my (CENSORED) ready for service only two days after it arrived in a crate from England. I don't know what I'd do without them.

I have to go now, dear heart. I miss you so much but I'll be back soon.

Please kiss Martin on his head from me. I do hope he has a little more hair than before.

I love and miss you so much.

Your husband

John

Censored by the unit commander

Jayne slowly folded the letter and put it back in its envelope. At least a few puzzles had been solved for her. Her grandmother was French and her grandfather was in the RAF. He must have been posted to France in the first days of the war, which suggested that he was a regular. As soon as she returned home, she would be able to find out more.

Jayne was touched by the tone of the letter. It was loving and gentle; her grandfather obviously missed his wife very much. But there was also a sense of adventure in the words, as if he were in some Boy's Own story. Perhaps that was the feeling in the early days of the war, before the reality of the brutality of conflict hit home.

She turned and looked at her reflection in the glass of the train window. Outside, it was dark with not a light showing. She remembered the ring she found in her mother's vanity case. Inside the initials J and M were inscribed surrounded by a heart. Was this John and Monique, her grandparents? Had Martin Sinclair given the ring to her mother on their wedding day?

She glanced back at the letters lying on the table in front of her. For a moment, a shiver of fear trembled through her body.

Could she read any more?

Chapter Twenty-Three

Friday, December 1, 1939
Flat 2, Albany St, London

The early days after John left were difficult for Monique. Although she was used to looking after children, having her own baby wasn't as easy as she thought it would be.

First was the continual desire for sleep. Martin was a hungry baby who was always waking up in the middle of the night to be fed. It meant that Monique could never sleep properly as she was constantly thinking about the young life lying next to her.

Second was simply getting around. Going out to the shops become a chore of preparing Martin; getting him washed and dressed and ready to go out. And once they were out, dodging the men filling sandbags or digging trenches was difficult when you were carrying a baby.

It didn't help that Martin was a particularly clingy child. If she were ever out of his sight for more than a few seconds, he would let out a howl to bring the walls of Jericho tumbling down. It meant when she was cleaning up or tidying the house, he constantly had to be with her, slowing her down and making it difficult to get anything finished.

The one time he seemed to quieten was on Saturday afternoons, when they went to the Dodds's house to see George. They had returned to London after the first scare of the declaration of war had subsided. Madame has soon returned to her gay social life whilst Mr Dodds worked his bowler hat to the brim at the ministry.

George was always pleased to see her and, for some reason, he had formed a bond with her child. Games of peek-a-boo would last hours, with neither boy nor baby ever becoming tired or bored of the predictability of the game.

And, of course, she missed John, worrying constantly that he would have an accident or, worse still, the war would finally erupt in France.

Mrs Dodds had taken to giving Monique the French newspaper that was provided by the Ministry to her husband. They were always a few weeks out of date, but at least there was news about her homeland. France seemed tired of the war, content to sit behind the impregnable forts of the Maginot Line.

She hoped it would always stay that way; a stand-off war, a phoney war. They would all grow bored and John would eventually come home.

The situation – her tiredness and perpetual unease – continued until one Saturday Mrs Dodds sat her down. 'I've found the answer,' she said, excitement in her voice.

'The answer to what?'

'To everything.'

Monique frowned. Whatever was she talking about? 'To everything?' she repeated.

'Yes, to help you out. Give you a hand with your child…' She could never remember Martin's name however hard she tried.

'I don't know…'

'Her name is Mrs Beggs and she used to be the Walmsly-Smythes' charlady but he's been posted to some godforsaken place in Scotland and Clarissa, for some unearthly reason, has gone with him.'

'But I don't know if I need a charlady.'

'Mrs Beggs is far more than that. She can clean for you and look after Martin if you want to take a few hours off to shop. Harrods has some lovely new things in. Cut for the war, you know, but still quite stylish.'

'I don't know…'

'And then you can come here more often. George misses you terribly and the new gal isn't a patch on you. Shall I set it up?'

'I don't know if we can afford it.'

'Surely John wouldn't begrudge you a little help. He's gone off to play soldiers in this beastly war, you need some help too. Look at what you did for me?'

Monique didn't have the heart to tell Mrs Dodds that there was no way she was ever going to emulate her. But the idea of having some help to do the washing and cleaning appealed, particularly as it meant she could spend more time playing with Martin or bringing him to see George. 'I don't know…'

'That's settled then,' Mrs Dodds said definitively, sipping the last of the China tea. 'I'll ask her to start tomorrow.'

Mrs Beggs tuned out to be a big, blousy woman, born and bred in Stepney. She quickly set to work on the flat, making it spotless and organised in less than a day. 'Babies is hard work,' she announced, 'I know, I've had six of them, with three grandkids.'

Martin took to her straight away too, happily sitting on her lap when she made a pot of tea for her elevenses.

Monique was glad of the break and having somebody to talk to. She'd forgotten how lonely it had been since John had gone away. Suddenly, there was the bright efficiency of Mrs Beggs every morning, except Sunday, to brighten up the day.

She still missed John, though. Lying awake at night in their bed, Martin swaddled in his clothes snoring gently beside her, she often wondered what her husband was doing.

When would he come back to her?

Would he come back to her?

Chapter Twenty-Four

Wednesday, December 27, 2017
Virgin Train from London to Manchester.

The train had stopped at Stoke on Trent; just thirty minutes left to Manchester.

Outside her window, the platform lights illuminated a soft rain falling on the old station buildings. Each drop was picked out in the light, like a cold diamond falling to earth. In the shadows, a man dressed in a thick parka and bobble hat sheltered under an eave, stamping his feet to keep them warm.

Jayne wondered where he was going that night. Was he going home or going out somewhere else? What urgent need was so important to take him from the comfort and warmth of his home in the Potteries to brave the rigours of the English weather just a few days after Christmas?

It was funny; London had been sunny but cold. The further north Jayne travelled the wetter it had become, as if she were entering into a different, harsher, damper world.

She pulled out the next letter from the pile tied with the ribbon. It was written on the same RAF notepaper as the first one and the address was in the same hand as before. She took a deep breath before she began to read the words written by her grandfather all those years ago.

My darling Monique,

I have some bad news, I'm afraid. It looks like I won't be home for Christmas after all. I know I said I would but it looks like everything has changed.

The CO announced this evening that all leave is cancelled for the foreseeable future.

I know this is a terrible disappointment for both you. I was so looking forward to spending Martin's first Christmas with the both of you. Just sitting by the fire and holding you, and him, in my arms.

How is Martin? Is he bigger and stronger? I would so love to see him. If you have time, perhaps you could go to a studio and take a picture of him? I could place it in my cockpit next time I go up.

Life continues on here as before. You will be pleased to hear my French is getting much better. Constant interaction with the locals plus a lack of any English on their part has made it totally necessary.

Practice makes perfect my old French teacher used to say. I wish I had listened to him a lot more when I was young!

We are still eating much better than we should. Monsieur Laplace looks after all the officers in his peculiar French way. I do feel guilty eating the best food there is here, whilst you will have to suffer rationing back in England in the new year.

I can't imagine queueing up for a measly two ounces of cheese. I could devour that small amount in one bite rather than make it last a week or more.

We are flying more sorties now and Jerry seems to have become more aggressive recently, but you shouldn't worry about me. We Sinclairs have the luck of the Gods and of all our ancestors.

I have to go to sleep now, darling, we have a recce in the morning. I always keep your photograph beneath my pillow when I am sleeping. It's as if we were still together even though we are separated by this beastly war.

Well, that's how I like to think of it. Horribly sentimental and not like me at all.

I miss you with all my heart, darling Monique,

Your husband

John

Chapter Twenty-Five

Monday, December 25, 1939 – Christmas Day
Hereford, England

Monique woke up late on Christmas Day. She had fed Martin in the middle of the night and then again at six that morning. He was now sleeping happily beside her, but still with a frown on his face.

It was a clear, cold day, with that wonderfully blue sky that only the English winter seems to provide.

She got up, trying not to disturb Martin, and quickly washed her face using the bowl and water provided last night by Aunt Betsy.

Myriad cooking smells were coming from the kitchen and suffusing the house with their aromas. In France, her Christmases had been quiet affairs spent at home with Maman killing a chicken to roast, but that was all.

Here in Hereford, Aunt Betsy seemed to have spent all her time in the kitchen since they had arrived on the 18th.

Monique checked that Martin was sleeping well, placing pillows on either side of him just in case he rolled out of the bed. She put on a dressing gown, quickly smoothed her bedraggled hair, and went out of the room.

'It's awake, finally,' shouted Aunt Betsy.
'What time is it?' asked Monique.

'Nearly noon on a bright, sunny Christmas morning. Did you have a good sleep, dear?'

Monique thought for a moment. She had slept well since she had arrived in Hereford. Perhaps it was the country air. Or the extra helpings of food that Betsy seemed to find even in the middle of wartime. Or the fact that Dan and Betsy spent hours looking after Martin, leaving her free to relax and nap. 'That smells wonderful.'

Betsy pointed to the oven. 'That? It's nobbut a goose. Farmer next door kills 'em for Christmas and I always picks a nice plump one from his flock. Would you like a cup of tea, dear?'

The English answer to everything.

A cup of tea. Since she had arrived in Hereford, Monique had drank gallons of the stuff.

'That would be lovely,' Monique answered.

'I'll make fresh. Dan's finished the pot.'

Dan looked up sheepishly from the table as Betsy bustled around.

'Now you drink this down and get yourself ready. Mr and Mrs Todhunter from the church are coming at one, and the vicar said he would drop in around then too. Likes his grub, does the vicar, a proper trencherman. Well, you only have to look at his expanding waistline to see the truth in that.'

Aunt Betsy could talk and brew tea at the same time, pouring the hot water unerringly into the pot without even looking.

'Here you go. Milk's in the jug on the table. And you be leaving that pot alone, Dan Sinclair – that's for Monique, that is.'

Monique sat down and poured out the brown liquid before adding just the right amount of milk. She knew it was the wrong way round, but she didn't care. This way she could get it exactly how she wanted it.

As she raised the cup to her lips, an almighty wail issued from the bedroom.

'His Lordship's awake then?' said Betsy. 'He'll be wanting his breakfast.'

Monique sighed, picked up her tea and went back into the bedroom.

An hour later, after dressing and fiddling with her hair, changing Martin and putting on his best clothes, she went into the dining room to find all the guests already there. The place had been decorated beautifully by Dan, with red crepe-paper streamers and Christmas crackers beside every place setting.

In the middle of the table sat a fat goose surrounded by roast and mashed potatoes, Brussels sprouts, buttered and glazed carrots, pork stuffing, winter cabbage, roasted parsnips, and a large gravy boat filled to the brim with a luscious brown gravy. On the sideboard was a selection of warm beer, plus a bottle of red wine from Bordeaux just for Monique.

Everybody gathered round her, peering into the bundle containing the sleeping Martin, careful not to wake him up.

'He's lovely, you must be so proud,' said Mrs Todhunter.

'A wonderful creation,' said the vicar. 'God's image in one tiny body.'

Dan had thoughtfully placed Martin's crib at one end of the table. Monique laid him down to sleep inside it.

The vicar stood in front of the table. 'Now, a short prayer of thanks before we tuck in to this wonderful food.'

They all bowed their heads in prayer.

'Thank you to Betsy and Dan for providing this wonderful feast. Even in the midst of war, the Lord and the land are still bountiful. Our thoughts go out to those who cannot be with us today…'

Monique thought immediately of John, stuck in some airfield in her own country. What was he doing now?

'…the soldiers, sailors and airmen defending this country from the hordes of Nazi Germany. Lord, we thank you for the feast on this, your birthday, in 1939. We bow our heads and give praise to you. Amen.' As soon as the vicar had finished, he sat down in his seat and said, 'Well then, Dan, get a move on with the carving before that bird decides to fly away.'

The rest of the day passed wonderfully, with Martin sleeping through everything, Christmas pudding and all. He only woke when Dan launched into his third rendition of 'Silent Night'.

Monique made her excuses and took him into the bedroom to feed him. As she lay there on the bed, with Martin suckling at her breast, she thought of John once more.

Today would have been perfect if he was there. She reached over to the cold side of the bed. How she missed him. Hopefully, he would be back soon, when this wretched war was over.

.

Chapter Twenty-Six

Thursday, February 22, 1940
Rouvre Aerodrome, France

John Sinclair sat in the Officers' Mess, an old Nissen hut that had been converted from a store to accommodate all the new arrivals. A half-drunk carafe of wine was in front of him.

Across from him, his friend, Flight Lieutenant Bob Barnett, was equally morose. His carafe was empty. He signalled the mess sergeant to bring him one more.

The rest of the mess was quiet, with other officers sitting in groups, drinking. The piano, salvaged from some old estaminet, lay closed and unplayed.

'Haven't you had enough, Bob?' John finally said.

'Not yet, not by half.'

The mess sergeant arrived with the new carafe of red wine, placing it down on the table. Bob Barnett signed the chit with a flourish. 'I haven't got started yet.'

'That will be your last one, Flight Lieutenant. We have to go up tomorrow and I want everyone sharp and awake. After today, we can't take any more risks.'

Barnett filled his glass and raised it. 'To the brothers we lost.'

The news had come through that a group of ME109s had jumped a flight of Hurricanes on their way back to the airfield. Three aircraft had been lost and none of the pilots had survived.

John Sinclair raised his glass half-heartedly and sipped the red wine. He glanced around the hut. The mood was sombre, as if it had finally hit home to all of them what they were doing in this foreign field of France.

The first six weeks had been monotonous. Escorting the Blenheim reconnaissance planes along the border, flying the occasional sortie out towards Luxembourg. Once they had even seen some ME110s in the distance, but they weren't given clearance to attack so they had to watch as the enemy aircraft, with their large black crosses on the side, simply turned for home.

The rest of their time was spent in training or looking after the planes to make sure they were in perfect running order when the day of action did come. For John was certain it would. Not today, perhaps, or tomorrow, or the day after tomorrow, but the day would come.

Christmas had been difficult. He had promised Monique he would be home, but in the end the squadron leader had cancelled all leave. He had written to tell her, hating every word he had put on the page.

Luckily, she had spent it in Hereford with Aunt Betsy and Uncle Dan. It sounded like she had a good time and at least she now had a charlady to help her around the house. Mrs Beggs was obviously a treasure, helping Monique care for their son.

He raised his glass of wine to his lips once more.

After today, he was certain the conflict would begin to escalate. The Germans had changed their tactics, becoming more aggressive; they would have to change too if they were going to survive. No longer waiting for orders to attack, but given carte blanche to roam the skies.

Barnett had nearly finished his carafe. John wondered if he should intervene. He decided to leave the man to continue to let off steam. One of his best friends had been shot down today, he was allowed one night to mourn the loss.

He pulled his RAF-issue letter pad towards him and unscrewed the top of his fountain pen. Time to write to Monique. He mustn't worry her.

Not now, not today.

After all, he had some more bad news.

Chapter Twenty-Seven

Friday, March 22, 1940
Flat 2, Albany St, London

Monique had just returned from taking Martin and George to the photographic studio in Trafalgar Square. She had promised John she would send him some pictures so, a week ago, she had dressed Martin in his finest sailor outfit and taken him along to have his picture taken.

He was not happy about it at all. Perhaps it was the place or the coldness of the day, but he just wouldn't sit still.

Finally the photographer had bribed him with a white rabbit, a toy Martin then refused to return. Monique shrugged her shoulders and ended up paying for both the toy and the portraits.

That morning she had gone back to pick up the prints. Martin looked wonderful but she appeared tired, with panda eyes. She would have to look after herself better.

They had returned through St James' Park. George wandered along, holding Martin's pushchair as Monique steered them both around the lake.

Both were fascinated by the blimps floating in the air above their heads, tethered to the ground by a long rope.

The soldier guarding one of them had become used to answering George's questions:

'How long is the rope going to the balloon?'

'Dunno.'

'How big is the balloon?'

'Dunno.'

'How high up is it?'

'Listen, sonny, I just guard the bloomin' thing, I know nothin' about it, okay?'

George carried on staring up at it anyway as they walked away.

After ice creams for her and George, and a bottle of milk for Martin, she took the young boy back to Morpeth Terrace before returning home herself.

The flat was wonderfully spotless and tidy, with a pot of Irish Stew bubbling away on the stove.

As the aromas of the cooking food drifted around the flat, Monique settled Martin down in his cot, careful not to wake him up.

This was her time. A quiet period when she could relax, read a French newspaper or simply listen to the radio.

Once again she thanked her lucky stars she had employed Mrs Beggs. Her charlady had become particularly useful once rationing had been introduced in January. Despite having an extra allowance because of Martin, Monique still found it impossible to find all the things she needed.

Queueing up for bacon, butter and sugar took time, while vegetables and meats were becoming more and more difficult to find. Even the local bakery, run by a Frenchman, stopped producing baguettes and went over to making a tasteless, white cotton-wool loaf, or the even-worse-tasting British loaf, which had the texture of dry sawdust.

Over elevenses one day, Mr Beggs told her, 'You just tell me what's you want, dear, and I'll get it for you. My son, Tommy, the one that's excused the Army because of his flat feet, well, he works at Smithfield.

A lot of stuff falls off the back of the lorry, if you know what I mean,' she said, touching her index finger to the side of her nose.

'Falls off the back of a lorry?'

'Drops into his pocket by accident, don't it?'

'But how can he fit vegetables in his pocket?'

'It's a turn of phrase, dear, ain't it? He has the ability, through his contacts, to hacquire certain foodstuffs which is otherwise difficult to find.'

'You mean he steals it?'

Mrs Beggs shook her head vigorously. 'Nah, dear, nothin' like that. He hacquires it, don' he?'

'But we're at war, isn't that illegal?'

'Well, they're all doin' it, ain't they? D'you ever see a skinny butcher?'

Monique shook her head.

'Or Old Higgins, the greengrocer, does he look like he's rationin' the eggs or bacon for his morning fry-up?'

Monique shook her head again.

'They're all at it, ain't they? Makes sense, don't it? You gotta use your contacts if you want something in life. That's what me old mum used to tell me, and she knew.'

It was later that day the post brought a letter from John. He had been in action that day. He couldn't tell her the details but, reading between the lines, she realised it had been a serious air battle.

She immediately sat down to write back to him, checking that he was okay and not injured. Knowing John, he would keep that sort of news from her.

When she had finished her letter, she kissed the photos of herself and Martin and put both into the envelope.

A reminder of home, and those waiting for him to come back.

Then, as the sun set over London and Martin slept quietly, she sat and prayed with all her heart for John to come back, imploring God to return him to her, safe and sound.

She knew he was listening.

Chapter Twenty-Eight

Friday, May 10, 1940
Rouvre Aerodrome, France

John was sitting in the ops room wearing his full flight gear, waiting. He was starting to feel uncomfortable now. The sun had risen on a bright early summer's day and it was beginning to get hot.

The others were feeling uncomfortable too. Some were on their feet, while others were walking around, a few more just sitting quietly and smoking their pipes.

The news had come through early that morning. The Germans had finally attacked and were pushing through Holland and Belgium.

'Why don't they give us some orders?' This was Bob Barnett speaking. Like the rest of them he was desperate to get into action. The waiting, the sitting around, was always the worst.

'I think the French are trying to work out what to do. You know it takes them years to work out what to order for dinner, never mind go to war.' This was from his other wing-man, Ron Treadwell.

'But the bombers should be flying now. It's when an army is on the move then it's most vulnerable. Everybody knows that.'

'Apparently not the French High Command,' interjected John, 'and besides, their air force is under the control of their ground chaps, so they haven't a clue how to use us best.'

An intelligence officer rushed in, handing the ops commander a note. They all sat up in their chairs.

'It's from HQ at the Advanced Air Strike Force, they are still waiting for orders.'

A collective groan went around the room.

Sinclair stood up and walked over to where the stationery was filed. He took a sheet of paper and an envelope from the rack and sat back down. This was the moment he had been dreading all morning.

He took the top off his fountain pen and began writing a short note.

My Darling Monique,

It looks like the scrap has finally started…

Chapter Twenty-Nine

Wednesday, December 27, 2017
Virgin Train from London to Manchester

The train was just entering Stockport when Jayne reached for the third letter. The first-class compartment was empty now; Jayne sat there all alone.

She opened the letter and began reading.

My Darling Monique,

It looks like the scrap has finally started. The whole show began this morning. I'm sure the news has already reached London and you will be aware of the German attack into Holland and Belgium.

Don't worry about me. We are doing nothing as usual. Just sitting around and waiting for orders. I'm sure the whole show will be finished before the French High Command realises it has a fighter force just ready and waiting to go into action. Jerry will be back behind his frontier and your countrymen will be lounging comfortably in their deep redoubts on the Maginot Line.

I'll write to you when I can, but this may be the last letter for a couple of days. You know how it is - wait, wait, wait, hurry up, hurry up, wait. That's the Air Force in a nutshell.

I hope Martin and yourself are well. I received the picture you sent to me. He looks like a bonny wee man, and you say he's teething now? The Sinclairs always seem to have a lot of teeth, more than our usual share.

Jayne smiled. It was true of herself too. She was always proud of her teeth never developing cavities or being forced to go to the dentist and suffer the pain of an extraction.

Make sure you look after yourself now the show has begun. Always carry a gas mask, and use the Anderson shelter if the Germans ever bomb London. It may never come to that, but it's always best to be prepared. The other place to go would be down into a Tube Station, but it can get very cold and draughty there so wrap up well.
Anyway, I have to go now. Looks like we are finally getting orders.
Bye, my love, and see you soon.

Lots of love,

John

Jayne Sinclair put down the letter as the train left Stockport station, reaching for another white RAF envelope, the last in the pile.

Chapter Thirty

Saturday, May 11, 1940
Rouvre Aerodrome, France

John Sinclair climbed into the cockpit of his Hurricane, adjusting his parachute so he could sit on it. He had already walked quickly around the aircraft and talked to the ground crew, checking if there were any issues he should be concerned with.

'She's raring to go, sir,' was Sergeant Crowther's only response.

He carried out his pre-start checks and then pressed the twin starter buttons. The engine coughed twice, the propeller reluctantly kicked into action and his cockpit was shrouded in a cloud of white smoke. He listened to the Merlin engine for a moment; it was running sweetly.

Sergeant Crowther unplugged the starter motor and gave him the thumbs-up before removing the chocks from beneath the tyres of the Hurricane.

John Sinclair went through his pre-flight checks quickly; contacts, pressure, petrol, radiator, trim, flaps, all okay.

A glance across to the rest of his wing; Flight Lieutenant Barnett and Flying Officer Treadwell. Both gave him a thumbs-up.

He was glad to be back in the air again after a debacle of indecision and procrastination on the day before. His wing had finally received orders at 13.30 yesterday. And, rather than escorting bombers to attack the German forces at their most vulnerable – in full marching gear on the open road – they had been tasked to escort a reconnaissance flight of Blenheims.

'Waste of bloody time,' said Treadwell.

'We should be bombing the hell out of them,' said Barnett.

'We follow orders, understand?' As he spoke John Sinclair felt far older than his twenty-seven years.

'Ours not to reason why, ours but to do or die?'

'Something like that,' he replied, before tightening his harness and marching out to his plane.

Now here he was, ready to do what they were supposed to do. The morning briefing had been clear. Provide a fighter escort for the Blenheims as they searched for the positions of the German army. More reconnaissance.

Of course, he had trained for times like this, but the reality was far different. An unreal reality, as if this wasn't happening to him but to somebody else. Some other John Sinclair.

He dove into the pocket of his flight jacket, pulling out the picture of his wife and child. They both looked so beautiful, sitting in the studio with a painted backdrop behind them. Martin staring directly at the camera whilst Monique looked down on him, the proud mother etched into every corner of her face.

He jerked the cockpit canopy forward and locked it into place, slipping the picture into the gap between the metal and the glass where it could look over him like some Russian icon.

The handbrake off, a light touch on the throttle, and the Hurricane began to move forward, bumping along on the grass of the aerodrome.

The familiar sense of anticipation flowed through his body.

It was always like this whenever he was just about to take off; a wonderful sense of elation where any fear or worry vanished in a total absorption in the moment and the workings of his machine.

Then, with tail trimmer set, throttle and mixture lever fully forward, the plane picked up speed across the grass, puffs of grey exhaust smoke clearing at maximum r.p.m.

There was no sudden surge of acceleration, but only a steady increase in speed, and a thunderous roar from the exhausts just ahead on either side of the windscreen.

And then he was free of the earth and rising into the air. The brown, yellow and green fields of France lay beneath him, stretching to the horizon.

He checked behind him; both wing-men were in position, slightly above on either side. Their mission today was to provide fighter cover for a photographic reconnaissance the Blenheims.

The flight proceeded smoothly. The sky was clear blue, one of those wonderful winter days when visibility was almost perfect with hardly a breath of wind and just a few clouds like cotton balls floating in the air.

After making their rendezvous with the leader of the Blenheims over Reims, they began to follow the railway line to Metz before heading up to the border with Luxembourg and then along that line to Sedan and home.

It was over Thionville, just before the Luxembourg border, that the trouble began.

Two ME109s came diving out of the sun on to the Blenheims flying beneath. Five others came straight for them.

'Bandits at ten o'clock!' John shouted through his radio.

He instantly rolled his plane and went after the leading ME, raking a short burst across his tail before the German plane vanished in a cloud of smoke.

Had he hit him?

He glanced around the sky. Above his head were the long white lines of contrails painted against the blue sky. Where were Barnett and Treadwell?

He could hear their voices over the radio but couldn't see where they were. He had to gain height.

Then a shout from Treadwell. A ball of flame erupted from the tail of a Hurricane above him, a canopy opened and a black dot fell head over foot from the plane.

For a few seconds, Sinclair watched as the black dot fell faster and faster towards the ground, before a parachute opened and a man began to drift slowly to earth.

The Messerschmitts had broken off the attack and headed back towards Germany. Sinclair glanced down at the Blenheims. The port engine of one of them was on fire. Slowly it drifted out of position and began to fall towards the ground.

He waited for the three airmen of the crew to jump from the plane.

Nothing.

The plane drifted down and down, closer and closer to the brown and grey fields below it.

'Jump, you idiots, jump.'

No bodies tumbled out of the plane.

'Jump!' Sinclair shouted through his radio.

The Blenheim crashed into a field just south of a wood. An orange and black fireball erupted into the sky, forming for a moment before vanishing into flames.

Sinclair looked away before gathering himself. 'Red Leader, status report, over.'

The crackle of a radio before an Australian voice answered. 'Where the bloody hell did they come from, over? A-OK here, will abort mission and return to base, over?' The remaining Blenheim banked to the left, turning for home and the safety of his own airfield.

'Okay, Red Leader. Over and out.'

All the time, Sinclair was watching as Treadwell's parachute slowly drifted down to earth, landing in a field next to an old church.

Was he in France, Luxembourg or Germany? Sinclair thought it was France but he couldn't be sure. 'Barnett, head for Rouvre, over.'

'Roger, Flight Leader. Is Treadwell okay, over?'

'I think so. He jumped out and landed well. No doubt we'll see him in the mess this evening, over.'

Then, out of nowhere, he felt his aircraft shudder under the impact of cannon and machine-gun fire. One ME109 flashed past in front of him. He kicked his rudder and dived after it, trying to centre it in his ring sight. He pressed the twin firing buttons and let go a short burst.

Then a finger of flame flicked past his right hand cockpit window. He glanced behind him. The rear of his plane was covered in smoke, flames erupting from the tail assembly. Pushing the nose down, he jerked the canopy lever back and prepared to bale out. He stood up in his seat, glancing behind him again. The flames had died out but smoke and oil filled the cockpit.

'Are you okay, Leader?' Barnett's concerned voice came over the RT.

Sinclair checked for any German planes. The sky seemed to be as quiet and still as that April Sunday when he'd had afternoon tea with Monique and George. It seemed such a long time ago now. A time of innocence. An age and half a lifetime away. 'Going to head back to base. Should make it with a bit of luck, over,' he announced over the RT.

'Will escort you, over.'

'No, head back. I'll make my own way, over.'

He throttled back and turned for Rouvre. The plane coughed a few times but the Merlin engine kept going. His forward vision was limited due to the oil and smoke, so he flew the plane by leaning his head to the right outside the canopy and staring through the whirring propeller.

He checked the oil pressure gauge; it was dropping quickly. One of the bullets must have hit his oil tank.

'Keep going, old girl, not long now.'

He looked over his shoulder. The canvas skin of the Hurricane was still smouldering but holding together. With a bit of luck, he should just be able to make it back.

Then the Merlin engine coughed twice and stopped.

Deathly quiet.

No engine roar.

No surge of power as he touched the throttle.

No whirr of the propeller as it cut through the air.

Just the sound of the wind against the flaps covering the gun ports. A whistling sound like a banshee calling out to the spirits of the sky.

The nose dipped and he started to descend. Staring out over the wing, he saw a farmer with his horse walking towards a large, open field.

He banked right and levelled out the plane.

He was dropping quickly now, gliding directly over the farmer.

The man looked up and took off his cap. Sinclair could see the thick moustache growing in profusion beneath his bulbous red nose.

The Hurricane hopped over a hedge and dropped into the soft earth, sliding along on its belly and veering right.

Sinclair braced himself, feeling the impact of the ground, hearing the bottom of his plane scrape along the freshly turned earth before juddering to a stop.

Smoke was now pouring from the engine. He released his parachute harness and jumped out of the cockpit, landing flat on his face. When he looked up, a pitchfork was pointing directly at him, at its head the farmer with the luxurious moustache and bulbous red nose.

'Je suis un aviateur Anglais,' muttered Sinclair.

'Eh, bien… Vous en voulez du vin?'

From his knapsack the farmer produced an enormous flagon of red wine, offering it to John.

'Cheers, just what I needed.'

The operations officer sent a car later that morning to take him back to Rouvre, as they were moving to Reims later that day.

He never did see Treadwell again. His friend's body was later found by the gendarmerie, still attached to his parachute, hanging from an ash tree like a piece of forbidden fruit.

Chapter Thirty-One

Tuesday, May 14, 1940
Reims Aerodrome, France

They had been fighting now for four days and everybody was exhausted. After the loss of Treadwell, a new wing-man had been flown in from England: Tom Howard, a Kiwi fresh out of Cranfield.

Their whole squadron was now down to eight serviceable planes and slightly more, but less serviceable, pilots.

John Sinclair was slumped in his chair, the weariness weighing down every muscle in his body. Beneath his kit, sweat dried and crusted on his body; the glass canopy of his Hurricane magnified the power of the May sun.

He had already shot down two ME109s, a Dornier and a Junkers 88 in the last four days, flown seven sorties, and crash-landed once more when his undercarriage had refused to descend. They had been forced to leave Rouvre by the advancing Germans and were now ensconced in the less comfortable billet at Reims.

'Right, you lot, gather round.' Squadron Leader Moore called all the remaining pilots over to him.

John Sinclair levered himself out of the chair and hobbled stiffly over to where a detailed map of northern France was laid out across the table.

'Today, we are going to escort Fairey Battles in their attack on the pontoon bridges at Gaulier, just north of Sedan. Here…' He pointed with his swagger stick.

'I didn't think there were any Faireys left, sir,' said Barnett. The group around him laughed. 'I mean the aircraft…'

'Playfair has been husbanding them for this attack. It's vital that they destroy the bridges. If the German army gets across, they will be able to break out from Sedan and fan out across France.'

'How have the Germans got so far, anyway?' asked Sinclair.

The squadron leader shrugged his shoulders. 'Your guess is as good as mine. Ours not to—'

Sinclair leant forward, pointing to the area around the bridges on the map. '—reason why.' Sinclair finished the sentence for him. 'The Flak is murderous around the bridges. When we escorted the French Brevets this morning, all of it seemed to be concentrated at Gaulier. The Fairey will be a sitting duck, it's too slow.'

'The pilots are aware of the danger and all have volunteered. Your job is to prevent the ME109s from disrupting the attack. Clear?' They all nodded. 'Your planes are fuelled and ready. Take care, gentlemen.'

They turned to walk towards their planes. Sinclair tightened the straps of his parachute harness before climbing on to the wing of his plane to enter the cockpit. A ragged bullet hole in the fabric covering his wing struts was still apparent from the action that morning.

'No time to patch this up, Sergeant?'

'No, sir. No materials. We're waiting for resupplies from England. The Whitley carrying them went down over the Channel.'

Sinclair nodded once, thinking of the poor pilot and crew who would have to brave the choppy waters and currents of the sea.

'Haven't been able to put the covers on the guns either, sir,' the sergeant added. He pointed to the open areas along the leading edge of the wings, where the blue steel of a machine gun could just be seen. 'It's going to be a bit noisy up there, sir,' said Crowther.

'I'll survive.'

John climbed into the cockpit and adjusted the parachute beneath him. He gave a thumbs-up to Sergeant Crowther and depressed the starter motor. The engine coughed into life, spewing forth a stream of white smoke before running smoothly.

After a thumbs-up to the other pilots, Sinclair placed the picture of his wife and baby in its place on the windshield and released the brake. The Hurricane rolled forward, picking up speed along the grass-covered runway.

Gradually the speed increased. He seized the lever, the flaps went down and the Hurricane rose into the air. He pulled up and raised the undercarriage, turning the plane round in a shallow curve.

He was aloft, soaring into the sky, trailed by two other planes.

The first thirty minutes were quiet, almost peaceful. They made the rendezvous with the Fairey Battles and headed directly towards Sedan and the bridges, using the brown ribbon of the Meuse as a guide. From above, the Faireys seemed small and insignificant, their long glass canopies glinting in the late afternoon sun.

The enemy was nowhere to be seen.

'Perhaps he's gone home for afternoon tea,' said Barnett over the RT.

'Keep radio silence, Barnett – and watch out, they are here somewhere.'

Then it happened. Five ME110s, up above to the right.

'Ignore them, stay in position,' John instructed.

Five seconds later, eight ME109s dived out of the sun straight towards the bombers.

Sinclair kicked the rudder bar and dived down towards the attackers. An ME109 appeared in his ring sights and he fired. The Hurricane shuddered as all four machine guns poured their metal into the enemy's fuselage. The ME109 pulled a hard right and Sinclair lost him in the smoke.

Down below, a Battle was burning along one of the wings. John watched as it flipped over and plunged nose-first towards the ground.

No parachutes or falling bodies emerged into the May afternoon.

He had to gain height.

He pulled up his stick and started to climb. As he did so, he noticed five of the ME109s working round behind him. He pulled a hard right and sighted on the nearest machine. He fired a burst and the ME109 immediately dived to escape.

He continued to climb, firing a deflection shot at three 109s that crossed in front of him.

Where were Barnett and Howard? They should have been behind him.

As he turned to check on the Battles below, John felt the Hurricane shudder and shake as cannon shells raked its frame.

He had to get away.

He dived down.

More gunfire, the shells hitting his left wing now. The rudder was not responding beneath his feet, the plane spiralling down towards the green and brown earth of France. The Meuse on his left, wending its way to join the Rhine as it had done for millennia.

He reached up to the canopy to pull it open, but it wouldn't move.

The whistling of the wind through the gun ports was loud now, the banshee calling out to the spirits.

In the seconds before his Hurricane plunged into the earth, he reached for the picture of Monique and Martin attached to his windscreen.

He would never see them again.

He would never touch them again.

Their picture fell from his fingers.

He scrabbled to look at it one more time. Where was it?

A flash of the green-brown earth of France, fought over by thousands of men down through the centuries.

Then blackness.

Chapter Thirty-Two

Wednesday, December 27, 2017
Virgin Train from London to Manchester

As the train pulled out of Stockport station, Jayne reached for the last envelope. It was the same as the others; white with the London address and name of her grandmother written in faded blue ink.

She peered in. There were two letters inside this time, and neither was on the thin white RAF stationery, more like onion skin than real writing paper. Instead, one was a dirty yellow colour, flecked with bits of brown as if the paper was reconstituted or reworked. The other was much finer; a brilliant, almost fabric-like white.

She took out the yellow paper and opened the single vertical fold.

IMMEDIATE MRS MONIQUE SINCLAIR, FLAT 2, ALBANY ST, LONDON
IMMEDIATE FROM AIR MINISTRY, KINGSWAY P4599 17/5/40

DEEPLY REGRET TO INFORM YOU THAT YOUR HUSBAND FLIGHT LIEUTENANT JOHN SINCLAIR IS REPORTED TO HAVE LOST HIS LIFE AS A RESULT OF AIR OPERATIONS ON MAY 14 1940

THE AIR COUNCIL PROFESS THEIR PROFOUND SYMPATHY LETTER CONFIRMING THIS TELEGRAM GIVING ALL AVAILABLE DETAILS FOLLOWS

UNDER SECRETARY OF STATE AIR MINISTRY. 8.30. A/17

Jayne stared into mid-air.

Above her head, she could hear the train manager announcing, 'We are now approaching Piccadilly station, Manchester. Please ensure you take all valuables with you before you depart the train. It has been a pleasure having you on board this train…'

Jayne zoned out the rest of the message and reached for the second letter in the envelope, expecting it to give the details of her grandfather's death. Instead it was a type-written note with the monogram of Buckingham Palace at the top.

The Queen and I offer you our heartfelt sympathy in your great sorrow.

We pray that your country's gratitude for a life so nobly given in its service may bring you some measure of consolation.

The note was signed in ink.

George R.I.

Jayne sat for a long time on the train, she didn't know how long, staring out of the window but not really seeing anything.

Finally, a guard approached and touched her shoulder gently. 'We've arrived in Manchester, madam, it's time to leave the train now.'

She gathered her things quietly. There was so much to do now, so much to research.

She had to find out the truth behind her grandmother's death.

For her own sake.

For Monique's sake.

And for the sake of this man who had given his life in the service of his country.

Who had betrayed his wife?

Chapter Thirty-Three

Friday, May 17, 1940
Flat 2, Albany Street, London

She let the yellow telegram with its pasted-on words tumble to the ground.

He was dead?

How?

He had promised her he would come back. Only last week he had written to her saying that whatever happened he was coming back. She read the telegram again.

DEEPLY REGRET TO INFORM YOU THAT YOUR HUSBAND FLIGHT LIEUTENANT JOHN SINCLAIR IS REPORTED TO HAVE LOST HIS LIFE AS A RESULT OF AIR OPERATIONS ON MAY 14 1940.

He can't be dead. He said he would return, wouldn't do anything rash, would make sure he would come back to them.

Alive.

Well.

Happy.

Martin began to cry in the bedroom. Monique wiped the tears from her eyes and went to pick him up, holding his body close to her chest.

All alone now, both of them, all alone.

She checked his cloth nappy. Still dry; he must have been dreaming. She patted his back gently, singing a lullaby to send him to sleep again.

Dodo, l'enfant do,
L'enfant dormira bien vite
Dodo, l'enfant do
L'enfant dormira bientôt.

Une poule blanche
Est là dans la grange.
Qui va faire un petit coco
Pour l'enfant qui va fair' dodo.

The sound of more letters dropping on to the mat in the hall interrupted her song. Still carrying Martin, she strode out to the mat and gathered them up.

One was from the Ministry of Food, another a circular from her local WVS. The third was white with John's handwriting on it.

He was still alive.

She tore it open and began to read. He was telling her the Germans had invaded that morning but he would be careful and look after himself. He described the weather and what he had eaten for breakfast. It was the same as all his other letters; chatty, informal and positive.

He was still alive.

It must have been a mistake. She had read about such things happening in the newspapers but never thought it could ever happen to her.

The radio had reported heavy fighting but they said the lines were holding and the British had already advanced into Belgium.

Nothing about the RAF, though. What was happening? She had to find out.

She put Martin back down in his cot, covering him over. He immediately grasped the soft rabbit lying next to his pillow, swallowed twice and then settled down to sleep, a puzzled frown creasing his forehead.

Quietly she tiptoed out of the room, closing the door.

The telephone was in the hall She checked the number and dialled it directly, her fingers trembling as the dial slowly wound its way back to 0.

The phone at the other end rang three times before a woman answered. 'Squadron Leader Strachan's office.'

'I'd like to speak to David Strachan, please,' she said tentatively.

'Just one moment, I'll put you through.'

Before Monique had time to thank her, David was on the line. 'Strachan,' he barked.

'This is Monique, David. I just received a telegram about John.'

The tone of his voice softened. 'I've been dreading this call. John was killed in action over France three days ago, Monique.'

'But you don't understand, David. I received a letter from him this morning…'

'I received the information from his squadron commander. His plane didn't return from a mission on the afternoon of May fourteenth.'

'But I received a letter this morning…' she repeated.

'The news was confirmed by Flight Lieutenant Barnett. He watched John's plane go down.'

'But that can't be true. How could he manage to write to me—?'

'Check the dates, Monique. His body was found in the wreckage of his plane by the gendarmerie.'

Monique put down the phone and walked over to where she had dropped the letter and the telegram.

He was alive. She knew he was alive.

The date on the letter was scrawled in his handwriting: May 10, 1940. A week ago.

She picked up the telegram from the floor and looked at the date again: May 14, 1940. The letter was written before the telegram.

She glanced down at the table. One of John's peaked caps lay on top of a pile of papers. She picked it up, seeing the stains from his hair oil on the leather band inside.

He was dead.

She sat down and, from the depths of her soul, a piercing scream of pain issued from her mouth and she began to sob uncontrollably.

For herself.

For her baby.

But mostly for John, the man she loved.

Chapter Thirty-Four

Thursday, December 28, 2017
Didsbury, Manchester

It was past midnight when Jayne arrived home in Didsbury. The trams had already stopped running, so she had been forced to take a black cab from the station. She joined the back of the queue and stood there.

Eventually she reached the head of the queue and waited and waited and waited.

Wasn't it always like that? she thought to herself. Once you reach the front of the rank, there were never any cabs to be found.

The wind was getting stronger, bringing icy air and the threat of snow to the station concourse. She dug a woollen bobble hat out of her bag and pulled it over her head. 'Sod fashion,' she said out loud, stamping her feet on the pavement to keep them warm.

Finally, after ten minutes, just before she froze to death, a cab arrived and she was rattled back home, accompanied by the complaints of the driver about Manchester United and the way they had been playing under José Mourinho. She was so tired she didn't pay attention to what he was saying, simply grunting now and then when there was a pause in his sentences.

As soon as she walked through the door, Mr Smith pounced. She bent down to rub his ears. 'I know, I know. You're hungry and you want to go out. Which is it to be first?'

Understanding her words, he slinked over to his bowl and smelled it as if to say, 'It's empty, woman.'

'Okay, okay.' Without taking her coat off she opened the fridge door, pulling out one of his gourmet pouches. After the cat had been fed, she took her coat and scarf off and made herself a cup of tea.

As the warm milky drink warmed her bones, she thought about what to do next.

Her grandfather had been killed in the early days of the war, the telegram made that obvious. But how, and why? 'I have to know,' she said out loud.

Mr Smith looked up for a moment, thinking she was talking to him. When he realised she wasn't, he lapped some water, stretched his back legs and ambled over to the patio doors.

'I get the message. But it's cold outside, are you sure you want to go out?'

He looked at her, then back at the glass door.

'Okay, but don't blame me if you freeze to death.' Jayne opened the door and a blast of cold air whistled into the house. 'Off you go then.'

The cat stood for a moment at the open door, his whiskers twitching, then he bolted out through the patio door into the garden, vanishing in the gloom of a winter's night. He would let himself back in through the cat flap when he wanted.

'Bye, Mr Smith,' she shouted after him.

Then, realising how ridiculous she sounded shouting to a cat, she closed the door and sat down in front of her computer, booting it up.

She knew from the telegram that her grandfather was an officer, a flight lieutenant to be exact. Not a high rank, which suggested he was a relatively recent recruit to the RAF. If she remembered correctly, the

Army records for World War Two had been released, but not the records for the RAF. For some reason, they had been retained by the Air Historical Branch of the Ministry of Defence.

Where to go to find out the details?

She logged on to the National Archives site. It directed her to the Gov.uk site for information on RAF casualties in World War Two. Records were available and, as a relative, she could obtain them free of charge but she had to complete a form and didn't know how long they would take to arrive.

Was there a quicker way?

She thought for a moment before typing in the address for the Commonwealth Graves Commission. This was an online register of all graves of the dead of both world wars. She typed in John Sinclair's name in the search box. There were 66 men with the same name who had died in World War Two. So many good men's lives wasted, she thought as she scanned down the list.

There he was, and the date was correct: May 14, 1940. He was buried at Choloy War Cemetery in Meurthe-et-Moselle, France. She clicked on his name. The information came up on a separate page.

Flight Lieutenant (Pilot)
SINCLAIR, JOHN JAMES
Service Number 38756
Died 14/05/1940
Aged 27
73 Sqdn.
Royal Air Force
D F C

Son of Martin James Sinclair, and of Emma Sinclair, of Alnwick

There it was in black and white. Her grandfather's death was confirmed. But even more, she now had his squadron, rank and army number, which would make any new search much easier. Plus she also had his parents' names and residence. With a bit of luck, she could go much further back in the family history.

One other thing she noticed was that he had been awarded the Distinguished Flying Cross. She quickly checked the unit histories site for the RAF. His name was on the site, along with his date of birth – June 20, 1913 – and his service history. She was disappointed there was no picture, but there was an extensive note on the reason for awarding his medal:

During the course of operations between November, 1939 and May, 1940, Flight Lieutenant Sinclair has displayed coolness, courage and a devotion to duty far above the normal behaviour required of him. In particular, in a reconnaissance sortie in the Peronne area on the 10th May, 1940, this Flight Lieutenant sighted seven enemy bombers about 5,000 feet above him, and while giving chase well into Germany, he was attacked from behind by an enemy fighter. Showing the finest fighting spirit, this officer out-manoeuvred the enemy and although his own aircraft was badly damaged he succeeded in bringing the hostile aircraft down. Thick smoke and oil fumes had filled his cockpit and although unable to see his compass, he skilfully piloted his aircraft, returning to a British aerodrome with useful information despite his machine being badly damaged. In all operations between the November to May, Flight Lieutenant Sinclair has displayed coolness, courage and devotion to duty.

Obviously, her grandfather was a very brave man – a man whose bravery have probably cost him his life.

She checked the time. 1.45 a.m.

It had been a long day, an unsettling day; travelling down early, meeting her father and discovering that her grandmother had been murdered. She hadn't even started that investigation yet. Where to go next?

'No more tonight, enough,' she said out loud. Today had been too long and too fraught; tomorrow would be another day. A better day.

She reached out and turned off the computer, but just as her hand was poised over the button, a thought hit her. Her grandfather was a pilot in the RAF. Perhaps he had obtained his flying licence before he had applied to join the Air Force?

She clicked on to the Ancestry.com website and typed in her grandfather's name in one of the record sets: the Royal Aero Club Aviators' Certificates 1910-1950.

She waited for a moment as the machine searched for a result. Three matches came back, but only one with the full name of John Sinclair.

She clicked on it and waited again.

And then she was staring at a picture of her grandfather.

She took a sharp intake of breath, as if somebody had punched her in the stomach. She had never seen her grandfather's picture before.

He was a handsome man; thick black curly hair, high forehead, a slight smile playing on the lips and large ears that stuck out from the side of his head. She recognised the ears; they seemed to be a family trait. He was dressed in civilian clothes; a neat suit and tie, and a knitted sweater.

Beneath the picture, a hand-written description simply gave his name, certificate number 9764, and the date he had received it: December 2, 1935.

She stared at the picture for a long time before finally turning off her computer. This man was her grandfather and she had just looked at his face for the first time. Looked back at her own past, an unknown past.

What was she going to do next?

Chapter Thirty-FIve

Friday, December 29, 2017
Somewhere in Whitehall, London

James Penrose put down his fountain pen at the sound of the gentle tap on the door. He turned the memo over so that its top-secret and confidential designation was hidden from view.

He tapped the space key of the computer on his desk and his personal page appeared. Everything was supposed to be routed through secure and encrypted channels, but Penrose and a few of his close colleagues still preferred the old-school method of communication; the hand-written memo. It was easy to conceal, could be restricted to his own elite group and, not being on the server, was unavailable to prying eyes from more senior management. He always thought the problem with having memos on a server was that they were there for ever; never changing, never being deleted, his and his colleagues' words and games available in perpetuity.

With a paper memo, one simply needed to set fire to it in the ashtray and the information had vanished for good.

Far more effective, low-tech and cheap.

He took his cigar from the ashtray and inhaled, rolling the mellow smoke around his mouth. Of course, smoking was officially banned in the office.

But unofficially, who would ever have the guts to report him?

Nobody.

Another gentle knock on the door.

He placed the cigar back on the brass cradle and shouted 'Enter,' in a loud, annoyed voice. Always better to intimidate the juniors before they even came in rather than bother doing it when they were actually standing in front of him.

A young man – Perkins, he thought his name was – popped his head around the door.

'Sorry to disturb you, sir.'

'What is it, Perkins?'

The man entered the room carrying a brown file. 'It's Proctor, sir. Perkins is in Eastern Europe.' He smiled, raising his eyebrows. 'Well, not actually there, he's in that division.'

'Get on with it, man.'

Proctor visibly quailed. 'Yes, sir. You asked to be notified. I sent you an internal note.' He pointed to the computer. It was well known that Penrose didn't use his computer, except to do the online Times crossword.

'Well, now you're here you can tell me in person.'

'Yes, sir. There's a note on the file saying you must be informed if anybody ever visits a Mr Martin Sinclair in Belmarsh, sir. The prison, HMP Belmarsh.'

'I do know what Belmarsh is, Perkins. Well?'

'Well what, sir? And the name is Proctor, like the people who monitor exams at Cambridge.'

'Actually, the etymology of your name is Anglo-Norman; procuratour, from the Latin prōcūrō, or "I procure". It's a title used in English in three principal contexts; in law, in religion and in education. But in your case, Proctor, I rather think it may have been used in vain.'

The man shook his head. 'I don't understand, sir.'

'Never mind, Proctor. Who was it who visited Mr Sinclair?'

Proctor opened his file and glanced at a note. 'A Ms Jayne Sinclair, sir. We have all the details from her application to the prison and it appears she is his daughter.'

Penrose stared into mid-air for a long time. 'I thought this may come to pass one day,' he muttered under his breath.

'Pardon, sir?'

'Yes, you are pardoned. The meeting was recorded?'

'It was bugged, sir, as usual.'

'I do hate the word "bugged", Proctor, it makes me think of cartoon characters rather than the serious work we do.'

'Yes, sir, I won't use it again.'

'Don't. Have the recording transcribed and sent to me.'

'Yes, sir. By internal mail or on paper?'

'What do you think, Proctor?'

'I'll do both, sir.'

'No, you'll just send me a hard copy. And only me.'

'But that's against protocol, sir.'

'Bugger protocol. Now get out and get me that transcript.'

'Yes, sir.' The young man retreated quickly towards the door, backing out of Penrose's room with his front facing the Director all the while, like a medieval courtier leaving the Tsar.

Penrose remained seated, the smoke from his cigar gently drifting up to the tanned ceiling of his office. 'I hoped this would never happen,' he finally said out loud.

Chapter Thirty-Six

Saturday, June 01, 1940
Flat 2, Albany St, London

The days after John's death passed in a blur for Monique.

The doctor prescribed some medication to help her sleep and she lay in bed unable to move, simply weeping into her pillow during the day and crying herself to sleep at night.

Even Mrs Dodds came to visit, trying to encourage Monique to go shopping with her, but to no avail. Luckily, Mrs Beggs was around to help take care of Martin, taking him out and trying to give his mother time to rest and recover.

Monique found it difficult to get up in the morning, as if it were easier just to lie in bed and sleep away the war and all its horror.

One day, Mrs Beggs came into the bedroom carrying Martin on her hip and tapped her on the shoulder. 'Right, this has gone on long enough, Monique. Your husband is dead, but a lot of women will lose their husbands before this war is finished. You have a son who needs you. If you really want to cherish your husband's memory, cherish his son. Do something to help this country. Whatever. But do something, don't just lie there and mope.'

'Leave me alone.'

Mrs Beggs walked over to the windows and pulled back the blackout curtains to reveal the bright sunlight of a June morning.

'Leave you alone? There's young men being bombed on the beaches at Dunkirk! I'm sure they'd want to be left alone too, but they can't. If we're gonna win this war, we've got to stop treating it like some country picnic or a day out at the Derby.'

Monique turned around, shielding her eyes from the bright light.

Mrs Beggs sat on the edge of the bed. 'Listen, dear, your son needs to go out. You need to go out. Staying here in bed will do you, nor him, no good. No good at all.'

Monique sat up in bed. She knew Mrs Beggs was right.

'What can I do?'

'Well, you can get up out of bed for a start and you can take your son out into the fresh air. If you want to help they're giving out tea and sandwiches at Victoria station for the soldiers arriving back from Dunkirk. Why don't you take Martin and go and help?'

For the first time since she had received the news of John's death, Monique felt there was something she could do. 'You get Martin ready and I'll get changed.'

Within five minutes, they were all set. Martin was in his pushchair, a smile on his face as the prospect of going out in the world once again made him happy.

They walked to Victoria station. Outside, a prominent sign from the Daily Sketch said, BEF EVACUATION PROCEEDING. Another trumpeted, FURIOUS DUNKIRK FIGHTING.

Monique hurried on to the concourse. A long table was laid out at one side. On it was a large metal teapot, an array of cups and saucers, and a pile of sandwiches wrapped in greaseproof paper. Two women were hurrying around tidying up another table where dirty cups and saucers and half-eaten sandwiches had been deposited.

Monique walked up to them. 'Can I help?'

The younger woman looked up at her and then down at Martin sleeping in his pushchair. 'We'll be okay, dear. Once the rush is on, you'll only get in the way with a child.' The young woman turned away to speak to her companion. 'Mavis, when are they due?'

The older woman checked her watch. 'Five minutes, but the station master said they were going to be delayed.'

'I'll take these through and wash them.'

'I don't know if we have time, dear.'

'Can I help?' Monique repeated.

The older woman stared at her for the first time. 'Are you French?'

Monique nodded.

The woman rushed out from behind the table. 'Wonderful, of course you can help. There's lots of French soldiers coming through and we can't understand a word of what they're saying. You can help Iris put out the sandwiches while I wash these cups. Just park your child on the right behind the table, I'll be right back.'

The soldiers arrived fifteen minutes later. Most looked dirty and tired, shuffling along as if sleepwalking.

'Sandwiches and tea for the returning soldiers,' bellowed Mavis every few minutes, followed by Monique shouting, 'Des sandwich et du thé pour les soldats ici. Venez mes compatriotes.'

Soon the table was surrounded by British and French soldiers, crowding round the table as Monique and Mavis served them tea and helped them take a sandwich. The younger woman, Iris, kept a running supply of fresh cups and saucers.

An English soldier hesitated before taking a sandwich. 'You want another, dear?' said Mavis. 'We've got plenty and there's a new batch arriving soon.'

'Thanks, pet, don't mind if I do,' answered the soldier in a broad Geordie accent.

'A cup of tea to go with it?'

'Aye, that'd be grand.'

'Sugar's at the end of the table, but be careful with it. It's rationed, you know.'

One French soldier was limping along, his arm around the shoulders of a comrade.

'Can you tell him there's a medical station quite close, just around the corner? Sorry, I didn't catch your name.'

'Monique,' she said, handing another soldier a cup.

'I'm Mavis. Can you tell him in French? It's just round the corner on the left. There's a doctor and nurses waiting to treat him.'

Monique explained the way to go, stuffing two sandwiches in the large pockets of the man's greatcoat.

Another young soldier, his face covered in oil and dirt, sat on the ground of the concourse with his back resting against a pillar, tears forming clear rivulets through the muck on his face.

Mavis stopped what she was doing and came out with a sandwich and a cup of tea.

'Here you are, dearie, get something warm inside you.'

He looked up at her for a moment, his green eyes wet with moisture. 'I never thought I'd make it home.'

'Where's home, dear?' asked Mavis, handing him the tea.

A look of confusion spread across the man's face. 'Here, England.'

'But whereabouts, dear?'

The man took a sip of the hot tea. A smile spread across his face and he rested his head back against the pillar. 'Manchester,' he finally said.

'Is that where you're going?'

He nodded.

'Well, take your time, dear, and drink your tea. I'll get the station manager to tell you when the next train is leaving.'

And the man fell asleep where he sat, the cup of tea still balanced on his lap.

For the rest of the day, they worked tirelessly as the trains arrived one after another into the station, disgorging troops returning to London, or transiting to the north and west.

Martin slept for a long while, then he played with Mavis as his mother served the tea and biscuits – by now, the sandwiches had run out.

It was only at six o'clock that they finally were relieved by new members of the WVS.

'You'll come again tomorrow?' Mavis asked as they were leaving. 'And bring Martin with you.'

Monique nodded.

She returned the following day and every day for the next week, until there were no more trains transporting the soldiers back from Dunkirk. Sometimes Martin came with her and at other times he stayed with Mrs Beggs until Monique arrived home, tired but happy.

In that week, she lost the despair that had overwhelmed her since John died.

Her fight back had begun.

Chapter Thirty-Seven

Saturday, September 07, 1940
Flat 2, Albany St, London

It was a glorious late summer's day when Monique woke up. The sun was shining and the sky was blue, with only a few cotton balls of cloud drifting across the south-east. There were a few aircraft contrails lined across the sky. The Battle of Britain, as the newspapers called it, had been fought for nearly three weeks now, but Monique had seen little of it, except for the inescapable white lines written by innumerable planes in the sky.

Every time she saw them she thought of a quiet man like John, all alone up there with the noise of his aircraft engine as the only company. Of course, she had listened to the radio with their talk of brave men and flying machines, but all she could think of was one man and his one machine.

A man who did not come back.

She had kept the thought of John from her mind by working hard. Since the evacuation from Dunkirk, she had been helping three days a week with the WVS, liaising with the French Army as her language skills came in useful. Martin was looked after by Mrs Beggs during the day. She seemed to love him as much as he loved her, waving goodbye to Monique as she went off to work with nary a care in the world.

Thoughts of John only came to her when she was alone in bed at night, Martin snoring beside her. Only then did she allow herself to weep.

This particular morning Mrs Beggs had taken the day off to be with her grandchildren in the East End, so Monique dressed Martin, saying,'Shall we go and visit George?'

At the sound of his friend's name, Martin gave a big toothless smile and mouthed, 'Jor.'

She placed his gas mask in her bag. It looked like the type of helmet sea divers wore, with the addition of a small pump at the side which she had to keep opening and closing like a small bellows.

Martin hated it.

She took it anyway. If one of the more officious Air Raid Wardens saw her without it, she would be scolded and possibly fined. Before leaving her flat, she draped her white gas-mask box over her shoulder and hurried to the lift.

It was a beautiful day. Perhaps they could take George to Hyde Park. For a second, the memories of ice cream with John intruded into her mind, before she banished the sadness by concentrating on pushing Martin down the steps to the street.

They emerged into bright sunlight. Despite it being early in the morning, everywhere people were wearing short sleeves and summer dresses. Even the office workers had their jackets draped over their shoulders.

She took the tube to Victoria. Inside was stifling, the heat amplified by the cluster of bodies inside the carriage. She was so glad to escape and carry Martin up the steps on to Wilton Road.

As she was walking across the street, with Martin gurgling happily in the pushchair, a droning noise filled the air. Monique looked up to see wave after wave of planes flying overhead. Most people stopped what they were doing and stared up at the sky. Were the RAF heading to Germany again?

Seconds later the air-raid siren began to sing, adding its high-pitched whine to the confusion and drone of the aircraft.

People began running aimlessly.

An Air Raid Warden called out to her. 'Inside here.' He gestured for her to enter a sand-bagged shelter. 'Hurry up! Can't you see those are German planes?'

He helped her carry Martin and his pushchair down the steps. Inside, the shelter was crammed with people. Some office clerks on a break, others ready to go Saturday shopping, a few carrying bags on their way home.

The door was shut and the electric lights switched on.

'Now, keep calm, everybody, don't panic. This won't be long.'

'Is it another drill?' asked one of the office workers. 'Only I've gotta go back to work. The boss'll kill me if I'm not there.'

The Air Raid Warden ignored him.

Outside, the droning from the sky was getting louder. Soon, the noise of bangs and soft crumps was added to counterpoint the sound of the aircraft engines. The ringing bells of fire engines added another high-pitched note, fading as they moved further away.

'Those are bombs, those are,' said the Air Raid Warden. 'I thought I'd never hear that sound again.'

The people in the shelter, about twenty in all, didn't say a word; they just listened to the noises outside.

Martin was quiet too. Monique took him out of the pushchair and held him close to her breast. He nuzzled into her, aware that something was wrong, but not really understanding what it was.

Along one side of the shelter was a bench. A man stood up to let her sit down and she thanked him. He raised a bowler hat in return.

A woman moved up along the bench. 'You sit here, dearie. He's a lovely chap, isn't he?' She rustled Martin's hair. He buried his face in Monique's body, studiously avoiding the woman.

The sound of the planes continued all afternoon, wave after wave going overhead.

Inside the shelter, tempers began to fray as the air became stuffy and the heat increased. Martin decided to fall sleep, only waking up once for a bottle and then promptly went back to sleep again.

Even when he was awake he stayed quiet, ignoring all the people around him, burying his face into his mother's body.

Monique stared straight ahead, listening to the sounds of the war outside the shelter.

Late in the afternoon, the all-clear finally sounded. Everybody in the shelter heaved a collective sigh of relief.

The Air Raid Warden opened the door and a breeze rushed in. Air that had a slight smell of burning attached to it.

He helped carry Martin's pushchair back up to the street. When they reached ground level, he stood up and stared out towards the docks.

'Will you look at that?'

In the east, an orange glow suffused the sky, like the early hours of dawn or the last throes of twilight. An eerie light that danced and swayed across the sky.

'They've bombed the East End. The docks must've taken a beating.'

The smell of burning drifted across on the wind.

Should she still go to visit George or return home? 'Will they come again?' she asked.

The Air Raid Warden stroked his greying moustache. 'Might do, you never know. The Germans were always very canny people.'

They both stared towards the docks. In the far distance, a large flame rose up to lick the sky before flickering back to earth.

'I'd go home, if I were you. And if the sirens sound again, make for the nearest shelter as fast as you can.'

The Air Raid Warden grunted and walked back down the steps to the safety of his underground cave.

Monique looked back across the road to Victoria. Should she go home? But she was so close to Mrs Dodds now. Even if they didn't get to Hyde Park this afternoon, Martin could still play with George.

She decided to push on. Walking quickly, she strode up Vauxhall Bridge Road, walking past the Palace Theatre; many a night she had spent there with John and the Dodds. Right into Carlisle Place and left into Morpeth Terrace.

The Dodds' apartment was just around a dog-leg corner. Martin was getting more excited as he recognised where he was going, rocking backwards and forwards in his pushchair, urging her to go faster.

She turned the corner and the Dodds' apartment wasn't there.

Just a collapsed wall that showed the inside of the living room, a picture still hanging on the wall, tilted at an angle. At the bottom of the building a pile of rubble lay heaped against the wall, fires glowing deep in its heart.

She shook her head. The rest of the terrace was intact. Just one building reduced to rubble.

The Dodds…

She pushed Martin along, running towards the building. A fireman blocked her way.

'You can't go inside there, love, too dangerous.'

'But my friends, George, they lived there.'

The fireman glanced back towards the smoking heap of rubble. 'If they were inside they didn't stand a chance, love. Nobody could survive a direct hit.'

Chapter Thirty-Eight

Tuesday, January 02, 2018
Somewhere in Whitehall, London

Penrose placed the transcript of Miss Sinclair's meeting with her father at Belmarsh Prison back on his desk. He adjusted the blotter so it was at exactly 90 degrees to the right-hand side of his desk. It did annoy him if things were out of place. Just as Miss Sinclair annoyed him. It would have been so much easier to let sleeping dogs – or in this case, sleeping prisoners – lie.

But it was not to be. Human beings had the awful tendency to disturb even the most carefully laid plans of mice and bureaucrats.

He picked up his half-smoked cigar and lit the end again, taking in a deep inhalation and rolling the smoke around his teeth. What to do next?

The transcript was maddeningly inexact; lacking the pauses, silences and hesitations that imparted so much meaning to speech. He would have to listen to the actual tape to get a feeling for the characters involved, particularly Miss Sinclair.

What was her motivation in all this? Of course, there was the obvious one of meeting her father for the first time – but what else was driving her?

He would have to see her police personnel file, of course. There would be something in there on why she left the force. Why would a woman with such a promising career pack it all in and become a family historian? He wanted particularly to see her psychological profile. There must have been an inciting incident that drove her to leave behind a good job and an even better pension for the uncertainties of life in civvy street.

He didn't have long to go himself before they put him out to grass. The thought of spending more time with his wife appalled him. It would be the peculiar hell of interminable games of bridge and the baking of Victoria sponges.

A shudder went from his Oxford brogues up through his Savile Row-clad body, exiting somewhere near his Cutler and Gross spectacles. Perhaps he could delay retirement? Plead a special case? The thought of leaving this particular matter in the clammy hands of Proctor and his ilk scared him more than facing a squadron of Cossacks on the rampage.

He pressed the intercom on his desk.

'Yes, Mr Penrose?'

'Get me Proctor or Perkins or Price, whatever he's called.'

'Yes, Mr Penrose.'

The knock on the door came three minutes later.

'Come.'

A head peered round the door.

'Come in, Proctor, you're entering my office, not burgling it.'

The man stepped through the door sharply. 'Yes, sir.'

'Get me the original tape of the meeting between the Sinclairs.'

'The transcript is not good enough, sir? I did it myself.'

'That explains it, Proctor.'

'Yes, sir.' The man turned to leave.

'And please arrange for Miss Sinclair's communications – mobile phone, computers, letters – to be monitored. I want to know who she's talking to.'

'No surveillance, sir?'

'Not yet. But track her mobile phone. We'll know from that where she is going.'

'Yes, sir.' The man hung around as if waiting to ask another question.

'Now, Proctor, not some time in the next millennium.'

'Yes, sir. And Happy New Year, sir.'

'Is it?'

'Are you doing anything? We have the inter-departmental Hogmanay tonight. I'm dancing a Scottish reel.'

'Sounds horrendous, Proctor. Don't cut yourself on the swords. I'll be having a wonderful time with Mrs Penrose, listening to her knit one and purl one. Always sends me to sleep. Well, what are you waiting for?'

Proctor scurried out of the door as if he were being chased by a sabre-toothed tiger.

'Heaven help us if the likes of Proctor are going to protect us in the next twenty years,' Penrose muttered to the closing door. 'You just can't get the staff these days.'

He then picked up his fountain pen to annotate the transcript once more.

He might have missed something important.

Chapter Thirty-Nine

Tuesday, January 02, 2018
Buxton Residential Home, England

The previous days had been trying for Jayne.

The good news had been that Robert was released from hospital and was convalescing at the Home in Buxton with Vera. They had spent a quiet New Year's Eve together before Robert felt tired and went to bed early. Jayne had spent a couple of hours to see in the New Year with Vera and the rest of the residents before heading back to Didsbury along a very quiet A6.

All in all, it was a subdued start to 2018.

The bad news was that Jayne wasn't certain how to proceed with the investigation into the lives of her grandfather and grandmother. This uncertainty was unusual for her. Normally, investigations proceeded smoothly, with each discovery leading on to the next. But in investigating her own family, she seemed to have stalled. There simply wasn't enough information to work with.

As she drove down the A6 to see how Robert was, tucked in behind an old dear who insisted on driving at 25 miles per hour in the centre of the road, she went through the case in her mind. Martin Sinclair had said his mother was betrayed, but how? It seemed she was a Frenchwoman who had married John Sinclair in 1938, having a baby on the first day of World War Two: September 3, 1939. That baby turned out to be her own father, Martin.

John Sinclair was killed in the first year of the war, flying for the RAF during the German invasion of France. A brave man, he had won the Distinguished Flying Cross. What had happened to her grandmother and how had she been betrayed? That's what Jayne didn't understand.

The woman in front finally signalled left and Jayne accelerated past her.

Where could she go next? She had looked in the Deaths Registry for Monique Sinclair and Monique Massat, her maiden name, but there was no listing. Surely she couldn't still be alive? She would be nearly one hundred years old if she were. And didn't her father say she was dead, and that he had been made an orphan?

She parked the car outside the Home, her brain still turning over the problem. Inside the reception, Rachel was manning the desk.

'How is he today?'

'Much better, back to his old self. Matron is very pleased with him.'

That was a turn-up for the books; the Matron being pleased with Robert for a change.

'They're in the lounge if you want to see them.'

'Doing the crossword?'

'Right first time. Or, in their case, right after about six hours working on the clues.'

Jayne smiled as she walked past the television room into the lounge. Vera and Robert were the only people there. She heard Robert's voice as soon as she entered. She could see them both sitting down on the couch with their backs to her. Robert had a shawl over his shoulders and was holding the newspaper.

'I don't think it's Glasgow, Vera.'

'It must be. Read the clue again.'

'"A short drink travels to the head of Wales for a place in Scotland".'

'A drink is a glass and if you shorten it, you get "Glas". "Travels to" could be "go" and "the head of Wales" is "W". A place in Scotland is Glasgow.'

'Aye, happen you're right, love. I'm so happy I married such a clever woman.' They both kissed each other on the lips.

Jayne thought it was time to let them know she was there. She coughed politely.

Vera turned round. 'Oh, hello, Jayne, we didn't hear you come in.'

Jayne walked forward to kiss Robert on the top of his head. 'How you feeling?'

'Much better now I'm out of hospital. It's funny, love, but when you leave a hospital you always feel better.'

'Perhaps it's being surrounded by sick people,' suggested Vera.

'And the smells. All that antiseptic and carbolic soap can't be good for anybody.'

'No more chest problems?'

'There's still a bit of wheezing there, but another couple of days of tablets should get rid of that,' said Vera.

'I feel like a bloomin' chemist, I do. I've got so many drugs to take, I could open up my own shop.'

Jayne sat down in front of them.

'Would you like some tea?' asked Vera. 'They'll be round in a minute with elevenses.'

Jayne shook her head.

'What's up, lass? You don't look at all well.'

'It's the investigation. I've discovered quite a bit so far but I'm nowhere near finding out the truth of why my father killed David Strachan.'

She spent the next thirty minutes taking them through what she had discovered.

'You've done well, Jayne,' Robert finally said. 'I didn't know your grandfather was a war hero.'

'I could go to the RAF and request his unit's history and find more about what he was doing in France, but...'

'But what, lass?'

'It doesn't get me any closer to solving the mystery of what happened to my grandmother. Why was she betrayed? And why did Martin Sinclair murder David Strachan?'

A shroud of silence hung over them for a minute before Vera spoke up.

'It seems to me, Jayne, there is only one thing you can do.'

'What's that?'

'You need to go back to see your father. You need to get more information from him.'

Robert stared at her. 'Happen Vera is right, lass. If you want to get to the bottom of all this, it's the right thing to do.'

Chapter Forty

Thursday, September 03, 1942
Hereford, England

They had saved up the eggs from their ration books and bought some more, plus some fresh cream from the side door of a farm, just on the other side of the road across from the cottage.

Martin stared at the three candles burning brightly on his birthday cake, the result of a long afternoon of baking by Aunt Betsy, assisted by Monique.

'Go on, make a wish and blow them out,' shouted Aunt Betsy.

Martin reached out for them instead.

'No, no, my sweet – blow. Like this…'

The candles wavered in her breath as she pretended to blow them out.

Martin puffed out his rosy cheeks and blew hard. One of them went out and he clapped his hands excitedly.

'Blow the others out too, dear,' Monique encouraged him.

He sucked in a lungful of air, and blew both out in one breath, clapping his hands again.

'Now, you are going to eat as much of the Victoria sponge as you can,' said Betsy. 'Them raspberries come from our garden, they do. The jam could be a little sweeter, but we couldn't get the sugar. Never mind, hey.'

She cut the cake, placing a large piece in front of Martin and smaller pieces on plates for Monique, Dan and herself.

Monique had been in Hereford for nearly two years now, slowly getting used to the rhythms of the countryside. After Mrs Dodds and George had been killed on the first day of the Blitz, she had stayed in London for a short time to help Mr Dodds. But gradually the bombing had become worse, with almost daily raids on London.

The final straw had come when the house two doors away in Albany Street was demolished one evening by a German bomb. They had been sitting in the Anderson shelter in the rear of the garden, waiting for the all-clear to sound. There were just five of them that evening: Mr Paterson from the ground floor and the Greggs from above her, with their baby girl. They had made sure to bring hot cocoa, buttered toast, and books, lots of books. It was five in the morning. There had been no sound of bombers since 2.30 a.m.

'They must have gone by now. I want to go back to a nice warm bed.' Mr Paterson opened the Anderson shelter's door. At the same time, a single droning sound could be heard overhead. Seconds later there was an almighty explosion. Mr Paterson was sent hurtling through the air, crashing against the bench, and the door was blown off one of its hinges.

Mr Paterson was winded but not badly injured. Somehow or other, Martin had managed to sleep through it all. They had gone out into the garden to see that the house two doors away had been blown to smithereens; all that remained was a pile of smoking bricks and burning timbers. The ARP wardens spent the next day looking for survivors but there were none. Seven people had died.

The next day Monique had written to Aunt Betsy, asking if she could come and stay with her in the cottage in Hereford.

That was nearly two years ago now. The time had gone slowly for Monique. In her years in London, she had become a town girl. The rhythms of the countryside, the time-worn traditions of doing certain things at exactly the same time every year, had no attraction for her any more. It was like living in a perpetual cycle of growth and death with short, sharp periods of activity in between.

Often she went on long walks. Inevitably, she thought of John and what could have been if the war hadn't come between the two of them.

Martin was happy living with Betsy and Dan. They loved him as the child they had never had and he, in return, loved them with all the artlessness of a three-year-old.

Dan became his substitute father whilst Betsy was far more than a substitute mother. She was a carer, a feeder, a person to cuddle. Martin had even taken to sleeping with both of them rather than his mother. It seemed as if Monique was the stranger, the distant relative in the relationship.

On her long walks, she often wondered if she were jealous of Betsy and Dan's relationship with Martin. And she realised she wasn't. Something had changed in her when John and George had died. It was almost as if something inside of her had died as well. The longer they stayed at the cottage, the more of a stranger she felt.

Yesterday, the day before Martin's birthday, she had finally made her decision.

'I'm going back to London, Betsy.'

The woman's face became crestfallen. 'I suppose you'll be taking Martin with you?'

Monique shook her head slowly. 'If it's okay with you, I think he should stay here. I've decided I have to help out in the war effort, I can't just sit it out here.'

'You can, you're always welcome to stay.'

'I know, but after John died I keep thinking I should be involved more. I should be doing more. Martin loves you and he loves Dan. He's happy here, and if I am doing war work, it won't be fair on him to live in London with me.'

'You know we'll look after him.'

She wrapped her arms round Betsy. 'I know you will.'

Betsy pulled her head away. 'Think about it a bit longer, will you?'

And she had thought about it. Seeing Martin smiling and happy, his mouth stuffed with Victoria sponge and his cheeks red with raspberry jam, had finally convinced her.

He would be happy here and she needed to do more.

That evening she sat in front of the mirror when everybody had gone to sleep, brushing her hair before she went to bed. She stared at her face; lined now, marked by the unhappiness of war before her time.

John gone.

Mrs Dodds gone.

George gone.

She looked at her left hand. Her wedding ring was still there, the old gold glistening in the light from the candle.

Slowly she took it off, wrapped it in paper and placed it in an envelope, addressed to Betsy.

That part of her life was over and a new one was about to begin.

She left early the following morning, kissing Martin on the head as he slept in Betsy's arms.

She thought about waking him up but decided that this way was for the best.

Closing the cottage door quietly behind her, she picked up her suitcase and strode out down the street towards the station without looking back..

Chapter Forty-One

Thursday, January 04, 2018
HMP Belmarsh, Thamesmead, London

Of course, Vera was right. Jayne did need to get further information from her father otherwise she could be spending years going round in circles. He must know more than he was telling her.

She was waiting in the prisoners' meeting room. The same guard as her last visit was on duty at the door. This time, though, there was another family at a table in the corner. A husband and wife, probably. The man was leaning over the table whispering to his wife as the child played with a red fire-engine toy next to her, not reacting to his father at all.

Jayne had travelled down that morning from Manchester, having left Mr Smith in the cattery yesterday. He was not a happy bunny when she left him in his cage, his paw clawing at the wire as if waving goodbye to her. But this time, she wasn't sure when she would be back from London. If her father didn't give her any new information then she would go to the National Archives and research the war diaries of her grandfather's unit.

The prison guard stepped smartly forward and unlocked the door.

Her father shuffled into sight. It had been less than a week since she had last seen him, but he looked smaller and thinner already, the cancer inside him already wreaking havoc on his body.

He sat down in front of her. 'Hello, Jayne, I didn't expect to see you here so quickly.'

She took him through her research so far. 'So that's as far as I've got.'

He made a moue with his mouth, the thin grey lips vanishing into an even thinner grey line. 'I would have thought you'd have done better, Jayne.'

'I need more information. The letters weren't enough. They only gave me my grandfather's history. But it's my grandmother you wanted me to investigate, Martin, wasn't it?'

He thought for a moment. 'We don't have much time. I'm dying, Jayne.'

'You told me that before,' Jayne said as casually as she could.

'So you have to work more quickly.'

'Help me.'

His eyes flicked up to the ceiling, like a cornered rat looking for an escape. 'She joined the SOE,' he said slowly, as if the words were being dragged from his mouth kicking and screaming.

'The Special Operations Executive? The wartime spies?'

He nodded. 'She abandoned me, a three-year-old boy, to go off and play soldiers.'

'But why?'

For a moment, her father looked almost human; a little boy trying to understand why his mother was no longer there to give him hugs and tuck him into bed at night. 'Don't you think I've asked myself that question every day since? Why did she leave her son to go to fight against the Germans? To liberate her country? To take revenge on those who had killed her husband, my father?' He shrugged his shoulders. 'I've asked myself so many times over the years but I've never found an answer. All I remember is waking up one morning and she wasn't there any more. Then Aunt Betsy died not long after and I was left with Uncle Dan.' He paused for a moment and his eyes glazed over as if was reliving those days. 'You know, I killed my first rabbit at six years old. Dan showed me how to break its neck. We used to go hunting together…'

Jayne needed to understand what happened to her grandmother. 'When did your mother leave?' she interrupted.

He stared straight at her, his eyes refocussed. 'I'm not certain. I remember her not being there but I'm not certain if that was when she left or if it was after a visit. I was so young, and time, like everything else in prison, tends to play tricks with the mind. But Uncle Dan told me she first went away in 1942.'

'And you never saw her again?'

A film of moisture appeared in his eyes. He looked old and tired and sad now. 'I can't remember.'

'When was the last time you saw her?'

And in a moment, the old, sad man disappeared and something more malevolent appeared in his place. 'That's for you to find out, Jayne. Do you expect me to do all your work? It's your turn to work out who betrayed her, who killed her.'

'But I've looked for her death certificate and there isn't one in the registers.'

'You're looking in the wrong place.' He stood up, pushing the chair back under the table and leant towards her. 'I've applied for a compassionate release, Jayne. With the diagnosis of cancer, the Governor thinks I have a good chance.'

In a move so quick she was unsure it happened, he thrust a piece of paper into her left hand, checking the guard hadn't noticed what he had done.

Jayne was so surprised, she mumbled, 'When will they let you out?'

'Soon, but I won't be totally free, they don't trust an old man enough. They may put me into a halfway house.'

Jayne had been to these places when she was a detective, usually to arrest somebody who had broken the terms of their probation or simply committed another crime. 'At least you'll be out of here.'

A look of madness crept into his eyes. He glanced around and leant closer to her. 'Don't you realise, I'll never me out of here.' His face softened for a second and Jayne saw the frightened old man hidden behind the tough exterior. 'Help me, Jayne. Help me find out who betrayed my mother.'

Jayne thought for a moment. 'But it happened so long ago. Can't you just forget about…'

'But for me it happened yesterday. Don't you realise that? The only way I can justify my life, justify all the years spent in here, is by finding out the truth.'

Then he shuffled back towards the door.

'Help me, Jayne,' he said as the the guard unlocked it

Martin Sinclair walked through without bothering to look back at his daughter.

Jayne glanced down at the piece of paper he had passed across to her. In a shaky hand, the words, 'They are watching us.' were written in blue biro.

Chapter Forty-Two

Monday, November 16, 1942
London, England

It took Monique over two months to get an interview with the Women's Voluntary Service. She thought it would be easy; just give them a call and then sign up to take part in the war effort. But no, despite being at war, the British had still not lost their love for slow-moving bureaucracy.

After calling them, she was told to pick up a form which she duly completed and returned.

Then she waited and waited and waited. London was quieter now; the continuous air-raid sirens and mad dashes to underground shelters had all but ceased. Even the news was better. El Alamein had been fought and the Germans seemed to be in full retreat, while the Americans had landed behind them in Casablanca. It looked like the tide had finally turned. Monique noticed a cautious optimism pervading the city, so different from two years ago at the height of the blitz.

Two months later, after staying back at her old flat in Albany Street, and calling the WVS virtually every day, she was allocated a time for an interview.

She turned up precisely ten minutes early in her two-piece suit, neatly fashioned using a whole year's worth of ration coupons. She didn't have any nylons so she used an eyebrow pencil to mark a line down the back of her legs. The last of her lipstick went on her lips in a thin layer.

She checked the mirror before she left. 'Beauty is a duty,' she mouthed to herself, repeating the theme on so many of the posters.

Eventually she was called to sit at a desk manned by an austere old lady with her hair in a bun and thick spectacles. The woman stared at the form Monique had filled in, then spoke in a rich, plummy, patronising voice.

'You say you were a nanny before the war... Mrs Sinclair?'

'That's correct.'

'Not much call for nannies in the WVS. We're here to support civil defence and provide services not catered for locally by other official organisations, such as organising evacuations, managing shelters, clothing exchanges, mobile canteens, that sort of thing. Ever done anything like that?'

Monique shook her head. 'I'm afraid not. But as a nanny one gets used to organising time.'

She sniffed. 'Your form says you have been living in Hereford for the last two years. What have you been doing?'

What had she been doing?

She laughed off her discomfort at the question. 'Not a lot, I'm afraid. Looking after my son Martin mostly.'

'You have a child?' The woman made a note on the form.

'Yes. He's three years old.'

'The father?'

Monique swallowed. Even after over two years the words were still so difficult to say. 'He was shot down in France in 1941.'

Not a trace of emotion or sympathy crossed the woman's face. 'I'm sorry to hear that,' she said mechanically before looking up from the form and staring at Monique. 'Do I detect a foreign accent?'

'I was born in France but married an Englishman.'

The woman nodded once before pushing back her chair. 'If you'd excuse me for a moment.' She got up and went through a door into the back room.

Monique wondered what she had done wrong. Would being a foreigner exclude her from joining the WVS? Nobody had ever mentioned it to her. Well, she would just join the ATS instead, or perhaps sign up for the WAAFs. She must be of use to somebody, somewhere.

Monique was just about to leave when the door opened again and the woman bustled out, followed by a man wearing the uniform of an RAF officer.

'Monique,' he said loudly.

She looked up. David Strachan stood in front of her.

'Well, this is a surprise, but it's wonderful to see you.' He kissed her on both cheeks. 'What are you doing here?'

'I want to help. Whatever you want me to do in the WVS, I'll be more than happy.'

'I'm sorry I haven't seen you since John died. I've had rather a lot to do. Tell me what's been happening to you.'

She told him about the death of George and Mrs Dodds, her life in Hereford and about Martin.

'You have been through an awful lot.'

'I just want to do something – anything, David. I can't stay at home any more and pretend the war doesn't exist.' She glanced across at the woman standing behind the desk. 'I'll work in the WVS, doing anything you want.'

'Oh, I'm not with the WVS. Another body completely,' he smiled. 'Something far more… adventurous.' He placed his hands on the table. 'To be honest, we're looking for native French speakers for some special work. When Miss Trubshaw here,' he pointed at the austere woman, 'heard you were French, she immediately contacted me. Listen, would you be interested in doing special work for the war effort? There is an element of danger, I'm afraid, but it is vital work.'

He sat back and waited for her reply.

'Yes,' she said straight away.

Chapter Forty-Three

Wednesday, December 16, 1942
The Victoria Hotel, London

A month after their meeting, David Strachan rang Monique and told her to go to the Victoria Hotel on Wilton Road, at 11 a.m. on a cold Wednesday morning.

As she walked to the hotel from the underground station, she passed the shelter where she and Martin had spent the first hours of the Blitz. So long ago now it seemed like it had happened to another person.

The Victoria Hotel was a slightly run-down, seedy building with an entrance covered in sandbags and guarded by a single stationary soldier.

She showed her ID and was met in the lobby, not by David Strachan, but by a dark woman wearing a severely cut tweed suit. 'I take you up to meet him on the fifth floor,' said the woman. She spoke with a foreign accent but Monique couldn't place it. Eastern European or something similar, she thought.

'Him' turned out to be a small, dapper, extremely courteous man wearing round tortoiseshell spectacles and a mauve cardigan. A man with all the military bearing of a pair of nylons.

'My name is Selwyn Jepson. Captain Selwyn Jepson. How do you do?' He held out his hand. The voice was educated but effeminate. 'I suppose you're wondering who I am and what you are doing here.'

'It had crossed my mind, yes.'

'Please sit down.' He indicated a couch opposite an armchair. The room was one of the hotel's suites, which had been gutted and turned into an office. But an office without desks, with all the feel of a gentleman's study.

After making himself comfortable and offering her tea, which she declined, he cleared his throat twice and then blew on his fingers before speaking.

'I represent a new organisation. One that has been especially created by the Cabinet Office to perform certain duties in the recently occupied territories…'

'Like my country?' she interrupted him.

'Exactly, like France. I'd like you to tell me about yourself, if you could.' He sat back and crossed his legs at the knees. She noticed he wore Argyle socks in an extremely garish pattern.

'What's there to talk about? I was born near Orléans in France in 1918. My father was a smallholder who fought at Verdun in the First World War.'

'Did he talk about his experiences?'

'Not often, no. But he was proud he had defended France. *Pour la Patrie* was very important to him.'

'And it's important to you.'

'Of course, I am French.'

He smiled. 'Please continue.'

'I came to England in 1936…'

'Why?'

She thought for a moment. 'Lots of reasons. My parents were dead, I had no close relatives. And an agency had introduced me to a potential client in London.'

'Mrs Dodds.'

She frowned. 'How did you know?'

He ignored the question. 'It must have been strange; you were in London, young, on your own, different food, different people, a different language… Quite adventurous for a woman from a smallholding in France.'

She thought about it for a moment. 'I suppose it was adventurous, but it didn't feel so at the time. I was busy every day with George and I had friends from the church—'

'Westminster?'

Again, she frowned – he seemed to know a lot about her. 'That's right. And Mrs Dodds was a kind if forgetful employer.'

'And then you met John Sinclair?'

She stayed silent.

'Your husband. He was killed in France in 1940, wasn't he?'

'Yes.'

'You have a child, Martin.'

'Yes.'

'Where is he now?'

'In Hereford with his aunt and uncle.'

'Yet you are here?'

'I decided I couldn't stay at home doing nothing any more. Martin is—'

'Three years old.'

'This has nothing to do with Martin. I have to do something. Don't you see I've lost my country, my husband, and my best friends? I can't just sit back and do nothing. We all have to make sacrifices, this is mine. And now the Germans have occupied the rest of my country.'

'Does that matter to you?'

'Of course it matters. How would you like to see England occupied?'

He was silent for a moment, as if working something out in his mind. Finally, he seemed to make a decision and pushed his glasses back up onto the bridge of his nose. 'Would you ever consider returning to France?'

'France? I don't know. I never planned to; what with marrying John, I thought I would spend the rest of my life in England.'

'Let me rephrase that. Would you return to France to work for us?'

She frowned. 'You haven't told me yet who "us" is…'

He smiled. 'I suppose I haven't. I represent an organisation created to conduct espionage, sabotage and reconnaissance in occupied Europe against the Axis powers, and to aid local resistance movements. Would you be interested in training for a role with such an organisation, Mrs Sinclair?'

'Yes,' she answered immediately.

'Even if it means dangerous, perilous work?'

'Yes.'

'Even if it means going into areas controlled by the Nazis?'

'Yes.'

'Organising sabotage and resistance?'

'Yes.'

'When you could lose your own life, leaving your child an orphan?'

She thought about Martin, her small child, alone in the world. 'Yes,' she answered finally.

He stood up, holding out his hand. 'Jolly good, we'll be in touch.'

'Is that it?'

'Yes, we're fairly informal around here and we tend to make decisions quickly. You'll be hearing from us shortly.'

A door opened at the side and the same woman who had escorted Monique up to the hotel room stood in the entrance.

'Mrs Atkins will get you to sign the Official Secrets Act before you leave.'

'So that's it? I'm accepted?'

The man smiled. 'Not yet, Mrs Sinclair, we have a few more checks to complete first.'

'This way, Mrs Sinclair,' the woman said firmly.

Monique left, not knowing what was going to happen in the future, but feeling that somehow or other she had just made the most momentous step of her life.

Chapter Forty-Four

Thursday, January 04, 2018
Somewhere in Whitehall, London

'This has become more serious, Proctor.'

Penrose looked up from the latest transcript of Miss Sinclair's meeting with her father at Belmarsh Prison.

'I totally agree, sir. After all these years in prison, the man is still hell-bent on revenge. Evidence of an acute psychopathology, if you ask me.'

Penrose sniffed. 'Well, luckily for Her Majesty's Government, Proctor, nobody is asking you. I want round-the-clock surveillance on Miss Sinclair.'

'But we're a little stretched right now; many people are still on their holidays.'

'I am aware of the date, Proctor. Mrs Penrose is still feeding me leftovers from Christmas. The joys of turkey fricassee await me on my return home this evening.'

'It sounds rather nice, sir. My girlfriend would rather die than cook me turkey fricassee.'

Penrose sniffed again. 'A feminist, is she?'

'A little, sir, but it's the veganism that gets in the way. We had Tofu Surprise for Christmas dinner.'

'Sounds delicious. I suppose the surprise was that you finished it?'

'No, sir, the surprise was there's no tofu…'

'I won't ask, Proctor. I have a feeling that discovering the details of your relationship with your significant other would be the mental equivalent of entering one of Mr Hawking's black holes in the Number Seven bus whilst reading the latest Jacqueline Susann novel.'

'Probably worse than that, sir.'

'So, back to business. Arrange the surveillance on Miss Sinclair. I want to know everything she does and everybody she speaks to from now on.'

'If you don't mind me asking, sir, why is this so important to the department?'

'I do mind you asking, but I will answer you anyway. Ever since the end of World War Two, this department has been charged with monitoring the service's reputation for efficiency, excellence and professionalism.'

He took a cigar out from its case, rolled it in his fingers and cut off the end, before lighting it with a gold Dunhill lighter.

He allowed the smoke to roll pleasantly around his mouth for a few moments before continuing his explanation. 'We took a severe hit with the Cambridge Spy case and the series of defections that followed. Mr Sinclair raised a particularly vexing issue for us regarding the performance of the SOE during the Second World War. We managed to keep it quiet even after he murdered one of our retired officers in 1979. In today's world, with its distrust of the Service, we need to continue to maintain the image we have spent so many years creating. I will not have the Sinclairs and their ilk threatening our work once more, is that clear?'

'Transparently, sir.' The younger man pointed outside the door. 'I'll carry on with arranging the surveillance.'

'Do that, Proctor. And one more thing – do we have CCTV images of the meeting?'

'Of course, sir, with audio.'

'I'd like to watch it, if I may. There's something not right about the transcript. It feels wrong somehow.'

'I'll send it to you over the internal mail, sir.'

Penrose glanced with distaste at the computer sitting on his desk. 'If you must, Proctor, if you must…'

Chapter Forty-Five

Sunday, January 10, 1943
Wanborough Manor, near Guildford, Surrey

The letter finally came to her flat in London a week later. It was on headed notepaper with the innocuous title of the Inter-Service Research Bureau, operating from 64 Baker Street in London.

She was instructed to proceed to Wanborough Manor near Guildford on Sunday, January 10. Attached was a movement order and a travel pass under the name of Monique Sinclair. There were no instructions on what she was to bring, how long she would be staying, or what she would be doing when she arrived there.

Nonetheless, on a cold and windy Sunday afternoon, she found herself collected from Guildford station by an uncommunicative WRVS corporal and dropped outside a large ancient Elizabethan house.

She stood there for a moment, her brown suitcase at her feet, staring up at the red-brick and aged-timber facade of the building.

What had she let herself in for?

The front door opened and a uniformed man came out. 'You must be Mrs Sinclair. I'm de Wesselow. Major de Wesselow. Pleased to have you aboard.' He picked up her suitcase. 'Let me show you to your quarters.'

And so began the strangest two weeks of her life.

She was introduced to her fellow students later that evening over a hastily arranged dinner.

There were six others in total, as Major de Wesselow announced that one had dropped out at the last minute. Three French people and three from England. The three English all had some connection to France in that they had either been born there or had spent their childhood in the country. All except her had some sort of recent military background, even though they held a wide variety of occupations in civvy street; a postman, opera singer, racehorse trainer, accountant, and fashion designer were all on the same course.

There was just one other woman; Yvonne Cormeau. She was a small, slight woman of a similar age to Monique and had spent the last two years in the WAAF at an airfield in Lincolnshire.

They immediately gravitated towards each other. Yvonne, Monique soon found out, spoke good French but with a strong British accent, having been born and raised in Shanghai.

Her spoken French came from a series of nannies and governesses appointed by her father to give her a rounded education. Like Monique, her husband had been killed too, but this time as a result of German bombing during the Blitz.

That evening, as they were getting to know each other, de Wesselow rose and tapped the water glass on his table. 'Gentlemen, and ladies, I welcome you to Wanborough Manor. Tomorrow, you will begin your training. In the first stages, we will improve your fitness, give you an introduction into the types of weaponry you will be using in the field, and assess your suitability – or lack of suitability – for the various roles that await you.'

He swallowed and then continued. 'Those of you who pass this initial training will then be sent to Scotland to a commando course, after which your future positions in the organisation will be assigned. The third section of your training is an in-depth study of these roles.'

One of the men put his hand up. 'What sort of roles?'

'There are four major ones that we use in our work in France. The first is to train group leaders. This will be for the men only, I'm afraid—'

'Why?' interrupted Yvonne.

The Major shrugged his shoulders and coughed. 'I'm afraid that decision has been made by those above my rank. The other roles,' he continued, 'are couriers, delivering messages and materials to the various cells; radio operators, coding and decoding messages to and from London; and finally, demolition experts, specialists at blowing things up. There are admin roles available here and in London for those whose temperament makes them psychologically unsuitable for work in the occupied territories.' He smiled and raised his glass. 'Anyway, enough of my blathering. Enjoy your dinner, ladies and gentlemen. Training starts at eight a.m. tomorrow morning.'

And it did, with a cross-country run that Monique found hard but most of the others seemed to handle with ease – particularly Philippe Lemaitre, one of the other Frenchmen on the course who quickly established himself as the leader of their group. The rest of the time was spent on the basics of being a spy. The fieldwork of dead letter drops and secret marks. How to follow a potential suspect without being spotted. Elementary map reading. The three different types of codes: double transposition, Playfair and Ironside. Lectures on life in Vichy and occupied

France, even though the latter existed in name only since the extension of German sovereignty the previous year. The importance of cover stories and ways to survive under interrogation and torture.

Finally, they were given lessons in the French language and culture, concentrating on the latest slang and the new rules and organisations introduced by the Germans. The latter Monique found particularly easy, but some of the others, including Yvonne, struggled. Her accent was very English despite having lived in France and marrying a Frenchman. They both decided that if she was sent on a mission she would have to become Belgian – or better still, Dutch – if she was to find an excuse for her poor French.

In the evening, the instructors would see how much alcohol their students could consume without falling over, and how they behaved whilst under the influence. Sometimes, when enough booze had been consumed, the instructors would throw in a night exercise for good measure.

Each night, Monique returned to her room exhausted but exhilarated. Gradually, the physical activity made her fitter and stronger, while the classroom work stimulated an interest in the complexities of being a spy. It also forced moments of self-doubt as she lay alone at night on her bed.

Would she be able to survive in occupied France?

Would she remember her training?

And what if she were captured? Could she handle interrogation? Or torture?

At the end of the two weeks, six of them – including Monique – were sent to Arisaig in Scotland for commando training, one of the men having dropped out with a badly damaged ankle, sprained not on an assault course but by getting out of bed one morning.

Monique loved the wild remoteness of the small village, nestled beside an inlet along the Morar Peninsula, its small stone cottages and turbulent seas a stunning backdrop to the wild inland moors. Once, in the middle of a map-reading exercise, she looked up and stared out across the cliffs, vowing to return after the war was over to visit this place once again.

It was in this village the recruits underwent intense training in living off the land, sabotage and demolition, practice with pistols and sub-machine guns, and numerous trials on assault courses – all to test their mental and physical strength.

One of the small-arms instructors, Gavin Maxwell, instructed her to read the signs of nature; the spoor of otters, the snap of a dry twig, the shape of trees. He also gave a precise description of the 'double tap' – the standard two shots of a professional assassination – but she couldn't imagine ever using his lessons. Imagine being faced with the awful dilemma of shooting somebody in the head!

Lessons in unarmed combat and silent killing were overseen by two former members of the Shanghai police: William Fairbairn and Bill Sykes, dubbed the 'Heavenly Twins'.

They concluded all sessions with the final instruction, 'and then kick him in the balls'. Fairbairn and Sykes issued Monique with a sharply-honed fighting knife, with which she could despatch her enemies with a delicate upward stabbing motion. She preferred to use it to peel fruit.

Many evenings she sat listening to Yvonne and the two instructors reminiscing about the wonders of Shanghai. It was another place she vowed to visit when all this was over. There was so much of the world she hadn't seen or discovered yet, so much life to enjoy.

Of course, she would think of Martin, wondering how he was doing in Hereford with Aunt Betsy and Uncle Dan, missing his hugs and the wrinkle on his forehead when he smiled. But she quickly banished him from her mind. It was important to remain focused. It would do her no good to worry about her child. There was a war on and her country to be saved. Her child and her dreams for the future would have to wait until the war was over, when her country was free again and life, in all its complexity, was back to normal.

One day at the end of the course, the head of Arisaig training, Colonel Malvers, addressed them.

'You have all done very well. The course is not easy, but you have passed it with flying colours. Lemaitre, you are to receive further training as a group leader. De Turville and White, you are to be trained as couriers and operatives. Mace, you are to receive further training in sabotage and demolition. Cormeau and Sinclair, you are to become radio operators. Thame House is full at the moment but they are sending somebody over to train you at the finishing school in Beaulieu. There's also some good news: you will all be given a week's leave before you start your final training.'

After the meeting was over, they buttonholed the Colonel before he had a chance to leave.

'Does that mean we're in?' asked Yvonne bluntly.

'No, it means you're going to finishing school,' replied Colonel Malvers.

'And why do the men become group leaders and demolition experts and we become radio operators?'

The Colonel smiled. 'It's partly about aptitude; we find women are more diligent than men when it comes to coding and decoding.'

'And?'

'And, to be frank, we find women handle the danger better.'

'Danger?' asked Monique.

The Colonel nodded slowly. 'In my view, the radio operator is the most important member of any network and their job is the most dangerous. They must send out signals and wait patiently for a reply from London, all the time knowing that the German detection units are looking for their signal, ready to arrest them at any moment.'

'You make it sound terrible, a nightmare.'

'It is.' He pursed his lips. 'You should understand, ladies, that I think being a radio operator is the most dangerous job in the whole of SOE.'

That night, Monique slept fitfully. Would she be up to the task?

Chapter Forty-Six

Sunday, March 07, 1943
Hereford, England

The week passed quickly for Monique; far too quickly. Martin had grown in her absence - he was nearly three and a half years old now. His English had the burr of the West Country; rounded vowels and drawn-out endings. When she first arrived, she tried to speak to him in French but he had forgotten most of the language, only remembering a few of the nursery rhymes and lullabies she had sung to him as a child.

There was also a distance between them.

Of course, he had run to her when she arrived, jumping up and putting his arms around her neck, excited to see her again. But the novelty soon wore off and he began to stay away from her, clinging more and more to Betsy. Monique tried to bring him out, taking him on day trips to town to go shopping or eat at the British Café. The distance still remained, however, despite everything she did.

The night before she left, when Martin was tucked up in bed asleep, she sat down with Betsy at the kitchen table.

'I've lost him, haven't I?'

'He'll be fine. He just knows you're going away again and he feels uncomfortable.'

She lit a cigarette, blowing the smoke up into the rafters of the cottage. It was a habit she had picked up in training. 'He's growing up very quickly.'

'Not surprising. A lovely boy, he is.' Betsy took a sip from her cup of tea. 'A sensitive boy, like his father, but more brooding. You know, he can sit and play for hours on his own without a problem. He doesn't seem to want to play with the other children at all. And when he goes fishing and hunting rabbits with Dan, he can sit there all day without moving.'

'Why did you never have children? You obviously love them so much.'

'We always wanted them but they never happened. Dan was gassed in the War, he blames that. I think it's God just playing an awful trick on us. The more you want something, the less inclined he is to give it you.' She took another sip of tea. 'Well, that's what I think anyway.'

Betsy stood up and began to rinse out her cup under the single tap above the kitchen sink. In the light of the oil lamp, her face looked troubled. Finally, she turned to Monique and said, 'You will take care with what you're doing, won't you? You haven't told me what it is and I haven't asked, but I'm guessing it's not something normal. They don't send you off to all these big houses in the country if it's just being a soldier, do they?'

Monique stayed silent.

'Do be careful, won't you?'

Monique sat up late into the night, smoking and drinking the last of Dan's whisky. She left early the next morning, kissing Martin on the cheek but not waking him.

It was the last time he was to see her.

Chapter Forty-Seven

Sunday, May 30, 1943
Beaulieu House, Hampshire

The last major test of Monique's training was about to begin. She had spent ten weeks at the finishing school at Beaulieu House, becoming adept at all the skills necessary for an SOE agent.

Most of the time had been spent on perfecting her Morse Code. Continually coding signals, sending them in Morse and then decoding the responses. So much work she now felt she dreamt in Morse, her fingers tapping the bedsheets in the middle of the night.

Her instructors had described her tapping technique as heavy but clear, and whilst she wasn't the quickest in the school, she certainly wasn't the slowest. That distinction belonged to a man from the Signals Corp who was as pedantic in his speech as he was in Morse.

But now the big day had arrived; the day of the final mission.

After her parachute training at Ringway in Manchester, she was to be transferred from Dunham Massey, where the SOE agents were staying, to a secret location.

Her mission was to find a job in Metropolitan Vickers, a factory in Trafford Park manufacturing

Lancaster bombers, photograph the inside of the factory and communicate the information to London.

All this without being caught and with local police being alerted that a parachutist had been dropped in the area.

She was taken by car early one morning, carrying her brown suitcase and another containing her radio, and dropped in Altrincham town centre. Luckily, she knew the area from her evening jaunts with the rest of the trainees to the Nag's Head, one of the local pubs.

She took the train to Stretford station and picked up a local paper, the Stretford Messenger. She checked the classified ads in it and found digs with a Mrs McPartland in a small but comfortable room on Urmston Lane for seven shillings and sixpence a week, half board. Her cover story was that she was Adele Richemont, a French refugee who had moved from Hereford to find work in Manchester.

The next morning she joined the thousands of others streaming towards Trafford Park, quickly finding the factory despite the total absence of signs. Earlier in the war it had been bombed, but now seemed relaxed in its security. A large board outside the factory detailed the job openings. Her luck was in; they wanted female operatives and the pay was two pounds ten shillings a week.

She went inside and was interviewed perfunctorily by an old man. After a few questions he asked, 'Right, when can yer start?'

'Tomorrow,' she answered.

'Report here at seven thirty a.m. Don't be late, mind. You'll be docked half a day's wages if yer late. We like to be punctual at Metro Vicks.'

The following morning she reported at the guard house, was given her factory ID and number, and was taken to the shop floor where she joined a gang of woman employed in sanding down the metal fuselage of the aircraft before it was painted in camouflage colours. Heavy, monotonous, back-breaking work.

During her lunch break she wandered around the factory unchallenged, surreptitiously taking pictures with a minute camera the Quartermaster had given her.

The evenings were spent on the radio to London, quietly tapping out her report in Morse and waiting for a reply.

Finally, she was ordered to return to Beaulieu after a week. Elated at her progress and her ability to create a whole new life for herself as a secret agent, she alighted at the station where she was met by a captain she hadn't seen before and three MPs.

'Mrs Monique Sinclair? You're under arrest,' they announced.

She was taken to a police station and placed in a cold cell.

What had she done wrong? Was this all a mistake? Where were the SOE leaders?

After two hours, she was taken into a darkened room.

'What were you doing in Manchester?'

'Why do you have a camera and photographs of the Metropolitan Vickers factory?'

'What are you really?'

'We know you're a spy, admit it and we'll let you sleep.'

'You're working for the Germans, aren't you?'

The questions came at her from a variety of voices and directions, continuing for the next four hours without stopping. They questioned her in English, they questioned her in French, they even questioned her in German.

She was becoming tired and disoriented. It was difficult to think straight. Who was she really? Was her name Adele or was it Monique?

She gritted her teeth and kept repeating her cover story. She was Adele Richemont.

Finally, after five hours, the lights went on and a major with a large moustache and gap teeth quietly said, 'Well done, Mrs Sinclair, you have passed with flying colours. One of the better results from this little training exercise.'

'I don't know what you mean, Major, my name is Adele Richemont.'

The bastards were never going to grind her down.

Chapter Forty-Eight

Thursday, January 04, 2018
Premier Inn, Blackfriars, London

Jayne stood on the platform, waiting for her train into central London. She had stopped off in a coffee shop in Plumstead and booked three nights in a relatively inexpensive hotel, the Premier Inn in Blackfriars.

It was a long way from the National Archives in Kew, but closer to the Imperial War Museum and the National Army Museum. Anyway, she preferred being somewhere in London with a sense of history, even though the area was being transformed with the creation of new skyscrapers. In the evening particularly, she enjoyed walking through the narrow alleys just off Fleet Street. Every time, she always had the sense of Pepys' London; a city of coffee houses, pubs and gossip, where danger lurked around every corner.

Her father's note had worried her. Was he clinically insane? A paranoid schizophrenic? How had he become like this? What had happened to warp his mind so? But, surely, if he were ill or deranged then the prison authorities would have put him in a mental hospital, or somewhere like Broadmoor.

The train arrived and she boarded. It was packed and, rather than fight for a seat, she stood at the end near the door.

What was she going to do?

If her grandmother had been in the Strategic Operations Executive, Jayne's first job would be to find out where the records were kept. She hoped they would be available, and not fallen foul of the one-hundred-year rule restricting access. She would hate to have her researches blocked because some faceless bureaucrat had decided the records could not be seen until 2045.

She also realised that, despite visiting her father twice, she was no closer to understanding why he had murdered David Strachan. She wondered if she should contact one of her old police friends in the Cold Case Division and ask them to access the files, if any still existed. But that would be a last resort. She hated asking for favours from her ex-colleagues.

The train arrived in Blackfriars and she strolled across to her hotel. It was a functional but comfortable address and she had stayed here before when she visited London. After checking in, she took a long shower to wash the stench of prison from her body.

Refreshed and invigorated, she started to research. She quickly typed in her grandmother's name, Monique Sinclair, then added a plus sign and the word 'SOE'.

A second later 127,349 results appeared.

She clicked the top one. A short Wikipedia entry for her grandmother.

Monique Sinclair, nee Massat

Little is known about this operative. She joined the SOE in January 1943 and was parachuted into Reims in July 1943, joining the Prosper network. She was arrested and executed in Dachau Concentration Camp in September 1944. The whereabouts of her grave is unknown.

The words struck Jayne like a blow to the chest. For a moment, she couldn't breathe. The small hotel room vanished around her and the words 'executed in Dachau Concentration Camp' seemed to loom out from her laptop, swallowing up everything else.

Her grandmother had died in a concentration camp.

Had someone betrayed her, like Martin said? This was what he was trying to avenge. Why hadn't he told her? Why hadn't he told the police?

Chapter Forty-Nine

Sunday, July 04, 1943
Orchard House, Baker Street, London

Monique was called into the SOE briefing room on a warm Sunday in July.

Around the table sat Maurice Buckmaster, the head of 'F' section; his deputy, David Strachan; and the woman she had met when she was first interviewed, Vera Atkins. Philippe Lemaitre was already sitting at the table facing the others in the opposite side.

As soon as Monique entered the room, she recognised a certain chill in the air. She wondered what she had done wrong this time.

'Ah, Mrs Sinclair, do please take a seat.' It was Buckmaster who rose as soon as she entered, and gestured to the place next to Philippe. 'So good of you to come in.'

She glanced at the Frenchman, getting a nod from him in return. The last time they had seen each other was nearly three months ago at the end of their course in Arisaig.

Strachan spoke next, taking charge of the meeting, his small moustache and large, round glasses giving him the air of a distracted bank manager. 'As we are all here, I'll begin the briefing. The mission we have decided for both of you will begin seven nights from now, on July eleventh, when you will be flown to France. Sorry for the short notice…'

He smiled one of those smiles that said he wasn't sorry at all.

Monique flashed back to David giving the best man's speech at her wedding. Now here he was briefing her on her mission into occupied territory in France. How the world had come full circle. For a second, John's face loomed into her mind; wearing his dress uniform, sitting next to her as David made a joke in French.

A moment frozen in time, the happiest day of her life.

She focused back on David speaking now.

'You will be dropping into a landing zone created by the local resistance near Reims…'

She would be returning to France, after all these years away. All the training and hard work had paid off; she was finally going to be doing something to get back at the Germans for taking away all that she held precious.

'…operational issues mean we have to act quickly,' he continued, 'and as the moon is at its best on July eleventh, that is the day it is going to be. Is everybody okay with that date?'

He looked up, waiting for assent. Both Monique and Philippe looked at each other before nodding.

'Jolly good. Philippe, you will have the code name "Boris", and Mrs Sinclair's will be "Nanny". In all your communications with us please use these code names. As I said, you will both be parachuting into a landing place to the north-west of Reims. Our organiser, Henri Dericourt, code name "Gilbert", has organised a spot for you and two other agents who will be accompanying you.'

'They will be working with us?'

Strachan shook his head. 'They have been assigned a different network near the German border. You will spend two nights in Reims and then you will be taken to Paris to join the Prosper network. There is an existing wireless operator for the network, Mrs Sinclair, and you will work in conjunction with her. In addition, you will be sending messages assigned to you by your section leader, Philippe.'

He paused for a moment as Monique asked a question. 'Two wireless operators? And why am I sending messages specifically from Philippe?'

Strachan glanced across at Buckmaster, who stared impassively into mid-air. His fingers tapped the wooden top of the table. 'We have heard there may be some issues with Prosper…'

'What sort of issues?'

'We have received reports the Germans may have infiltrated it and placed an agent or agents on the inside.'

'May have?'

'Both myself and Buckmaster have discounted the reports but, nonetheless, they need to be checked. That job will be done by Philippe, with you relaying messages back to us from him. Is that clear?'

'So let me understand. You are sending us both to work with a network that may already have been compromised?'

'As ever, Mrs Sinclair, you have hit the nail on the head.' Buckmaster spoke for the first time. 'However, we believe the reports are incorrect. Prosper is one of our best-run networks, stretching across most of northern France, from Le Havre in the west to Reims in the east. Its leader, Francis Suttill, code name "Prosper", is one of the best we have and the rest of his team have been performing exemplary work in the most trying conditions…'

Strachan interrupted his boss with a gesture. 'If it's any consolation, Mrs Sinclair, we don't think there is anything to worry about, just the usual paranoia which infests agents when they have been in the field for a long time.' He pushed his glasses back up to the bridge of his nose. 'Is everything clear?'

They nodded.

Strachan moved brusquely on. 'Mrs Atkins will continue your briefing and, of course, you will receive the usual preparations for a mission in France. Any questions?'

'My radio. Will I use one in France or take one with me?'

Mrs Atkins answered. 'You will be carrying one on the flight. An existing agent, code name "Madeleine", is using the one with the network at the moment. You will not meet or share call signs. For added security, we will be instituting a two-step verification process for you.'

'Which is?'

Mrs Atkins searched in the file on her desk, pulling out a brown index card. You will tap out "rain" before the third word, and the tenth word will be repeated.'

Monique memorised the verification code and wanted to ask more questions, but Strachan and Buckmaster had already risen from the table. The latter had his hand out. 'Good luck,' he said, shaking Monique's hand, 'break a leg.'

She smiled. She certainly hoped she wouldn't, not on this parachute jump anyway.

Chapter Fifty

Thursday, January 04, 2018
Premier Inn, Blackfriars, London

Jayne finally closed her laptop. She was tired and it had been a long day, what with travelling down to London, meeting her father, and discovering the appalling news her grandmother had been executed at a concentration camp.

The rest of her research had revealed little that was new. Most of the articles or information on her grandmother had used the information from Wikipedia, simply repeating it without adding anything else.

She had discovered more about the SOE, though. It was founded as Winston Churchill's pet project, to take the war directly to the countries occupied by the Axis powers. Exactly 117 members of the SOE had been captured and executed by the Germans, and this list contained such celebrated war heroes as Violette Szabo, Noor Inayat Khan, Nancy Wake, Yvonne Cormeau and Diana Rowden. Brave women, all of them.

She had also found out that some of their personal histories were available for research at the National Archives. However, many had been destroyed in a fire at the SOE's headquarters in 1946. A fire which some commentators suggested may have been started deliberately to cover up the organisation's activities during the war. As ever with spies, there were enough conspiracy theories to fill a false-bottomed suitcase.

As she lay in bed that evening, it suddenly hit her why her father had contacted her. It wasn't any sense of paternal pride. It wasn't any desire to see how his daughter had developed. It wasn't any great wish to meet her after all these years.

It was simply because the documents that would prove who had betrayed his mother were not online. They could only be accessed by visiting the National Archives in person. More importantly, when he was jailed they were not available at all, not having been vetted or released by the government department which decided such matters until 2003.

For a moment, in the dark of her hotel room with only the rustling of the water pipes for company, Jayne felt immensely sorry for herself.

Her father complained of being abandoned by his mother so she could join the SOE. But hadn't the same happened to Jayne? Hadn't her father abandoned her in his relentless pursuit of whoever he believed had betrayed his mother? A desire for revenge that still burned strong inside him despite his mother having died nearly seventy-five years ago.

A wave of immense sadness washed over Jayne. Why should she still have to suffer his madness? She was her own person. A former policewoman and now a successful genealogical investigator. Why did these family issues still continue to haunt her after all these years?

The answer came to her in the voice of Robert, her real father. 'Because they do, lass. Until we sort them out, until we resolve them, they will always be there, like the executioner's axe ready to swing down on the back of our neck.'

Well, she wasn't going to let this continue any more. Despite her father, and despite his madness, she was going to find out what really happened to her grandmother in 1944, come hell or high water.

Or she'd die trying.

Chapter Fifty-One

Sunday, July 11, 1943
Just outside Reims, France

She sat at the edge of the hole and looked down. Eight hundred feet below her, the fields of France zipped past in a dark blur.

'Three minutes.' The dispatcher held up three fingers. 'You guys go on the order,' he shouted over the engine noise. 'One and two on the first pass,' he tapped Philippe and Monique on the shoulders, 'second pass, the containers. Third pass, three and four. Then we're outta here. If you don't jump, you comin' back with us to Blighty. Capiche?'

They all nodded. Monique adjusted her position. The jump suit she was wearing was uncomfortable on top of her French day clothes. A static line stretched from the rear of her parachute to a hook on the fuselage of the plane. At least opening the chute was one less thing to think about.

The beating of her heart in her chest increased in intensity, threatening to burst through the skin. Above her head, a red light flashed on. The young dispatcher put both thumbs up, mouthed 'thirty seconds' and stared at her as if he expected her to refuse to jump.

She nodded back at him, reusing to be intimidated, shuffling forward a little more so her legs were dangling down into the Joe Hole.

The green light went on.

She saw Philippe jump through the hole and then vanish. She hesitated for a moment and felt a shove in her back and then she was falling, falling. A rush of air removed her cap, whipping her hair across her face. She tried to remember to keep her arms across her chest and her feet pointed straight out below her.

But her feet weren't beneath her, they were level with her face. She panicked; what was she to do?

And then a solid jerk beneath her shoulders and a white cloud opened above her head. Her fall slowed down, the wind still rushing past her head, but a strong breeze now, not a gale. Above her head, the moon shone brightly, its pitted face a dappled grey.

She looked down. Three lights in the form of a triangle were shining up at her from below. A welcoming committee or the Germans? She would soon find out.

Off to her left, Philippe was drifting towards the darkest part of the forest, his parachute reflecting the rays of the moon.

She drifted straight down towards the lights. The ground wasn't far away now. She braced for the landing, but it came earlier than she expected, driving her knees up into her chest. She tried to roll as she had been taught at Ringway but the breath was knocked out of her and all she could do was grunt and lie on her back, fighting for air.

A man appeared above her.

'Are you okay?' he said in French.

She had never been as glad to hear her mother tongue.

He helped her to her feet, releasing the fastening on her harness.

'My name's Gilbert. It's actually my code name. If you want you can call me Henri, everybody else does.'

A hand appeared in front of her. She shook it, the palm and fingers clammy to her touch.

'Boris?' She used Philippe's code name.

'Okay. His landing was rougher than yours, but he'll survive. Quick, get out of your jump suit and pack the parachute into this.' He handed her a rough canvas bag.

Above her the drone of the Liberator was getting louder.

'Second pass – the containers,' she said, pulling in her chute like one would reef in the sail of a ship.

'Go and wait by the second light.'

As she ran towards the torchlight, three more parachutes opened above her and lazily drifted down to earth. Philippe was waiting for her, standing next to a man with a large antenna sticking out of his backpack.

'We're here, back in France, finally.'

She stared at the man with the backpack, who was talking into a fixed microphone in front of his lips.

'Direction-finding equipment. He's talking to our pilot. Otherwise we'd never find this place,' Philippe explained.

Four men ran past them to gather in the containers, dragging them back to the lights.

'I need my radio, it's in case two,' she said.

They undid the latches on the black containers. Inside the second one was an innocuous-looking brown suitcase. She took it out and flipped open the latches. The radio equipment filled the case, with a pair of headphones nestling in an alcove to one side. It looked undamaged but she would only know when she sent her first message to London.

Henri ran up, pushing two bicycles. 'Use these to cycle to the safe house. I will join you this evening to check your documents are in order. Here's the address.' He gave a piece of paper to Philippe. 'Your contact is Mrs Delorme. You are to tell her you are the cotton spinners from Charleroi. You got that? The cotton spinners from Charleroi.'

Above their heads, the drone of the aircraft was getting louder as it returned for the third time. Philippe glanced at the address.

'Raymond over there will guide you.' He pointed to a young boy, no more than thirteen years old, sitting on a bike at the edge of the field. 'Leave now.'

'But what about the equipment and canisters?'

Above their heads, the cream parachutes of Elviron and Wallace could be seen drifting to earth.

'Forget them, leave now!'

The both looked at each other and then grabbed the bikes from Henri. They mounted them and rode across the rough field to the young boy.

'Let's go before the noise of the plane attracts Jerry.' The boy kicked his bike through a gate at the edge of the field on to a tracked path. 'If we are stopped, you've heard there's work in Reims and that's why you're cycling here this morning. I'm your nephew who's showing you to the factory, okay?'

They both nodded. It felt strange to be given orders by a thirteen-year-old boy, but he was professional and had obviously done this before.

They rode in silence as the sun gradually rose above the surrounding fields. The air smelt so different from London and Hereford. She had forgotten how it was in France; fresher, more natural, the fragrance of wood smoke tinting the air like a hint of colour on a white wall. Barely there, but definitely noticeable.

There is nothing so pretty as the fields of France in the early hours of the morning, before the sun has risen to warm the earth.

After thirty minutes riding down country lanes, the boy signalled left and they deviated down a small alley, avoiding the main road into the centre of the town. They kept to the narrow streets and alleys for the next twenty minutes as the boy expertly guided them through the old town, heading unerringly towards the cathedral.

The town was waking up around them. The shutters of cafés being opened. Street sweepers removing the last bits of rubbish from the night before. The smell of fresh coffee – real coffee, not the ersatz stuff they served in England – mingling with the aroma of baking bread and croissants. A postman, also on his bike, wished them good morning as he went on his rounds, taking a small glass at every café he stopped at.

It was wartime, but the inhabitants of Reims were not going to let a little war disturb the rhythms of their morning.

The boy pointed to the cathedral, its elegant, tall spire dwarfing the houses surrounding it. 'You'll be staying close to there, in an apartment on Jean-Jacques.'

He was pedalling faster now, trying to get them to their destination before the town woke fully and the streets began to fill with people. Finally, he stopped in front of a door on one of the streets close to the cathedral. He pushed it open and, covering his lips with his finger, indicated they should be as quiet as possible. They rolled the bikes down a narrow pathway approaching a set of steps. The boy leant his bike against the wall, indicating that they should do the same, then he tapped gently on the glass next to the door.

It was answered immediately by a small, mousy woman who had obviously just woken up.

Philippe stepped forward and pronounced the sentence he had been told to say. 'We are the cotton spinners from Charleroi.'

'Yes, yes, I know who you are.' She waved her hand as if swatting a fly. They were ushered into a small kitchen-cum-dining room with a large, round table at the centre.

The woman spent a few moments examining them up and down. 'You look like foreigners. Your clothes are too good, too new.'

Monique was suddenly conscious of her two-piece suit, made last week by the SOE tailor in London to match the fashions that were supposedly popular in Paris.

'I'll give you some older clothes,' said Mrs Delorme. 'We don't want you sticking out like Napoleon's ears. Would you like coffee? I'm afraid it's mostly chicory but we can't get anything else these days.'

'But I smelt fresh coffee as we rode in, and croissants,' said Monique.

'Bof,' the woman blew air out of her lips, 'that's for the Boche, not for us. Sit down and have some anyway, at least it is warm.'

She went to put the hot water on a two-ring gas stove.

Monique looked around the kitchen. The house was obviously that of a wealthy man but it had an air of seediness, as if it hadn't been occupied for many years.

Mrs Delorme returned with a bowl of hot brown water that tasted vaguely of coffee, and some bread sliced up into neat rounds. 'It's last night's bread, I'm afraid. I'll make you something more substantial later when Henri arrives. You will sleep soon, yes?'

Both Philippe and Monique nodded.

After drinking her coffee and eating the bread, Monique was shown to a small room at the back of the house with just a single bed and a small dresser.

She took off her shoes and lay down on the bed. At five she would have to transmit her first message to London, before waiting until seven for the answer. But until then she was going to sleep.

As her eyes began to close, she wondered how long she would manage to survive in France. The country seemed so different, and yet so much the same.

One last thought flitted through her mind before she drifted off to sleep.

Was the Gestapo waiting for her?

Chapter Fifty-Two

Sunday, July 11, 1943
Rue Jean-Jacques Rousseau, Reims, France

Monique woke up with a start. She glanced at the watch given to her by the SOE: 4.00 p.m. Somewhere nearby, a clock was just striking the hour; four solid chimes of a bell.

She had slept most of the day but it was now time to get to work. She set the radio case down on the table and opened it up. Everything looked fine despite being dropped from 800 feet.

She attached the wire to the transmit head and the receive wire to its separate head. Taking both wires, she walked to the window, opening it to tape both ends to opposite sides of the frame.

She plugged the radio set into the mains - the Mark 11 worked off a 6-volt battery or the mains - and she decided that she would try to save the battery for later if she could. Finally, she attached the Morse key to its port on the radio.

Now was the moment of truth. Had the radio transmitter been damaged when it was dropped from the plane? Had it survived the landing? She crossed her fingers, said a quick prayer to the local saints, and switched it on.

There was a small flicker of light behind the dials and then the machine suddenly surged into life.

Good, it seemed to be okay. She would only really know after she had sent and received her first message.

She took out her double decryption codebook and began to encode her message.

ARRIVED REIMS RAIN SAFELY STOP. MADE CONTACT WITH GILBERT STOP STOP. WILL GO TO PARIS DAY AFTER TOMORROW STOP. NETWORK IN GOOD ORDER STOP.

She added her code name, NANNY, putting the word 'rain' before the third word and repeating the tenth word as her verifications. It had been drummed into her again and again in the week before she left that these identifiers were important in case the Germans ever tried to send a message pretending to be from a particular agent. The double decryption keys could be stolen but agents were told never to reveal their identifier, whatever happened.

With the encoded letters and numbers in front of her, she glanced at her watch: 4.45 p.m. Should she start sending now, or wait?

She decided to wait. Another lesson drilled into her training was to keep regular hours of transmission. It was another signal to London that everything was going well.

Her watch took an achingly long time to tick around to five o'clock. The house itself was quiet, just the creaking of the wooden floorboards as they cooled, breaking the silence. Was Philippe still sleeping or had he gone out with Madame Delorme to reconnoitre the town?

She didn't know.

The minute hand of her watch reached the twelve and she began tapping out the signal in Morse code.

In the quiet house, the sound of the two metal contacts meeting as she transmitted the message sounded immense. Her instructor had told her she had a heavy hand, and now she knew he was right.

She finished the message and waited before sending the end code. She hoped she hadn't made too many mistakes in either the encoding or in the sending. And, if she had, they had a bright listener at the other end who could work out what was missing from the message.

She now had to wait two hours before London sent her a reply. Two hours during which time she was especially vulnerable with the radio unconcealed, the wires outside the window attached to the wall and her codebooks and Morse transmitter lying on the table.

There was nothing she could do. She went to lie down on the bed again. Perhaps she could nap until seven o'clock.

She had just closed her eyes when there was a noise outside the door. She quickly rose from the bed, closed the lid of the case and stuffed the codebook down the back of her dress.

A knock.

'Who is it?' she asked.

'Henri, can I come in?'

The door opened before she answered. Henri stood there wearing his street clothes and carrying a brown fedora in his right hand. He looked different from this morning, more furtive, less in control.

'Transmitting already?' he asked. 'Any response from London yet?'

Monique ignored the question. 'Where's Philippe?'

'He's gone to meet a courier from St Quentin. He'll be back soon. Have you eaten yet? We could go into the town.'

Monique suddenly felt hungry. The thought of food enticed her but she shook her head. She had to sit here and wait for the reply from London.

'Suit yourself. Can I take a look at your documents?'

She searched in her bag, pulling out her identity and ration cards.

He examined them carefully, his forehead creasing into a frown.

'What's the matter? These were created in London. They are copies of the latest cards.'

He held up her Carte d'Identité. 'It's the paper, it's too good. We haven't seen paper like this since the beginning of the war.' He took out his own cards. She could see the difference immediately. His cards were printed on a flimsier, rougher stock.

'How could they make such a simple mistake?'

He shrugged his shoulders.

'Will they pass an inspection?'

'I don't think so. But don't worry, I know someone in the Mairie. They'll be able to make you another set. Do you have photos?'

She dug out the extra set of shots London had given her. 'When can you get them?'

'Don't worry, he's quick. Tomorrow at the latest. You're going to Paris the day after.'

'Am I?'

'To meet Frager, the deputy head of the Prosper network. Raymond will travel with you.'

'Raymond?'

'The young boy who brought you here this morning.'

'Won't that be dangerous for him?'

'But less dangerous for you. Travelling as a family will make the Boche and the Milice less suspicious. He will have documents to match yours.'

'Courtesy of your friend?'

'Voilà. It's how it works. And if you want to stay alive, you'd better get used to it.'

Monique didn't like this man. He had the air of the braggart about him, as if he were the only one who knew anything. She heard the sound of tapping from her headphones. London was early.

She ran over to her radio and placed the headphones over her ears, transcribing the Morse as it came through. When the message had finished she typed the code for 'received' and then packed up the set, bringing the wires in from the windows. If a German listening van was nearby, the last thing she wanted was for them to pick up her signal with a long message.

'Where can I hide this?' she asked.

He shrugged his shoulders again. 'Ask Mrs Delorme, how would I know?'

She placed the suitcase under her bed. Not the best place to hide it but it would do until Madame returned. Time to decode the message from London. She pulled out her one-time pad and began the slow, tedious process of double decryption. Luckily, the message was short.

'What does it say?'

She paused for a moment, wondering whether to share it with this man, before finally deciding she would. After all, he was one of the heads of the Prosper network. 'It's quite short: "Congrats on safe landing and meeting Gilbert stop. Still no news from Prosper stop. No contact with Elviron and Wallace stop. Did they arrive safely stop?"'

'That's all?'

'That's it.'

'We sent them both directly to Jacqueline. They are to head out to the Vosges the day after tomorrow.'

'They probably haven't set up the radio yet. I'm sure they'll send a message soon.'

As she finished speaking, she heard the noise of the door being opened and slammed shut. She rushed downstairs to find Philippe bent over the kitchen table, breathless, with Mrs Delorme peering out into the main road through the net curtain.

Monique rushed to him. 'What's wrong?'

'German patrol with Milice… Asked for papers… Thought I was a goner.'

'His French isn't good enough,' added Mrs Delorme. 'I had to tell them he was my Belgian cousin who'd left his papers at home. They asked for my address.'

'You didn't give them it?' shouted Henri.

'I had to, it's on my identity card…'

Chapter Fifty-Three

Friday, January 05, 2018
The National Archives, Kew, London

Jayne walked from the hotel to the Underground past one of the pubs she loved to visit when she came to London: The Blackfriars. Not this time, though – the amazing art-nouveau reliefs would have to wait for another visit.

She walked into the modern station, buying a day return and then descending to the District line. The deeper she went, the more the air thickened with the smell of people, lots of people.

Despite it being 9.30 a.m., when the train arrived it was crammed. She squeezed between a man reading the Financial Times and a student with a rucksack bigger than herself, hanging on to the overhead strap for dear life as the train rattled and wobbled its way to Kew Gardens station.

From there it was only a short walk to the National Archives, hurrying past the fountain to enter the main entrance. After passing through security, Jayne immediately took off her coat, making sure she took a pencil and notepad from her bag before placing them in a locker.

In front of her was a row of computer terminals with a big 'Start Here' sign hanging above them. She sat down behind one of the terminals and typed 'SOE' into the Discovery section of the catalogue.

2622 hits. If she wasn't going to spend till next Christmas here, she had better narrow down her search.

She typed 'Monique Sinclair' into the search field.

53 records. Much better. She scanned the list quickly. Most records related to the name Sinclair, including family records and papers. She took a quick note of the listing numbers for when she had time to discover which branch of the Sinclairs she was descended from.

Suddenly, one record shouted out to her.

Monique SINCLAIR, nee MASSAT, aka Suzanne FEVRIER, born 20.03.18, died 13.09.44.

Special Operations Executive: Personnel Files (PF) series. Information on individual subjects and access conditions is available at…

For the moment, seeing the actual date of her grandmother's death shocked Jayne. She caught her breath and her hand came up to cover her mouth. It was there in black and white. Her grandmother had died in September 1944, just eight months before the end of the war.

She clicked on the link and was taken to a separate page.

You are in;

The National Archives' catalogue
HS - Records of Special Operations Executive
HS 9 - Special Operations Executive: Personnel Files (PF) series

HS 9/812 - Special Operations Executive personnel files. Information on individual subjects and access conditions is available at item level.

This record (browse from here by hierarchy or by reference):

Catalogue description

Monique SINCLAIR, nee MASSAT, and Suzanne FEVRIER, born 20.03.18, died 13.09.44

Ordering and viewing options:
Date: 1939-1946
Held by: The National Archives, Kew
Legal status: Public Record(s)
Closure status: Open Document
Access conditions: Closed until 2003
Record opening date: 11 April 2003

She ordered the file, bringing up another form and reserving a seat in the Document Room. Then she entered the document numbers from her notepad. A timer showed the documents would be available in twenty minutes.

She checked her reader's ticket was still in her wallet and went upstairs to the second-floor Document Room. Sitting at desk 4b, she put her notepad and pencil down on the old wood and stared across at the lockers on the far wall.

She just had to wait. It was not something she was very good at, but it was impossible to rush the archive clerks. They would get her documents to her just as soon as they could.

Opposite her, a young researcher was reading through some old documents. She twisted her head slightly to see what they were. Government papers on the Partition of Ireland in 1921, apparently.

The researcher caught her looking and covered up the papers on his desk. She smiled, embarrassed, and looked across at the lockers where her documents would be deposited.

She checked her watch. Five more minutes. Then she would be able to find out more about her grandmother and what she did in the SOE.

A clock on the wall inched slowly, agonisingly, to 10.30.

She got up and walked over to the locker. Inside was a large brown internal folder, used to send documents from one bureaucrat to another. The front was lined, and on the lines some dates and document numbers had been written.

Jayne took a deep intake of breath and reached in to pull out the sheaf of documents.

The cover page simply said:

MONIQUE SINCLAIR, nee MASSAT, aka SUZANNE FEVRIER, NANNY.

Chapter Fifty-Four

Friday, January 05, 2018
The National Archives, Kew, London

Jayne stared at the first document. It was a copy of the Official Secrets Act, dated 1939. It seemed pretty standard; the document hadn't changed much even when she was bound by it as a police cadet. She scanned down the clauses until she came to a signature: Monique Sinclair.

Her grandmother's signature. Once again, Jayne was astounded at the effect such a simple mark with a pen had on her. The handwriting style was definitely French, much more rounded than English with the characteristic long serifs. A date in her hand indicated when it was signed. This must have been the time she had just joined the SOE. So where was Jayne's father then? Was he in Hereford?

She put it aside and pulled out the second document. It was printed on flimsy wartime paper and had yellowed with age, but the typewritten statements were easy to read.

INTERVIEW REPORT

Interview No. 564   Jepson/11/42

    Particulars: Potential recruit
    Name by which known: Mrs Monique Sinclair nee Massat

Nationality: French
Living Relatives: One son, husband deceased

Report

Mrs Sinclair is an attractive woman in her mid-twenties with a ready smile and charming manner. Throughout the interview she answered the questions thoughtfully and honestly, perhaps too honestly. I expect a little more subterfuge and less openness from our agents.

Her demeanour was confident, sitting erect in the chair despite obvious nervousness at the strangeness of the situation.

Physically, she seems a little weak and not as robust as some of our other candidates. She may have problems with some of the active elements of the course. And despite being born on a smallholding, she seems more at home in the city rather than the country. Her hands were soft and well manicured, not those of your typical farm girl.

Her French is impeccable, with no obvious accent or shortcomings, unlike some of the recruits. She displays an obvious pride in her country and its culture. A patriot rather than a nationalist though.

Her one obvious weakness is her son. When questioned on leaving him behind while she went off to war, her answer was forthright: 'We all have to make sacrifices, this is mine.'

Despite this frankness, I believe her attitude to her son needs to be monitored throughout her training.

In conclusion, I would recommend she commence training at Wanborough in the New Year, with the caveats I have elucidated above.

Signed

Jepson, Captain

It was signed with a large open 'J' dominating the rest of the letters.

'I wonder who Jepson was,' said Jayne out loud, receiving a stare and a 'shhhh' from the researcher opposite.

She reached for the next document in the file.

TRAINING REPORT

S.T.S. No. 02.   Party No.6.

School No.OB.13.
Particulars: Agent Initiation
Name: Mrs Monique Sinclair

Report

Completed training satisfactorily, despite initial problems on the obstacle course. Showed determination to overcome the lack of physical prowess. However, has an aversion to firearms which could prove problematic. Did not want to fire the Webley or the Sten and only did so under threat of expulsion. Her reluctance seems to be moral rather than physical. She refuses to discuss it, but it may be an issue with her Catholicism. It obviously may create problems with her training in the future.

She was popular amongst the other attendees, forming friendships easily and effectively. Her social skills are well-formed, allowing her to talk easily to different levels and strata in society.

Recommended for further training with the above reservations.

De Wesselow, Major
Head of Training, Wanborough Manor

Jayne remembered back to her own days in the police force as a cadet. During the training in Stockport, she had wanted to quit so many times. Only the thought of her mother's gloating face telling her, 'I knew you weren't good enough,' had kept her going to the end.

She wondered if her grandmother was the same. What kept her going through all this? She was obviously feisty, though, refusing to fire her weaponry. The pressure to conform in the training was so strong, she knew how difficult it was to resist.

The more she thought about it, her grandmother reminded her of her own character. Perhaps that's where she had inherited her stubbornness?

She reached for the third document in the folder. What secrets did this one hold for her?

Chapter Fifty-Five

Tuesday, July 13, 1943
Rue de la Faisanderie, Paris, France

After spending two sleepless nights in the Delorme house, they left for Paris on the afternoon train. As good as his word, Dericourt had produced documents for them which looked far flimsier and less new. For Monique, the Carte d'Identité and the Ration Card both bore the name Suzanne Fevrier. Philippe was now Henri Darlat, and the young boy was a nephew of Monique's, going to stay with them in Paris. Henry Frager was to meet them in the Café Chez Touret on Friday afternoon at 2.00 p.m.

They purchased tickets easily and boarded the train without a problem. However, after thirty minutes a section of the Milice, headed by a plainclothes officer, began inspecting documents.

As they examined hers, Monique held her breath. The uniformed officer looked at her picture and then called his plainclothes colleague to join him.

Monique pushed the suitcase with the radio inside further under the seat with her heel, praying they wouldn't ask her to open her luggage.

For a few seconds, the plainclothes policeman examined the photo.

'You look far younger than your age appears on your documents, mademoiselle.'

She looked up at him and smiled. 'I look after myself, monsieur, the secret to looking young.'

'Perhaps you should give some tips to my wife.'

'A woman's secrets are hers and hers alone, monsieur, but I could give her the name of my beauty spa in Paris?'

'No, no, please no.' He handed her back her Carte d'Identité. 'She spends enough on herself as it is. My poor salary cannot afford anything more. And the boy?' He pointed to Raymond.

'My nephew. His parents died in 1940.'

The Milice man nodded once. 'Au revoir, mademoiselle.' He touched the rim of his hat and turned to examine the documents of another passenger.

Finally, Monique breathed out.

Fortunately, the rest of the trip passed uneventfully, with Monique staring out of the window as the train approached Paris. She had visited the city many times with her parents when she was young, but it seemed different now, as if it were under a perpetual cloud of mourning.

This was her first visit since she had passed through as an innocent eighteen-year-old girl on her way to England to work for the Dodds and meet young George.

On arrival at the Gare de l'Est, they quickly passed through ticket control without their documents being checked.

Together, they boarded a taxi to their new address: 18, Rue de la Faisanderie.

She continued to stare out the window of the taxi as Philippe and Raymond sat silently by her side.

The place depressed her. Everywhere German uniforms walked the streets as if they owned them. Buildings sported Nazi swastikas hanging down in long flags from their balconies. Well-dressed and coiffeured women openly consorted with German officers, hanging on their every word as they ate in restaurants or drank in the many bars.

The ordinary people, on the other hand, had a look of despair etched into their faces, shuffling along the streets, their string bags empty but for a few morsels they had been able to afford in the markets. Over the whole city hung an air of resignation, like a blanket of unhappiness. Gone was the jolly, carefree city she remembered from before the war. In its place something more sombre, more Germanic, had taken over, occupying all the warmth and happiness.

Raymond knew the apartment. He led them up to the third floor, producing a key from his pocket to open the front door. 'This is where you will stay for the next couple of days,' he announced with a seriousness that belied his age. 'Someone will come to talk with you later.'

And then he was gone. Monique never saw him again, and she often wondered what had become of him.

The apartment was typical for that part of Paris and a Haussmann building. The rooms were small, the ceilings high, the pipes noisy, and an aged concierge guarded the entrance downstairs like she was guarding Buckingham Palace, peering out through her door as people entered.

They were on the third floor, so at least Monique didn't have too many stairs to climb, but it also meant there was only one way in and out. If the Gestapo knocked on their door, there would be no way of escape.

Her next radio *sked,* or schedule, was that evening. Accordingly, she set up the radio and sent her transmission while Philippe slept. The answer from London came back two hours later.

BRINGING FORWARD TRIP STOP. WILL ARRIVE PARIS JULY 22 STOP. URGENT WE MEET STOP. STRACHAN STOP.

She looked at the decoded message on her pad. What was so important and so urgent that London would fly out the second-in-command of the section into the heart of enemy territory?

Chapter Fifty-Six

Wednesday, July 14, 1943
Café Chez Touret, Paris, France

The following day she met Frager, along with Philippe, in a café on a street in the eighth arrondissement.

They walked in separately, Monique first, with Philippe joining five minutes later. She was to recognise Frager from the ancient brown leather briefcase on his table.

He was already there when she arrived. A small, dapper, bald-headed man sitting in the corner reading a newspaper.

She walked over and spoke the code sentence. 'I've been waiting for my uncle for six months. Do you know where he is?' She felt slightly ridiculous saying this to a complete stranger.

He glanced up from his paper. 'Take a seat, I've been waiting for you.'

That wasn't the agreed reply. She hesitated. Should she sit down?

'Please take a seat, mademoiselle. Oh, in case you are wondering, I am supposed to say, "I saw your uncle near the Champs-Élysée yesterday".'

He smiled up at her. 'Now we've got that rigmarole over and done with, please take a seat. You will be far more comfortable than standing there.'

This man wasn't what she expected. He seemed to have a flippant, almost ironic attitude to the basic tenets of tradecraft.

He leant forward and whispered, 'If you continue to stand in front of me like that without saying anything, you will simply draw attention to yourself. See, the barman is already looking at you.'

She glanced over her shoulder. The barman was staring at her as he polished a wine glass. She quickly sat down.

'Good, I'm glad we have the ridiculous introductions out of the way. My name is Frager. The British refer to me as "Architect".' He coughed and smiled. 'The British can be so trite with these things. You will call me Frager, everybody else does. A glass of wine? I'm afraid the coffee is ersatz, the sweepings off the streets. The best stuff is reserved for the cafés the Germans frequent, not places like this.' He waved his arm to indicate their surroundings.

Monique looked around her. It was a typical working-class café, the sort of place people dropped into for breakfast or a drink after work. The overall colour scheme was brown, with just tinges of an ancient red paint to brighten things up. 'Thank you, but I'm fine,' she finally answered.

'You have to drink something, dear, remember we are friends meeting to catch up over old times.'

'A glass of wine, then.'

He raised his arm. 'Gaston, two more glasses when you are ready.'

The barman nodded.

'Luckily, Gaston still has his contacts in Bordeaux. The Germans do not have a monopoly on wine yet. If they did, France would revolt immediately. And if they ever touched our cheese…' His hands went up in the gesture of an explosion.

Monique watched him as Gaston poured out two glasses of red wine at the table. Was this man really the second-in-command of the network in northern France?

A shadow hovered over their table.

'My uncle—' began Philippe.

'Yes, yes, I've been through all that with your companion. Please sit.'

The leader of her group took his seat next to her.

'Gaston, another glass— No, let's have a bottle to celebrate meeting old friends,' Frager shouted loudly across the café.

Gaston brought a bottle of Medoc over to the table with an additional glass for Philippe.

Frager raised his glass. 'To the success of our endeavours, and the demise of our enemies.' He drank the glass down in one and reached for the bottle to replenish his wine.

As he poured it, Monique noticed his hand was trembling, spilling a little of the wine on the table top.

'And now to business, shall we?'

'You know my instructions?' said Philippe curtly.

'I am aware of them, yes. I fact, it was myself who raised my suspicions when I last visited our friends three months ago.'

So it was this man who had frightened London into believing there was a traitor in his organisation.

'What raised your suspicions?'

'My contacts in the Abwehr warned me that the SD were—'

'SD?' asked Philippe.

'*Sicherheistdienst*. The intelligence operation of the SS.'

'Not the Gestapo?'

Frager sighed loudly. 'I thought our friends would have briefed you properly. There are three German intelligence operations in Paris. The SD is the intelligence wing of the SS, the Gestapo is the police operation for the SS, and the Abwehr is German military intelligence. In the game of spying, all three chase us. Luckily, they hate each other just as much as they hate us.'

'You have contacts in the Abwehr?' asked Monique.

'They hate the SD, the SS and the Gestapo. We play one off against the other.'

'A dangerous game.'

'The game of secrets always is.' He fixed Monique with a strange look, as if he could see into her soul.

'So you believe your organisation has been undermined by the SD?' interrupted Philippe.

The man shook his head. 'I *know* my organisation has been compromised by the SD. Our friends overseas, however, think I am wrong.'

'Not exactly true,' said Philippe. 'They have full confidence in the man you named as the chief suspect. That's why I am here.'

A man named as a suspect? That wasn't part of the briefing. Then it hit Monique that maybe she didn't know everything about this mission. What had they not told her?

'Good,' said Frager.

'This may be speaking out of turn, but if you have a suspect, why don't you interrogate him? And if he confesses, get rid of him?' she asked.

The man shook his wrist in that French way that registers surprise. 'Bof, women. Always the most ruthless in our group. I suppose you would be the first to volunteer to execute the man too?'

Monique stayed silent.

'Our friends overseas placed him in our organisation, that's why. He is their man.'

'Why do you suspect him?'

'Too many coincidences. Arrests of key agents in Paris and the north-west. The discovery of radios just as they begin broadcasting.'

'It could have been the detector vans…'

'True, but the Germans seems to know what we are doing even before we do it.'

'Have any of your agents been turned?'

'There was a woman last year,' he glanced across at Monique, 'a wireless operator. She became the mistress of the head of the Abwehr.'

'You closed down all the cells that she was working with?'

'Of course, do I look like an idiot? But still the arrests continue.'

Philippe appeared to think for a moment before he said, 'Monique, I think you should return to the apartment.'

She stared at him. Was she being dismissed?

'There is no point in you being here. It is too dangerous. You have met Frager now.'

'If you need to contact me, just leave a message with Gaston,' Frager added, pointing to the barman polishing wine glasses.

She looked at both of them. She was being dismissed. 'I think I should stay her with both of you. What would happen to the mission, Philippe, if you were caught?'

'The mission would be terminated and you would be sent back to our friends. It is better that you leave now,' he said emphatically.

'I have arranged for a Mrs Ysette Treville to help you move to another location, three days from now. You mustn't stay too long in one place. The detector vans have been particularly active recently…' added Frager.

There was no point discussing it any more. Monique rose from the table. 'I'll wait for her to contact me.' She held out her hand and in a loud voice, said, 'It was a pleasure meeting you again, Jean.'

He stood up and reached over to kiss her on both cheeks, whispering, 'Only the English shake hands when they say goodbye. You must be more careful.'

Chapter Fifty-Seven

Wednesday, July 14, 1943
Rue de la Faisanderie, Paris, France

Monique made her way back to the apartment.

Dusk was descending over Paris, the sky a vivid orange burnished with streaks of green and grey. At any other time, she would have loved to be here, strolling along the boulevards hand in hand with John, stopping off in the cafés for a glass of milky Pernod and a bite to eat. Or wandering down to the Seine and watching the heavily laden barges plough their way downstream, understanding that thousands had done the same before them and thousands would do it again in the future.

But she was not here with John. She was on her own, alone and afraid, surrounded by the enemy. So she held her handbag in front of her, skulking in the shadows as the German soldiers and their French girl-friends laughed gaily, drank in the cafés or bought the latest fashions from the modistes on the Champs-Élysée.

She was so relieved when she finally returned back to the empty apartment; running up the stairs past the startled concierge, fumbling with the key in the lock before hearing it eventually click into place, then hustling through the door, and slamming it behind her as fast as she could.

For five minutes she leant with her back against it, trying to catch her breath and willing herself to be calm.

Gradually, she retained control, breathing slowly and deeply. 'Time for tea,' she said out loud walking to the kitchen. Then she realised there was no tea, just a dark brown powder made from acorns that resembled coffee.

She lit the gas, putting a saucepan of water on to boil and emptying the brown contents of the jar into the water. It would have to do, at least it was hot and wet.

Sipping her hot sludge, she checked the time: 6.45 p.m. In fifteen minutes, she would have to make her *sked* for the week.

She brought out the radio from its hiding place in the wardrobe, spited it on and attached the wires to the correct terminals.

Quickly she tapped in her call sign and the message Philippe had given her regarding the contacts they had made.

Then she sat down to wait for the reply. She knew this was the most dangerous time for her. Any minute now she might hear the growl of an engine in the street below as one of the radio-detector vans honed in on her position, followed by the sound of boots on the stairs and banging on the door.

But strangely, she was calm now. The nerves of walking on the street, surrounded by Germans, had vanished in the detail of coding messages and the mechanics of being a wireless operator.

This was her job, what she was trained to do. Unlike the streets, it held no fears for her.

Two hours later, the headset began to vibrate with the message from London. She wrote it down, using her one-time pad to decode it.

GAMEKEEPER AND USHER ARRIVING 22 JULY STOP. WILL CONTACT YOU ON 24 JULY EVENING STOP. GOOD NEWS ON BORIS STOP. ARCHAMBAUD STILL ON AIR STOP. IMPERATIVE HE BE CONTACTED STOP.

'Gamekeeper' was David Strachan and 'Usher' was Jack Hartsoumanian, an agent she had met briefly at Beaulieu. He had started Prosper with Francis Suttill and, along with Gilbert Norman, alias 'Archambaud', they had grown it to cover most of northern France.

Philippe came in just as she finished decoding the message. She passed it to him and then carefully switched off the radio, dismantled the aerial wires and placed everything back in the wardrobe.

If the Germans ever searched the apartment she knew they would find it quickly, but in a cursory search it might be missed. And besides, should the concierge come into their place while they were out, it would be better not to have radio wires sticking out of the window.

After she finished putting the radio away, Philippe sat her down.

'I talked with Frager after you left. He hasn't seen Prosper, Archambaud or Whitebeam for the last three weeks.'

'Is that normal?'

Philippe made a moue with his mouth. 'It happens, he said, particularly if they have an operation with another cell in Normandy.'

'But all three missing at the same time? London says Archambaud is still transmitting to them.'

'Is he? Perhaps they are in Normandy.'

'Or the Germans are using his transmitter and his codes…'

Philippe scratched his head. 'We must wait now for Strachan to arrive. Only a week away.'

She stared at him.

'There was one more thing from Frager. He asked you to be careful. If the Germans have Archambaud, then you are in grave danger. It means they know the frequency we are broadcasting on.'

Chapter Fifty-Eight

Friday, January 05, 2018
The National Archives, Kew, London

Jayne pinched the skin between on the bridge of her nose. Reading these documents with their tightly typed pages was giving her a headache.

She glanced at the clock. 12.05. Across from her, the man researching the Irish documents had already left for his lunch. Should she go to eat, give herself a break?

She shook her head. She had to carry on, get to the bottom of the mystery, she might never have the chance again.

Once more Martin Sinclair's words reverberated through her mind. 'Help me, Jayne. Help me find out who betrayed my mother.'

She reached for the next document in the folder.

TRAINING REPORT

S.T.S. No. 10.   **Party No.28.**

School No.OB.8.
Particulars: Agent Field Training
Name: Mrs Monique Sinclair

Report

An interesting candidate.

She has become steadily stronger as the training has progressed becoming more and more confident of her abilities. She has coped particularly well with the rigours of hand-to-hand combat displaying a resourcefulness with surprised her instructors. After initial reservations regarding the use of firearms, she has gradually become better in their application, overcoming many of her moral scruples. She will never be a great shot but at least she has reached a level of competence which should see her in good stead should the need arise.

Her relations with her fellow trainees have, on the whole, been good. Indeed, she seems to have been the one person that most of the others would like on their team. A kind lecturer would ascribe this to her skills and her natural ability to get on with people. A less kind person than myself would put it down to her attractiveness.

Her social skills are not to be underestimated. In the fraught atmosphere of an overseas assignment, the ability to work calmly as a member of a team could turn out to be a valuable asset.

However, there are two areas that give me a cause for concern. The first is her Catholicism. She insisted on attending mass every Sunday during training. Whilst the school tries its best to accommodate the religious sensibilities of its students, there are often times, as there would be in the field, when this is impossible. Mrs Sinclair was adamant that her wishes should be obeyed.

Perhaps, the death of her husband has led her to reach out for spiritual consolation?

The second is the more worrying. Mrs Sinclair has a young son in Hereford. During the course, she continually tried to send him letters and cards. It was explained to her this was not allowed as it would jeopardise the security of our establishment. She still persisted. Again, in the field and under interrogation by the Germans, could her son be a source of weakness they could exploit?

To summate; Mrs Sinclair is an exceptional candidate who I believe, even with the two concerns outlined above, should be considered for further training as a Radio Operator. However she should be monitored in the future. The concerns I have outlined above could become serious weaknesses in a operational situation.

Malvers, Colonel
Head of School, Drumbo House, Arisaig.

Chapter Fifty-Nine

Saturday, July 24, 1943
8 Villa Leandre, Montmartre, Paris, France

They moved every three days to a new hideout. First to an apartment on the Rue Du Colonel Moll near the Arc de Triomphe, which Monique hated, and then to a pretty little terraced house in Montmartre, not far from Sacré-Coeur. It was situated in one of the many lanes that lined the top of the hill.

Strangely, she felt safer in this area than in the centre of Paris.

Firstly, there were fewer German soldiers on the streets and she wasn't constantly being faced with grey-clad men every time she ventured out of the apartment. Secondly, she spent most afternoons in the white church itself, finding solace and relief in the burnished wood, the burning candles and the aromas of incense. She even made friends with one of the priests, a young man from the Auvergne in his first posting in Paris. He had a simple faith in God, which she found comforting. Even better, he asked her few questions, accepting without question her cover story of being a poor farmer's daughter from Orléans looking for work in the big city.

The messages from London continued to arrive as per her *sked*, becoming more demanding in tone every time she contacted her handlers.

ARCHAMBAUD IN CONTACT STOP. WANTS TO MEET ON 26TH AT MARTINE'S 5PM STOP. RETURNED FROM MISSION STOP. HAS GOOD NEWS STOP. URGENT MEETING NEEDED STOP.

She walked back to the house. Philippe was waiting for her. 'I was worried for you. You shouldn't wander off on your own, it's too dangerous. on the streets at the moment.'

'I have to get out of the house, the atmosphere is so oppressive here.'

'Where did you go?'

'The usual place. Sacré-Coeur.'

'How many times did they tell us in training not to adopt a routine? Routines are dangerous, people will notice you if you go to the same place again and again.'

'Nobody notices me,' she lied. 'I sit at the back and pray.'

Their argument was interrupted by a knock on the door. In an instant, Philippe was across the room, peering out of the net curtain.

She watched his shoulders visibly relax as he turned to her. 'It's Strachan.'

She ran to open the door. David Strachan bustled inside with two other men, both of whom Monique recognised - Henri Dericourt and Jack Hartsoumanian.

'It's great to see you, David,' she said.

'You don't know how happy I am to be here, away from London.' He glanced across at Philippe. 'Evening, Philippe, how are you?'

Philippe was sitting in the corner, a stern look on his face. 'Fine. Shall we get down to work?'

'This arrived from London for you yesterday.' She gave David the decoded message.

He took it in quickly. 'Martine's is one of our safe houses on the Rue de Rome, close to the Gare Saint-Lazare. Has anybody been in touch with Archambaud recently?'

Both Philippe and Monique shook their heads. 'And Frager hasn't seen him, Prosper or Whitebeam for three weeks.'

David sat down. 'That is worrying. But London is still convinced the messages from Archambaud are genuine. The codes and call signs are correct.'

'He could have been forced to give them up,' said Monique.

'Perhaps, but the information he has given us recently is accurate regarding Normandy. Not something the Germans would let us know if he had been turned.'

Philippe sat up. 'They could be playing us. Letting us have snippets of information so we think the messages are genuine.'

David thought for a moment. 'There's only one way to find out. I have to meet him.'

'You can't,' said Jack.

'It's the only way to find out.'

'It's too dangerous.'

'I was sent by London to discover what happened to the network. I'm not going to do it by sitting on my arse waiting for the Germans to find me.'

'I'll do it,' said Monique. 'They won't be expecting a woman.'

'Impossible,' answered David. 'Archambaud has never met you, why would he trust a woman he has never seen before? It has to be me.'

Henri spoke for the first time. 'I agree, it should be David.'

Jack stepped forward. 'You're wrong. It has to be me.' He began counting off his fingers. 'Firstly, I know Archambaud by sight. I can recognise him immediately. When was the last time you saw him?'

David looked down. 'Over a year ago.'

'Secondly, you're too valuable to lose. Capture you and the Boche would know our organisation in London, and all our agents in the field. Thirdly, if I go missing, you will know Archambaud has been turned and can report to London in person and they will believe you. I have been talking to the centre about moles in the operation for six months now and still they delay. You are the only one they will believe.'

David laughed. 'I can't believe we're arguing which one of us wants to walk into a possible death trap. Okay, I agree. Philippe and Monique, you will accompany Jack but don't go in. Stay outside and watch what happens. Only when Jack calls you forward are you to move. Henri, you need to go back to organise the next drop from London.'

'It's on Wednesday. We're also sending agents from the Symphony network back to London. They're bringing in a Lysander.'

'Good.'

Monique stepped forward. 'If I give you a letter, Henri, will you give it one of the agents to take back.'

'Just a postman, me. Can you give it to me now?'

'Five minutes, ok?'

Henri nodded.

'And now, gentlemen – and lady – I need to sleep. We have a busy day ahead of us tomorrow.'

'*À demain*,' said Jack laconically.

Chapter Sixty

Monday, July 26, 1943
Rue de Rome, Paris, France

A half hour before the meeting, Monique took up position in a small café next to the entrance to the apartment block. Just three other tables were occupied; two men in earnest business discussions, a couple obviously in love despite the war, and a man wearing a brown trilby, nursing a glass of wine who had obviously been sat there for a long time.

Monique sat down at one of the tables at the front, so she had a clear view of the road in front of her. Philippe stood on the other side of the road, outside one of the side entrances to the Gare Saint-Lazare, standing under a clock as if he were waiting for somebody.

She sipped a coffee tasting of sawdust and ate a croissant that had been fresh two days ago. She had asked for jam but the waiter had looked at her strangely.

'Jam, madame? We haven't had any jam for three months. None of the cafés have jam.'

She mumbled a quick apology, explaining that she had only just arrived in Paris by train.

He seemed to accept it, grumbling about outsiders invading their city as he walked away to serve somebody else at another table.

She still had to get used to living in France again. There were so many things that were different, so many foods that were no longer available. A Parisian would know these things; she would have to learn them or some smart Milice would soon work out she wasn't who she said she was.

She checked her watch. Five more minutes. On the other side of the road, Philippe was pacing up and down, his nervousness getting the better of him. A truck full of armed Germans passed in front of them and parked on the road beside the station.

What were the Germans doing? Had they been betrayed?

Then a Feldwebel undid the back of the truck, shouting for the troops to get down. They did, forming an orderly line before marching into the concourse of the station.

Monique breathed a sigh of relief. She glanced down at her table. The remains of the croissant lay shredded on the plate. She quickly gathered up the crumbs and placed them in her handkerchief.

'Another café, madame?' It was the waiter again.

Should she order one more? But it was undrinkable. What would a Parisian do?

She shook her head, waving him away as if swatting a fly. 'Drinking more of this muck would make me sick.'

'As you please. The better coffee will be here tomorrow morning at eight o'clock, but it runs out quickly.'

He danced away between the tables, back into the dark interior.

On the opposite side of the road, she saw Jack approaching from the direction of the station. He was wearing a worker's flat cap and blue jacket, carrying what looked like a tool box in his right hand. He walked past Philippe without acknowledging him and crossed the road towards her.

For a moment, their eyes met and she could see he was afraid. Very afraid.

She glanced away, pretending to finish the last of her coffee. He passed in front of her table and turned left to enter the apartment block.

The man with the trilby got up from his table and vanished inside the cafe leaving his half drunk glass of wine.

The road was quiet. Next to her, she could hear the voices of the two businessmen discussing the price of tyres and the possible numbers they could sell to the Germans.

She jumped as a chair scraped along the street making a screeching noise. The couple from the table next to her stood up and walked away towards the station holding hands.

She glanced across at Philippe. He was staring up at the second-floor apartment where they were to meet, looking for a signal.

Out of nowhere, a Mercedes slid to a stop in front of him. Two men jumped out, both carrying a revolver in their right hand.

Philippe glanced to either side, looking for an escape route, saw there was none and fumbled inside his jacket to pull out a revolver of his own.

A single shot rang out and Philippe fell forward slowly, as if in slow motion.

Monique sat there transfixed, staring at the action in front of her like watching a film in a theatre. The waiter rushed out to the street, saw what was happening and ran back into the café.

The men were bending over Philippe's body now, turning it over to look at the face.

Philippe didn't move.

Another car accelerated to a stop outside the apartment block, right in front of Monique.

She sat up, ready to run, but three plainclothes men ran past her into the building.

Inside the car, a German officer with the insignia of the SS on his collar was calmly smoking a cigarette. He looked across at her and smiled. The smile of a tiger seeing a goat tied to a tree.

The man with the trilby walked calmly out of the cafe and spoke to the German officer pointing up at the window and the across at Philippe lying motionless on the street.

The officer opened the door of the car and glanced across at her one more time, before throwing the butt of his cigarette to the ground and walking over to the spot where Philippe's motionless body was lying.

He stared down at it for a minute or so before ordering the men, in German, to pick up the body and put it in the car.

Monique didn't know whether to run or stay where she was.

She glanced down the street towards the station. It was suddenly quiet and empty. People had immediately decided to vanish from view on hearing the first sounds of gunfire.

Seconds later, Jack was hurried out of the apartment door, manhandled by two burly guards, his wrists handcuffed behind his back and blood dripping from a cut on his forehead.

For a second, his eyes caught hers, before a large hand grabbed his head and shoved it beneath the top edge of the car door.

The man in the trilby bundled him into the back and the car accelerated away from the kerb, leaving a cloud of exhaust in its wake.

She looked across the street. The other Mercedes had vanished too.

The waiter and the customers from inside the café wandered cautiously out into the road.

But there was nothing left to see.

Monique was suddenly surrounded by people, but she had never felt more alone in her life.

Chapter Sixty-One

Monday, July 26, 1943
8 Villa Leandre, Montmartre, Paris, France

She didn't know how she got back to Montmartre.

The whole trip was a blur as, time and time again, she replayed the terrible death of Philippe in her mind.

David was waiting for her when she returned. As soon as he saw her face he knew something had gone wrong. He rushed over to her and grabbed her shoulders roughly. 'What happened? Tell me what happened.'

'Philippe's dead,' she mumbled.

'What?'

She sat down, taking a few deep breaths and trying to pull herself together. He brought her a glass of brandy. 'Here, drink this, it will help.'

She swallowed a mouthful, feeling the spirit burning the back of her throat.

He knelt down in front of her, placing his hands on her knees. 'Now take your time and tell me exactly what occurred.'

She took a deep breath and told him everything, from the moment she sat down at the table in the café to the time the car accelerated away from the pavement with Jack imprisoned inside.

When she finished, David stood up and began pacing the room, firing off questions as he thought of them.

'You're certain Philippe is dead?'

'Yes. At least, I think so. He wasn't moving when they put him in the back of the car.'

'And Jack was in handcuffs?'

'Yes.'

'Were they waiting for him or did they arrive to search the apartment when you were there?'

'A man with a trilby was sitting outside the cafe. He spoke to the German officer in the car.'

'Was he watching? An observer?'

'I don't know…'

'Think woman,' he shouted.

She replayed the events in her mind. 'I'm not sure, but I think he was watching. He vanished into the cafe and could have made a phone call…'

David squatted down in front of her. 'Did he make a phone call or not?'

'I couldn't see from where I was sitting but a few moments later, the cars arrived. The occupants of one car attacked Philippe while the other sent men up to the apartment. She closed her eyes and relived the events in detail. 'I think the men who arrested him were not the same as those who arrived in the car.'

'Be clearer. Which is it? They were or weren't the same men?' he shouted the question at her.

'I don't know,' she answered, 'why is it important?'

He stopped pacing and turned to face her. 'Because if they were waiting for him inside, they either knew about the meeting, or about the safe house.'

'Who else knows of the existence of that place?'

'Prosper, his team, myself, and obviously all the people who were here yesterday.'

'A lot of people.'

He nodded.

'And if they arrived after Jack went into the building?'

'It means they were tipped off, either from somebody watching or from somebody within the network who knew about the meeting.'

'But not many people knew…'

'Exactly. Just us two, Philippe, Frager, Henri and Jack himself.'

'You're saying one of us is the traitor?'

David didn't answer, slumping down on the sofa and remaining motionless as if in a trance.

'We need to leave here. We're not safe,' Monique said finally.

He sat up with a start as if suddenly realising the importance of her words. 'Get the radio and your things together, we're going now.'

'Where?'

'Another safe house.'

'But it might be compromised…'

'We have to take the risk, we can't stay here any longer.'

She went into her room, throwing her clothes into a suitcase and recovering the radio from its hiding place.

David was ready and waiting for her when she returned to the living room with the cases.

'Where are we going?' she asked.

'To the Bois de Boulogne. It's the only place left I know.' He paused for a second before continuing, 'With Jack captured and Philippe dead, it means the traitor must be Frager or Henri.'

'You know, I had a bad feeling about Henri the first time I met him.'

David shook his head. 'He may be a little wild, but he's a good chap. I hired him myself. Without his organisational and pilot skills, the delivery of agents into France would be impossible.'

'So you're saying that leaves Frager?'

He didn't answer, simply picking up the suitcases and walking towards the door. 'Let's go. We have to get there before curfew at eleven.'

She stood still for a moment. He was wrong. It had suddenly occurred to her that there was one other person left who could have betrayed them.

David himself.

Could he be the traitor?

He turned back to face her. 'What are you waiting for? Let's get moving.'

Slowly, reluctantly, she picked up the radio case and her own suitcase. She would have to be careful from now on.

Very careful.

Chapter Sixty-Two

Friday, January 05, 2018
The National Archives, Kew, London

The man had returned from his lunch. Jayne watched him as he rearranged the papers on his desk, put two sharpened pencils on the left hand side, burped twice and then began work.

She loved watching people in libraries and archives. It was almost as of the presence of the past stripped them bare of pretence, revealing the real person with all their quirks and eccentricities.

She glanced down at the folder. Just a few more files to go. She turned over the next sheet of paper.

FINISHING REPORT

S.T.S. No. 34.   **Party No.37.**

School No.OB.37.
Particulars: Full Agent Training plus W/X Course
Name: Mrs Monique Sinclair

Security Code: 'Rain' before the third word and the tenth word repeated.

<u>Report</u>

This agent has passed the course with flying colours. Her initial training passed smoothly and she was transferred to Arisaig for outdoor, combat and field training. While competent in fieldcraft and combat training, she found it difficult to come to grips with firearms training. She finally found the necessary application and passed the course in a competent manner. Accordingly, she was assigned to be a Wireless Operator in F Section.

In her final training, we found she had an intelligence and an aptitude for radio work and coding. Her transcriptions were extremely accurate and her speed at Morse was described as outstanding even if her hand was a little 'heavy'.

Her final field exercise was instructive. She managed to find employment, scout and photograph a factory in Manchester, remaining undiscovered even though the local police had been warned she was in the area. She managed to stand up well to post-training interrogation, maintaining her cover story throughout.

Our recommendation is that Mrs Sinclair be assigned to a network as soon as possible. She has that rare ability to be active and passive at the same time, being able to sit still and be patient and then to jump into action at a moment's notice. And, although she could be classed as pretty, it's not a beauty that draws attention to itself, but is able to fade into the background when necessary. A classic English Rose, even though she is French.

One worry is the presence of her young son living with her late husband's relatives in Hereford. In an operational situation, her concern for her son may be used against her and should be regarded as a major weakness. Indeed, she has asked her instructors what will happen to him if she is sent to France. I have attempted to allay her fears but it is obviously a worry that preys on her mind.

I would unstintingly recommend Mrs Sinclair for active service.

William Marquand, Major
Commandant, B Group

Appended to the type-written report was a handwritten note scrawled in the margins.

Nonsense.

It was signed in block capitals.

BUCKMASTER.

Jayne had already googled this man's name in her research. He was in charge of the SOE's F Section, running every agent in France from his office in Baker Street.

Why had he put such a curt note in her grandmother's file?

Jayne read the report again. She couldn't help feeling that she was reading about herself, the sort of report she would have received whilst training as a police cadet in Manchester. It began to dawn on her that her grandmother's and her own characters were remarkably similar. She recognised the ability to be patient for long hours and then suddenly spring into action. It described her style of working to a T.

Also the facility with codes and coding. After all, that was exactly what she did as a genealogical investigator; poring over documents and working out what lay behind them, not merely the facts on the page. It was the code written into everybody's life that she was adept at understanding.

She began to like this woman, her grandmother.

What else would her documents reveal?

Chapter Sixty-Three

Tuesday, July 27, 1943
Bois de Boulogne, Paris, France

They moved to a new hideout in Boulevard Richard Wallace, not far from the Bois de Boulogne. David warned her to be careful in this area, as many SS officers kept apartments for their mistresses in the locality. Every time Monique went outside to buy food or meet one of her contacts, she couldn't help feeling that she was being watched. She knew it was all in her head, but still the feeling persisted, like the after-effects of a hangover.

The messages from London continued to arrive as per her sked: three times a week, on Tuesdays, Thursdays and Saturdays. With the absence of Archambaud, she became the group's second wireless operator, the other being an Indian woman whom she had met at Beaulieu – Noor Inayat Khan, code name 'Madeleine'.

Frager and Henri came frequently to the apartment to meet with David. Together, the three of them would sit with their heads close together, whispering to each other.

Occasionally, one of them would pass her a message which she had to encode and send to London. In her free time, she would write letters to her son, giving them to Henri to get back to London. The man always took them reluctantly as if he were doing a big favour.

But other than that, there was little interaction with her, telling her nothing about what they were planning or doing.

Finally, she had enough. One day, after they had gone, she cornered David before he went out.

'What's going on?'

He was putting on his coat. 'What do you mean?'

'You know exactly what I mean, David.'

He stopped what he was doing and looked at her properly for the first time in days. 'Henri and Frager have their contacts in the Abwehr. Apparently, Jack and Archambaud are both being held by the SD in Avenue Foch. We are trying to minimise the impact of their arrest, moving any agents they knew to fresh locations.'

'Has anybody else been arrested?'

He shook his head. 'Not since Jack was taken.'

'Perhaps he hasn't talked.'

'Not many people are able to resist interrogation for ever.' A knowing look passed over David's face. 'We've managed to minimise the damage so far.'

'And Prosper and Whitebeam?'

He shrugged his shoulders. 'Nobody has seen them. We must assume they have been taken too.'

'Why haven't you told London?'

He sat down and ran his fingers through his hair. She could see he had a large bald spot in the middle of his crown. 'We can't be certain yet that they have been taken. Perhaps they have just decided to lie low.'

'Without telling anybody? And you said Frager could be the traitor.'

'He has convinced me he wasn't. I don't know if there ever was a traitor. Perhaps the Germans just got lucky. They were watching a known safe house, saw

Jack going inside and decided to arrest him. You said yourself that a man with a trilby was watching the entrance.'

'And what about Philippe?'

'He reacted too quickly giving himself away.' He looked up and stared straight at her. 'There are two things that convinces me it was just bad luck.'

'And they are.'

He pointed at the two of them. 'Us. If the German's had known about the meeting, they would have arrested you too.

Monique wasn't so sure.

'And if they had known, I would have been arrested by now. Yet the streets are quiet and our sources in the Abwehr say they are presently working against a group in Le Havre. If there was a mole, I would have been snatched up by now.'

'Perhaps the Germans are being clever. By not arresting you, they make us think that there is no mole.'

He smiled. 'You have been reading too many spy novels, Monique, the Germans are not that clever. No, I am convinced now – the rumour that there was a mole was spread by the Boche to sow confusion in our ranks, to create suspicion.'

He glanced up at her standing in front of him, licking his moustache. 'Look, Monique, you may as well know… I've decided to go back to London. I've done all I can here, my work is completed. There is no mole in the network. Security has been too lax, and Frager is tightening up. Henri is organising a Lysander to come and pick me up. You need to come back with me.'

'No.' The words were out of her mouth before she realised she had spoken them. 'I'm staying here,' she said firmly. 'This is what I was trained to do, this is where I belong. My country, this network needs me.'

'They have Madeleine.'

'And what if she gets taken? There is more than enough work for two wireless operators.'

He shrugged his shoulders. 'I can't force you to come back with me, but—'

'My mind is made up, David.'

He stood up, placing his hands on her shoulders, his face close to hers. 'If this is about John…'

'It's not,' she said, moving away from him. 'It's about me. I'm a good wireless operator. I can help this network, help Frager, aid my country. If you were in my shoes, what would you do, David?'

He didn't answer her question. 'Just think about it, Monique, please think about it.'

She gritted her teeth. 'I'm staying, David, I don't need to think about it.'

Chapter Sixty-Four

Sunday, August 15, 1943
1 Boulevard Malesherbes, Paris, France

It was a hot, bright, blue August day when David left.

They had been moving from apartment to apartment, constantly trying to dodge the German detector vans.

The continuous shifting of abode was beginning to wear Monique down. She realised that her home, the place she lived, mattered to her; her clothes neatly folded in the correct cupboard, the kitchen utensils hanging out to dry on the same hook, being conscious of the times for mass at the local church. All these small, simple things kept her feet on the ground and gave her a sense of security.

She knew such a feeling was false; staying in one place was the most insecure thing she could do. But she didn't care. She vowed that once David left she would settle down in one place, probably Montmartre – at least there she felt at home.

In the three weeks since the death of Philippe they had moved once every two days, occupying different apartments in the various arrondissements of Paris. Sometimes they stayed in the same place twice, much to the muttered annoyance of David, who thought it was extremely bad tradecraft.

Gradually, he relaxed a little as the threat of arrest waned. He went about his duties; meeting leaders of the resistance in the suburbs surrounding the city, continually digging for news on Archambaud and the others, setting up new groups as far afield as Saint-Quentin and Rouen.

As the threat lessened, the hunt for the mole also decreased. David became more and more convinced the arrests had been bad luck. 'They were just in the wrong place at the wrong time.'

Monique didn't agree, but kept her counsel to herself. There was no point arguing any more, his mind was made up.

When it wasn't one of her *sked* days, Monique spent the time reading or in church, finding peace in the mundane tasks of washing her clothes, listening to mass, or hunting in the shops for fresh fruit, vegetables or bread. Coffee was a luxury she spent hours trying to obtain, often asking the resistance leaders if any could be found.

On *sked* days – still Tuesdays, Thursdays and Saturdays – she stayed at home, patiently encoding the messages given to her by David or Frager, waiting for the eventual replies from London. The evenings were spent listening to the BBC with the volume turned down as low as possible, checking that the messages were transmitted correctly by the announcer in London.

'Aunt Phyllis has a bad cold this morning.'

'Two bad tyres were left on the road last night.'

'The apples will fall from the tree.'

All these messages broadcast in clear English over the BBC held a particular meaning for one of the networks. A parachute drop of supplies, a shipment of arms, the arrival of a new agent or courier.

On the day David left, they said a quick goodbye.

'Are you sure you won't come with me? There's room on the Lysander.'

She shook her head. 'Where are you leaving from?'

'Just outside Reims. Henri has arranged the landing strip.'

He put on his dark beret and hoisted a workman's backpack over his blue jacket. 'Be very careful, Monique,' he said, leaning in to kiss her cheek, 'you need to watch out for Jerry.'

'I will. Here's a letter for my son and another for a cousin who's with the Free French forces in Plymouth.'

She passed over both letters.

'I didn't know you had a cousin living in England.'

'Neither did I until just before I left.'

He placed the letters inside a compartment in his backpack. 'London will message you after I have arrived.'

He turned to walk towards the door.

'David,' she shouted. 'Watch out. I don't trust Henri.'

He held his arms out wide. 'I've not been taken so far. The luck of the English. And without Henri I wouldn't be leaving tonight. Bon chance.'

He hesitated for a moment, about to speak, as if something were troubling him. Then he hitched up the backpack and was gone, leaving a stillness in the air.

Monique slumped down on a chair.

* * *

Two days later, just after she had transmitted the latest reports from Frager, she received a short, coded message from London.

PACKAGE ARRIVED SAFELY STOP. GAMEKEEPER HOME STOP. MISSING FRESH BREAD STOP. MORE MESSAGES TO FOLLOW STOP.

He was back in London.

She didn't feel any sense of joy, or exhilaration. Not even a celebration that he had arrived home safely.

Instead, there was a feeling of disquiet that hadn't left her since he had departed.

A feeling she couldn't shake no matter how hard she tried.

Chapter Sixty-Five

Friday, January 05, 2018
Somewhere in Whitehall, London

Penrose was worried.

He had played and rewound the recording of Mrs Sinclair's meeting with her father again and again and again.

It was obvious the father had passed something to her as he was leaving. But what was it?

A message?

New information?

His cell had been searched numerous times over the years. The guards had found the old letters from John Sinclair to his wife. They had even found copies of all the old birthday cards he had sent to his daughter. But had they missed something? Had Martin Sinclair been hiding something all these years?

A slight tap on the door disturbed his thoughts.

'Enter,' he shouted irritably.

Proctor sidled in like a burglar gaining surreptitious entry to a darkened house. 'Sir…'

'What is it Proctor?'

'The surveillance team have reported on Mrs Sinclair as you requested.'

'And?'

Proctor checked his notes. 'She spent last night in Room 235 of the Premier Inn, Blackfriars. She was online working on her computer. I have requested a log of the sites she visited from that IP address from GCHQ. Unfortunately, many other people in the hotel were also online using the same IP address.'

'It doesn't matter, Proctor. Analyse the information and isolate her sites.'

'Yes, sir. This morning, she woke up at 6.35 and had a breakfast of coffee, croissants and jam…'

'I don't want to know what she had for breakfast, Proctor, where is she now?'

'At the National Archives, sir. She has requested the files of her grandmother from the clerks. These files were cleared for release in 2003.'

'Has she requested any other SOE files?'

Proctor checked his notes. 'Not that I know, sir. Perhaps…'

'This is becoming serious,' Penrose interrupted his junior, 'I want reports every hour on her activity, the files she requests and the calls she makes.'

'Yes, sir. Shall I ask the clerks at the archives to stop the release of the documents?

'No, of course not.'

Proctor looked quizzical. 'Why not, sir?' he asked tentatively.

Penrose sighed and then explained in a voice one would use to a seven-year -old. 'Because, Proctor, if we stopped the release of the documents, we would never know what was hidden inside that was potentially harmful to the department.'

Proctor's eyes lit up. 'So Mrs Sinclair is going to find out for us, sir.'

Penrose sighed again and waved Proctor away imperiously. 'Just get on with it, man.'

Chapter Sixty-Six

Sunday, August 29, 1943
8 Villa Leandre, Montmartre, Paris, France

As she promised herself, she moved into the house in Montmartre the day after David left. Neither Frager nor Dericourt complained, in fact, they both seemed to approve of the move.

She recognised the danger of staying in one place, always taking a roundabout route to the house when she returned home. She checked out the local streets, staring at the residents until she recognised their faces. She noticed the way the people opposite lived their lives – when they went to bed, when they woke up, when they went to work – in order to see if their daily routine changed in any way.

She also found a hiding place for the radio; in one of the old fireplaces that had been bricked up. Frager helped Dericourt to pull it apart and create a false door, behind which she could hide her equipment and her codebooks. It was awkward to access but at least it gave her some peace of mind that the radio might not be found if the Germans ever discovered her.

She even decided to avoid the local shops, going out of her way to different areas of Paris on the Metro to buy her food. It meant she was never sure what she would find, but she could live with that if it gave her a greater sense of security.

She continued to go to Sacré-Coeur, however. The priest became quite friendly with her, stopping to talk if he saw her knelt at a prie-dieu in one of the alcoves.

He continued to call her 'Jeanne', as his private joke. He never once asked her why she was able to spend such a long time praying in church during the day, when she was supposed to be looking for work. Perhaps he thought she had her priorities in the right order.

Frager visited her daily, sometimes bringing food but always giving her new messages to send. Dericourt came less often, travelling as he did to Reims and Le Havre.

Before the last journey, she had given him a letter for her son and another for her Aunt Sonia in Leamington Spa.

She never expected any replies from these letters. They were her way of keeping in touch, keeping her memories alive for the day she returned. She had a morbid fear her son would forget her, forget she ever existed. With the letters, at least he would know she thought of him and missed him.

One day, she would hold him again, hugging him in her arms, never letting him go.

In the meantime, she concentrated on her work; collecting the messages, encoding them and sending them to London, receiving answers in return two hours later.

She was always meticulous in her coding and her Morse, finding solace and comfort in the task. By concentrating on the job in hand, it stopped her thinking of danger, or the possibility of detection and discovery.

It even stopped her thinking about John and their son, Martin.

She missed the boy terribly; his smile, the way he held his head, the seriousness with which his little body attended to even the most mundane tasks.

He was like a smaller version of her.

* * *

The end of her time as an agent came one Sunday morning.

She woke up early as she always did, walking to the window to pull back the curtains to let in the morning light.

It was the lack of noise that gave them away.

Outside her window, there was always something happening even this early in the morning. A car going down the street, a child playing a game, a cat prowling, a postman whistling the latest ditty from the radio.

That morning, there was nothing.

Silence.

She put on her slippers and raced downstairs to the living room, across to the window looking out over the street.

There was nobody there.

Her neighbours hadn't stirred yet. The postman had not been on his rounds. The child opposite had not left for church. Off to the left, a dog began to bark.

The loud squeal of brakes as a car slid to a halt. The slamming of doors. Hob-nailed boots on the cobblestones.

Then, a few seconds of silence, followed by a fist banging on the front door.

Monique grabbed a jacket from the hall and ran upstairs to the attic, still wearing her slippers. She paused for a moment on the landing.

A German officer was shouting through the door. She couldn't make out what he said. Two soldiers ran in from the left and swung a heavy sledgehammer against the lock. The sound of splintering wood echoed through the house.

She had planned for this day for so long.

She threw open the attic window, climbing out on to the roof. Below her, the door crashed inward and boots thudded up the stairs.

She climbed up to the apex of the roof and began to scramble up to the ridge line. Her slipper slipped on a tile, her knee crashing into the hard surface.

More shouting in German in the house below her.

She scrambled up to the ridge line and stood up, keeping one foot on either side of the tiles.

Walking along the ridge, she passed over the neighbour's roof and kept going. The street was one continuous terrace, ending in a L-shaped corner house. She shuffled as fast as she could towards the corner, keeping her arms stretched out to her sides for balance.

At one point, her slipper snagged on an upstanding nail, cutting open the ball of her toe and making her tumble forward.

Her knees scraped the sharp tiles, and she felt a tab of pain shoot up from her foot.

She glanced backwards.

A soldier had stuck his head outside the window and was pointing at her, shouting something gutteral in German.

Standing up again, ignoring the screaming pain in her foot, she raced along the L-shaped roof, sliding down to a lower level at the end.

She couldn't see the soldiers any more but she could hear their harsh voices.

She picked herself up quickly and hobbled across a flat roof overlooking an interior courtyard.

At the end in the middle of gable wall was a red, metal door.

She tugged at it.

Locked.

She could still hear the Germans shouting behind her but couldn't see them. Another door lay across a stone parapet.

She climbed onto the ledge.

Look up, don't look down.

She looked down.

Below her, a cobblestoned courtyard was strewn with rubbish and discarded metal. For a moment, she imagined falling, her body landing on the scrap, being sliced open by the sharp edges.

She shook her head.

Think, Monique, think.

She ran along the edge of the roof, her arms open wide. Behind her the soldiers' shouts were getting louder.

Jumping down from the parapet, she hobbled towards the door, trying not to put any pressure on her foot.

She tugged it open as far as she could, hearing the metal scrape against the concrete floor. Wheedling her body into the small gap, she squeezed through, pulling the door tightly closed behind her and bolting it.

Steps led down to another internal door.

She had never come this way before. What if it were locked?

She stopped for a second, catching her breath. Behind her, the soldiers began pounding on the metal door, the sound echoing off the white walls of the landing.

Saying a quick prayer and crossing herself, she placed her hand on the wooden knob and turned it.

The door opened easily, revealing more stone steps heading down.

She took them two at a time, holding on to the mahogany banister and trying not to put weight on her foot. At the bottom, the concierge was just putting out rubbish into a metal bin.

'Bonjour, madame,' said Monique.

The woman looked up but didn't try to stop her as she walked past.

A large wooden door gave on to the street. Rue Caulaincourt. If she could get to the Metro, she would be able to escape. Where she would eventually go, she didn't know, but anywhere would be better than here.

Monique pulled open the door and peered out.

The street was quiet. A baker putting his bread into the boulangerie window. A café with three customers enjoying a morning drink. A postman on his bike, a red-veined nose betraying his love of good wine. A few cars with well-dressed women sitting in the back, driving to church. A workman putting up a colourful Dubbonet poster on a wall using a long brush.

She stepped out, pulling the jacket across her chest to cover her nightgown. She was conscious she looked odd in a pair of slippers but hoped nobody would notice or, if they did, they might at least pretend not to notice.

She walked right down the street as casually as she could, trying to minimise her limp.

Past the boulangerie.

Past the café.

Past the lavanderie.

Past the leather shop and the greengrocers.

She was beginning to relax. She could hear the noise of lorries and shouting but it seemed to be far behind her.

Up ahead, the famous blue sign for the Lamarck-Caulaincourt Metro.

Not far to go.

She checked in her pocket. Her wallet was still sitting there with her *Carte d'Identité*.

Where would she hide?

She thought for a moment.

Gaston and the restaurant. He would know how to get a message to Frager and hide her until she could leave France.

As she crossed Caulaincourt Square, a man moved silently out from the shadows. 'What are you doing here so early in the morning?' he asked.

She stopped and turned slowly towards him. 'Oh, just looking for a present for a friend. It's her birthday and I forgot.'

He pointed down to her slippers.

'We're having lunch and I thought I'd look for it this morning. I live close by and—'

'Why don't you have lunch with me instead?'

She tried to move away but was grabbed from behind by a pair of powerful arms and lifted up in the air.

'You really shouldn't run, you know. It's most unbecoming for an Englishwoman.'

A hand clamped across her mouth and she was bundled into a waiting car.

Chapter Sixty-Seven

Friday, January 05, 2018
The National Archives, Kew, London

Only two documents remained in her grandmother's file. Jayne was reluctant to open them, knowing they could only contain bad news. Her hand hovered over the folder.

'Get on with it,' she said out loud, drawing a stare from the researcher opposite.

She stared back at him until he looked away, and then she turned over the document. It was an internal memo sent by David Strachan to Maurice Buckmaster, the head of the French section of SOE.

I 397/France(11)/B.1.a./DS
10th October 1943

Dear Maurice,

I enclose herewith a decoded signal from DERICOURT received last night from the radio operator of the SYMPHONY network.

NANNY WAS ARRESTED AT VILLA LEANDRE. STOP. DETAINED BY SD. STOP.

NETWORK ALERTED AND WILL GO UNDERGROUND. EXPECT FURTHER ARRESTS. STOP.

The message is necessarily terse and to the point.

We have requested further details from DERICOURT AND FRAGER but have received nothing to this point.

The arrest of Mrs Sinclair gives me cause for concern in the following areas;

1. The **PROSPER** network has been severely compromised and now has no radio operatives.
2. We are uncertain if the arrest was as a result of a leak, a spy or simply bad luck.
3. Mrs Sinclair was warned not to return to that particular safe house. She seems to have ignored those warnings.
4. The status of our agents and the local resistance on the network must now be in doubt.
5. Under interrogation, Mrs Sinclair may reveal the location of safe houses and other operatives.
6. **FRAGER** and **DERICOURT** are at risk.

I therefore recommend;

1. We shut down **PROSPER** immediately.
2. **FRAGER** is to go into hiding.
3. A new network is to be created with new operatives, radio operators, and couriers sent from London.

4. DERICOURT is to remain in place for the foreseeable future, organising the arrival of the new operatives.

yours sincerely,

D.Strachan

Copies to V Atkins.

DS/AEG

In the margin of the memorandum, somebody, presumably the addressee, had scribbled '**Agreed**' in pencil.

So that was it. The war must go on. Her grandmother was captured by the German's and there was no concern for her welfare or her fate. Simply, a desire to move on and protect the network.

Jayne understood this was a war and pragmatic decisions had to be taken, but she was shocked by the ruthlessness of the memo. This man had been the best man at her wedding, for god's sake.

There was only one document left in the folder. Jayne dreaded the information it might hold, but she turned it over anyway.

Chapter Sixty-Eight

Monday, August 30, 1943
84 Avenue Foch (HQ of the Sicherheitsdienst/SD), Paris, France

Monique was thrown into a cell on the fifth floor of the SD building on Avenue Foch.

On the journey in the car, she was forced to bury her head into the seat, a rough hand on the back on her neck.

The officer who arrested her talked continuously in accented, but perfect, English.

'We know who you are, Mrs Sinclair, we've known for quite a while. How is your son? What was his name? Ah yes, I remember now – it was Martin, wasn't it? Shame about your husband John, he was a brave man. But weren't they all, those flyers who were sent on a mission knowing they would die?'

There was a slight pause, followed by the striking of a match against sandpaper, the flash of a flame and then the unique aroma of Turkish tobacco filling the car.

'Such a waste of a life, don't you think? If fact, when you consider it further, a waste of three lives. Ah well, the fortunes of war. Or should I say, the misfortunes?'

More smoke filling the air. The hand pressing on the back of her neck increased its pressure.

'You will tell us everything you know. Everybody does in the end. Like canaries, some sing earlier than others, but every one sings for their supper eventually.'

The car jerked to a halt in a squealing of brakes.

'I do hope there won't have to be any unpleasantness between us. I'm here to help. Think of me in that way: somebody who is here to help.'

A black hood was placed over her head and two burly arms grabbed her, half-walking and half-dragging her out of the car and up the steps.

They threw her in a cell where she lay on the floor, listening to the sounds around her. The scraping of something against a plaster wall. Tapping on a pipe. A German guard talking to his comrade. A woman sobbing nearby.

Her breathing, shallow and uneven.

She sat up slowly, taking off the hood.

The cell was small, damp and cold, with a single small pane of glass placed high up on the far wall through which she could see the battleship-grey sky.

She pulled the thin jacket around herself. Underneath it, she had nothing on but the thin cotton nightgown she had worn in bed. Somehow, one of her slippers had come off. Her right foot was filthy, the toenails caked with dirt.

For some reason, the condition of her feet troubled her more than anything else. She wanted to wash them now, dry them with the fluffiest towel and cover them in warm talcum powder.

It wasn't going to happen, though.

Not today.

She looked up at the single square of grey sky and wondered if this was deliberate by the Germans. Letting a prisoner see just a small piece of the world outside, tempting them with the possibility of freedom.

A key in the lock. The door opening. Two burly guards dragging her out by the hair along a corridor and throwing her into a room.

'My men sometimes can be far too rough, Mrs Sinclair.'

She felt a soft hand under her arm, helping her up into a chair.

'My name is Kieffer, Major Kieffer. I chastise them continually, but do they listen? Never. What can one expect from East Frisians, though?' He scratched his nose. 'A joke for you. An East Frisian is walking home kicking old bottles, when a genie pops out of one. "I can grant you three wishes," says the genie, "so choose wisely." The East Frisian says, "Give me a beer that'll never run out." A bottle appears in the Eastie's hand and he downs it, but when he pulls it away from his mouth it's still full. The happy Eastie continues walking home. The genie shouts after him, "Hey, you still have two wishes left!" "Oh," says the Eastie, "gimme two more of these!"'

He then proceeded to laugh uproariously at his own joke. 'Gimme two more of these,' he repeated. 'You know, Mrs Sinclair, it reminds me of the British, they keep sending me agents. I wonder if the genie will ever stop giving me presents.'

'I don't know who you're talking about. My name is Suzanne Fevrier.'

He waved his finger at her. 'Very good. I saw what you did there. A little pretence for the dumb kraut, huh?' He nodded at the guard.

Monique suddenly found her head jerked back by the hair and a hairy forearm pressed against her Adam's apple.

'Hans here is not the most subtle man on this earth. With women he has an almost neanderthal approach. It seems to be effective, though, they love chatting to him.'

Monique felt the forearm press harder against her throat. She began to gag, but the forearm tightened and tightened and tightened. She found she couldn't breathe any more, grabbing the arm to try to pull it away. It simply became tighter. Her feet began to kick out as she struggled in vain to break the grip.

She was losing consciousness. The world was blurring round the edges of her vision, becoming less and less focused.

Kieffer was looking at his watch. 'Despite his lack of intelligence, Hans has done a scientific study on the length of time it takes a woman to suffocate. So far, our best time has been two minutes and thirty-eight seconds. She was Polish, though, and it's a well-known fact the Slavs have stronger neck muscles.'

Kieffer waved his hand and the pressure suddenly eased.

Monique leant forward, coughing, desperately trying to suck air into her chest.

Kieffer picked up a file from the table in the corner. 'Let us not waste any more time, Mrs Sinclair.' He began to read from the file. 'You arrived in France on July eleventh, parachuting in from an American Liberator. Your code name is Nanny and you are a wireless operator for the Prosper network.'

'My name is Suzanne Fevrier, check my *Carte d'Identité*. I've never heard of this Mrs Sinclair.'

Kieffer nodded at the man standing behind her.

This time the pressure across her throat was instant. A hand on the back of her head was forcing it forward against the forearm. She struggled to breathe as her throat constricted.

No air.
No air.

No air.

She felt herself begin to black out and lose consciousness… Falling into a dark abyss.

And then the pressure eased and cool air flooded into her lungs.

'This is incredibly boring, Mrs Sinclair. Eventually, I will lose patience and Hans here will have the pleasure of ending your life. Or I will misjudge when to tell him to stop. Or he may mistake the amount of pressure to use, crushing your hyoid bone by mistake. *Quel dommage*. Another life snuffed out in the blink of an eye. So it goes. Rather than let this happen, it would be much easier if you talked to us.' He picked out her codebook from the file. 'Could you tell me what this is?'

'I've never seen it before.'

'Yawn, yawn. It's a double-encryption codebook, Mrs Sinclair.' He held up a notepad. 'And I presume these are the notes from your last message. Shall we take a look?'

Monique's decodings from last night were still written on the page. She should have thrown them away.

'We have been sloppy. Here is the message you received from London last night. "Three agents dropped near Le Havre stop. Arrange meeting with Frager stop. Gilbert will bring to Paris on August 30 stop." You have been lax, Mrs Sinclair. We will pick these men up right away.' He smiled. 'Or we may simply follow them and let them show us their contacts. Now, when is your next *sked*? We should send your masters a message from you.'

'My name is Suzanne Fev—'

She didn't finish her sentence before the arm came round her neck and began to squeeze.

Her world went black.

Chapter Sixty-Nine

Thursday, September 02, 1943
84 Avenue Foch (HQ of the Sicherheitsdienst/SD), Paris, France

For the next three days, Monique wasn't allowed to sleep.

Every couple of hours she was wakened by a bucket of cold water being thrown over her. Four times she was taken to be interrogated, and asked the same questions over and over again.

What was your mission, Mrs Sinclair?
What have you been doing, Mrs Sinclair?
Who are your contacts?
Who is the leader of your network?

Finally she was carried back to the interrogation room. Kieffer was there, along with a tall man wearing round, metal-rimmed glasses.

'This is Captain Goetz, our radio expert. He runs our *Funkspiele* operation. "Radio Game" would be a good translation in English, I think. You will help him, yes?'

Monique stayed silent, barely able to keep her eyes open.

'Now, Mrs Sinclair, this is becoming tiresome.' He opened the file again, producing pictures of the SOE training centres in England. 'Here at Ringway, you did your parachute training. In this one, Beaulieu, you completed your wireless course.' He pronounced the name the English way: *Bewlay*.

Monique looked at them and said, 'I don't know what the hell you are talking about, my name is Suzanne Fev—'

She hadn't finished the sentence before the punch struck her on the side of the face. She saw Kieffer's face contorted in anger before it subsided into the smug smile he normally displayed.

'How much longer are you going to keep this up, Mrs Sinclair?' He turned to Goetz. 'We must show her everything, Ernest.'

Goetz produce a black file. 'Here are your recent signals to London, Mrs Sinclair, plus the letters you have written home since you arrived in France. By the way, your Aunt Sonia sends her love.'

He passed over a sheaf of papers to her. She glanced down at them. Copies of her signals and, even worse, the letters to her son.

How did they get them?

'David Strachan is now back in London. We hope he enjoyed his visit to our capital.'

'You knew David was here?'

'Of course, Mrs Sinclair. It was a lot of fun to follow him and see where he went. He led us to many of your agents.'

'But—'

'You are going to ask me why we didn't arrest him?'

It was almost as if he could read her mind. She was exhausted, not thinking straight.

'What would be the point of doing that? We know all about the SOE in England. You have a fine training operation. Shame you have such...' he stumbled over the words for a moment, '...such fools running it,' he finally said.

Monique couldn't help herself, her tiredness ruling her mind. She blurted out, 'You know everything, you must have an agent in London.'

'Perhaps, Mrs Sinclair, or perhaps we have one here in Paris. Goetz here also has your codes and your call signs. Next time, I would not leave so much paper in the house. My rats found plenty in your rubbish.'

She was exhausted and defeated. They knew everything, what was the point of fighting any more? All she wanted to do was sleep. Sleep for a year and a day.

Goetz stepped forward, adjusting his glasses. 'We have already been in contact with London, disguised as you, of course. Here is the message we sent.'

Through half-closed eyes, she stared at the printed message.

HAVE MOVED RAIN LOCATION STOP. VILLA LEANDRE NO LONGER SAFE STOP. PLEASE SEND NEW CRYSTALS FOR RADIO STOP. CONTACT AT 18.00 HOURS TODAY STOP. NOT AVAILABLE ANY OTHER TIME STOP.

'London was kind enough to reply almost immediately.'

She stared at another message as it swam in and out of focus.

YOU HAVE FORGOTTEN YOUR DOUBLE SECURITY CHECK STOP. BE MORE CAREFUL IN THE FUTURE STOP. WILL CONTACT AGAIN AT 18.00 HOURS TOMORROW STOP.

All the air went out of Monique's lungs. Her body felt as if her spine had collapsed and turned to mush. She felt herself falling forward off the chair on to the floor. How could they have been so stupid? She had sent over 120 messages and had never forgotten her security code before.

Kieffer ran forward and picked her up gently, sitting her back on the chair and smoothing down her sweat-stained clothes. She found a glass of water pressed to her mouth and she drank the cool liquid down.

'It must have been a shock for you, Mrs Sinclair. London are amateurs. It's not a game at public school any more — this is real life, where some agents work with us, and some agents die. Which are you going to be, Mrs Sinclair?' He produced a picture from the top pocket of his uniform. 'Is this your boy? He does look a strapping lad, the spitting image of his father. You would like to see him again, wouldn't you?'

Looking at her son, Monique began to weep, the salt in the tears stinging her red-rimmed eyes. The sobs wracked her body. It was as if nothing in the world mattered any more except the young boy in the picture.

'You will help us, Mrs Sinclair. It is the only thing you can do if you want to see your son again.'

She looked into Martin's eyes, seeing the joy and happiness and innocence inside. What sort of world would Martin grow up in? One inhabited by the Kieffers and the Goetzs of this world? Or something better, something full of love and happiness? The words of David Strachan at her wedding came back to her:

'Love is like flying. It's overcoming obstacles, facing challenges, holding on and never letting go. It is soaring high into a blue, blue sky and reaching for the stars... together.'

She thought of John and their love. How different their world could have been without the war.

She raised the picture of Martin to her chapped lips and kissed the image. She hoped he would understand her decision.

Letting the picture fall to the floor where it lay in her blood and sweat, she said, 'My name is Suzanne Fevrier. I was born in Chartres in 1918…'

Chapter Seventy

September, 1943 - August, 1944
Fresnes Prison, Val-de-Marne, south of Paris, France

Monique was tortured for five days after her refusal to speak.

Her legs were burnt with hot irons, and electrodes connected to a car battery attached to her breasts. She was severely beaten daily, and each time she was asked, 'What is your name? What have you been doing?'

She kept repeating the words that remained fixed and imprinted in her mind, refusing to think about anything else, ignoring the pain that seared through her body.

'My name is Suzanne Fevrier…'

On the sixth day, she was carried bodily down the stairs and thrown into the back of a van, where she lay unmoving at the feet of the guards.

Once or twice they kicked her in the head just to ensure that she was still alive.

She made no sound when they did. To cry out would only have encouraged them to kick her harder.

She was taken to the main prison in the south of Paris at a place called Fresnes. An old brick-built fortress, constructed to house the most dangerous criminals in France, it smelt as ugly as it looked.

There she was kept in isolation for the next three months, seeing only a guard twice a day when he brought her a bowl of gruel in the morning with some water and her main meal in the evening: a bowl of something resembling soup along with a hunk of gritty bread.

It was difficult to move off the thin mattress that covered the concrete bed. Her legs were useless now, all the muscles weakened by the red-hot irons placed on her skin and between her toes. But she shuffled over to retrieve her food, determined to eat and regain her strength. She tried to exercise too, forcing her legs to walk the three steps across her cell, backwards and forwards until she was exhausted. She had once watched an animal in London Zoo do exactly the same. A repeated movement over and over again, as if in some sort of trance.

She knew why now.

In the physicality of movement, she kept herself alive.

The rest of the time she spent inside her head, reliving days with John in all the detail she could remember. Or feeling the touch of Martin as he held her close when they slept together. Or that day in Regent's Park, when George brought herself and John together by nearly falling in the pond after being chased by the swans.

Her memories were her friends and her boon companions, holding her close and keeping her warm at night.

In the cold nights of December, she also thought about who had betrayed her and the other members of the Prosper network.

Henri Dericourt?
David Strachan?
Henry Frager?

Or somebody else?

She went over and over the details in her head, reliving what Kieffer had told her and putting together the pieces of the jigsaw puzzle until she was certain she knew who it was. One little mistake had given him away, she saw it now. Or rather, one thing Kieffer had said.

When she was released, she would bring him to justice, making sure he was tried for his crimes. Until then, she would wait and get strong, preparing for the day when she would be free again.

Of course, she tried to pray, creating a little prie-dieu in the corner with one of the soiled blankets and the wooden side table. But it was no use. God seemed to have deserted her when she was first arrested. She tried to talk to him, but a little voice in her head kept saying, 'What sort of God is it that would leave you here in prison at the mercy of the beasts of the SD?'

She never had an answer to the little voice, so she stopped praying.

She did sometimes manage to communicate with the inhabitants of the adjacent cells by simply tapping on the walls and shouting questions, hoping they would be carried along the pipes. One woman had been incarcerated since 1942 for the heinous crime of hoarding food.

Another time, the cell next to her had been occupied by a SOE agent, Peter Churchill. Together they tapped away in Morse as quickly as if they were talking to each other. For the first time in a long while, Monique felt human again. In talking, albeit through tapping, she regained her spirit and her joy. But the guards must have heard because he was taken away one evening, never to return.

Where had he gone? Had he been executed? She didn't know.

After three months, she was allowed out of her cell to exercise and meet other prisoners. She found it strange to be surrounded by people after such a long time alone.

Even more, her incarceration had made her distrustful. Would she be betrayed again? So she kept herself to herself, not even spending time with the other SOE agents who were kept in Fresnes.

She only allowed one woman to be her friend. A Dutchwoman, Florence Koolmans, detained in the jail for smuggling on the black market.

'It was only a few cigarettes,' she told Monique one day.

'How many?'

'Twenty thousand. I could smoke those myself.'

'Where did you get them?'

'A German officers' mess. It didn't help they still had the stickers of the Waffen SS on them.'

Monique laughed, the first time she had found something to smile about in months.

'And I suppose the boxes of chocolate, coffee and wine didn't help either.' Florence stopped for a moment. 'You know we could have a hell of a party with that stuff. Even in here.'

Monique was still dressed in the jacket and nightdress she had worn in Montmartre what seemed like a lifetime ago. Her body was painfully thin, and she found it difficult to walk for long periods. The exercise in the cell had helped a little, but without proper nutrition she was never going to rebuild her strength.

Florence helped her find some new clothes, discarded when a prisoner had died. 'They're not much, but at least they are better than what you have,' she said as Monique dressed painfully and slowly. 'You know the one thing I miss most?'

Monique shook her head.

'Lipstick. I miss looking in the mirror and applying my lipstick. It made me feel like a woman, you know, that last touch-up before you go out, staring in the mirror, knowing you are able to face the world.'

'There are no mirrors in prison.'

'I know, but I'd still like the lipstick, just for the taste of it on my mouth. And you, what would you like?'

Monique thought for a moment. 'Paper and a pen,' she finally answered.

'Why? Not much use in here.'

'I'd like to write a note to my son, to ask him how he was and tell him what has happened.'

A week later, Florence sidled up to her and whispered in her ear, 'I have something for you.' She opened her coat to reveal a half sheet of pristine white paper and a pencil.

'Where did you get that?'

'A guard. He wanted a quick feel and who was I to say no? But I made him pay for it. I remembered you wanted paper so this is what I asked for. Couldn't get a pen, though, so he gave me a pencil.'

'But... you shouldn't. You can't—'

'I can do what I want. So here, take it. Quick, a guard is coming.'

Monique found the paper and pencil in her hand. She looked all around before folding it up and hiding it in a hole in the lining of the jacket from the dead woman.

That night, when everyone was asleep and there was a full moon, she composed a message for London and for her son. Perhaps it would never get back there, but she had to try. They were the ones who had to know the truth.

Two days later, she pulled Florence aside and pressed the folded square of paper into her hand.

'Keep it safe. If you ever get out of here, give it to SOE in London. They will know what to do with it.'

Florence passed it back to her. 'You give it to them. You heard the news, the Allies are not far from here. We will soon be liberated.'

'Then keep it for me, just in case. But promise to give it to London.'

Florence shrugged her bony shoulders. 'If you say so, but—'

'Thank you.'

* * *

One evening in early August, when the heat in the prison was stifling and the place stank of all the rancid decay of thousands of unwashed humans, a guard came to her cell. She recoiled immediately, expecting a beating or worse. Instead, he stood there with a stupid smile on his face.

'You are leaving us.'

'Am I?' she croaked, the sound of her voice different to her now, like that of a stranger. Had her vocal cords been damaged by her torture?

'Tomorrow,' he told her bluntly, 'but don't look forward to it. You're going to Germany. A place called Dachau.'

Then he locked the door and was gone.

Chapter Seventy-One

Thursday, September 14, 1944
Dachau Concentration Camp, Bavaria, Germany

The following day, Monique was moved to Dachau, escorted by two guards. She was accompanied by four other SOE agents; Madeleine Damerment, Elaine Plewman, Yolande Beekman and Noor Inayat Khan.

They were driven in a van with no windows to Strasbourg, stopping only occasionally when the guards needed a break.

The women hardly spoke to each other on the journey, each in their own little prison, unwilling to speak lest the guards heard and uncertain if any of the others were spies.

Finally, when the van had stopped and the nearest guard was far away, Yolande spoke first: 'I don't know about you, but I could murder a steak.'

'For me it would be a roast potato. I have dreamt of a roast potato for the last year; crisp on the outside, soft inside.'

'A scone, dripping with Devonshire cream and strawberry jam, washed down with a good, strong cup of tea. Heaven.'

'A glass of fine wine. A good claret or a rare Burgundy. Just the one glass, no more, it would be enough,' said Noor. 'And what would you have?'

'One last kiss from the lips of my son. No food, just the taste of his lips on mine,' said Monique.

They talked more after that, sharing their experiences of the SOE when the guards weren't listening.

After four weeks in Strasbourg jail, they were put on a train to Munich, escorted by two SS guards.

As they sat in their seats, the other passengers studiously avoided looking at them, as if by not acknowledging the existence of the bedraggled women, they could pretend such things never existed.

A whole nation gone blind.

On arrival in Dachau, they were separated and handcuffed to iron chains in individual cells.

That night, a guard went into each one of the cells and beat the women until they were black and blue.

The following morning, each of them was taken out of their cell and led to an outhouse.

Yolande Beekman spoke German to the officer in charge. 'What are you going to do with us?'

'You are to be executed for spying.'

'Can we see a priest and make our peace with God?'

'Nobody is available.'

They were forced to kneel on the ground in front of a guard.

Monique found her hand being taken by Elaine Plewman. She lifted her head and stared at the blood-splattered wall in front of her.

The image of John, his RAF peaked cap set at a rakish angle and a smile playing on his face, appeared on the wall.

'Hello, John,' she whispered.

Her husband was joined by a laughing George and Martin. They all held hands and together they reached towards her.

She stood up and took the hands of her husband and George, walking down a long country road towards a setting sun.

'We've forgotten, Martin,' she said.

'He'll come afterwards,' her husband replied.

Behind her head, the metallic click of a pistol being cocked.

It was the last sound she ever heard.

Chapter Seventy-Two

Monday, January 05, 2018
The National Archives, Kew, London

The last document in the folder was another memo, this time from a J H Martell to another civil servant or member of the security services.

Jayne tried to work out who these people were from their titles but was unsuccessful. Just two bureaucrats following up a request from one of their seniors.

**K 176/France(13)/F.6./JHM
11th November 1945**

Dear John,

Following the request from Sutcliffe, I have received information from the US Forces in Stuttgart. As you know they have been interrogating former Gestapo and Sicherheistdienst operatives as and when they turn themselves in or are captured.

One such operative, Christian Ott, has reported on the deaths of five SOE agents at Dachau Concentration Camp on 14th September, 1944. I enclose herewith an extract from the report de-

tailing the events leading up to their execution, compiled by our American friends.

Jayne caught her breath. Her hand came up to her mouth and she stopped herself from crying out. The use of the word 'execution' after the bland functionality of the rest of the memo, hit her like a punch to the stomach,
She forced herself to continue reading.

'This statement was given on October 29th at the Stuttgart Detention Centre to Captain Michael Ridge, Judge Advocate General's Office.
"A Gestapo man named Max Wassmer was in charge of prisoner transports at Karlsruhe and accompanied the women to Dachau. I spent some time working with him later in the Karlruhe office of the Geheime Staatspolizei. One afternoon, he told me he volunteered to accompany five women to Dachau as he wanted to visit his family in Stuttgart on the return journey.
The five prisoners had come from the barracks in the camp, where they had spent the night, into the yard where the shooting was to be done. Here he [Wassmer] had announced the death sentence to them. Only the Lagerkommandant and the two SS men were also present. The German-speaking Englishwoman (the major) had told her companion of this death sentence. All five had grown very pale and wept; the major asked whether they could protest against the sentence. The Kommandant declared that no protest could be made. The major had then asked to see a priest. The camp Kommandant refused this on the grounds that there was no priest in the camp. The five prisoners now had to kneel with

their heads towards a white wall and were killed by the two SS, one after another by a shot through the back of the neck. During the shooting the women held hands. For four of the prisoners the first shot caused death, but for the German-speaking Englishwoman a second shot had to be fired as she still showed signs of life. After the shooting of these prisoners the Lagerkommandant said to the two SS men that he took a personal interest in the jewellery of the women and that this should be taken into his office."

It all seems pretty clear even it though it is a secondhand report. I think we can conclude the agents died in Dachau on the date stated.

Yours etc

John

Jayne found her eyes filling with tears. She stood up from her desk and ran past a startled archive clerk.

She discovered the ladies on the left and ran towards it, bursting through the door and finding an empty cubicle. She sat down on the toilet and began to sob, her shoulders heaving.

She was crying for herself, for her grandmother and for a world that could be so cruel.

Chapter Seventy-Three

Monday, January 05, 2018
The National Archives, Kew, London

After twenty minutes of sobbing for her grandmother and for herself, Jayne sat up straight. 'Pull yourself together, Sinclair,' she told herself, 'you're the strong one and you still haven't found out who betrayed her to the German's. Finish this, finish this now.'

She fixed her hair and make-up in the bathroom mirror and marched back to the Archive computer.

She was going to discover who betrayed her grandmother and nothing was going to stop her.

She went through every single item in the SOE archive, ordering every one that could be of possible use in her search. It was a long shot but she was determined to find out the truth.

Back in the reading room, she went through all the files: The SOE activity reports for Northern France. Buckmaster's notes. The 'Prosper' files. Postwar analyses of SOE's performance.

Even a whole raft of memos, reports, analyses and commentaries on the possibility of a German mole. They had investigated three possible suspects; Frager, the deputy head of the network, Dericourt, the person in charge of organising all agent arrivals into France, and Strachan, the second-in-command of F section. All were cleared of wrongdoing. Or rather, no case was proven against them.

If they couldn't discover who the traitor was back during the war what chance did she have now?

Jayne glanced at the clock. 4.50. The archive would soon close for the day. Opposite her, the other researcher was packing up his stuff noisily. She stared at him and he looked away but became much quieter.

She pulled the last file towards her. On the cover was a bland title. 'Dutch woman's message re female agent.' It was the same as the description in the catalogue.

She couldn't remember why she had ordered this particular file. Had it been delivered by mistake?

She opened it and found another memo.

G/SOE/H.1./SS
13th April 1948

Dear Arthur,

Attached please find a message from a Dutch woman, Florence Koolmans, passed to our embassy in the Hague. Apparently, this woman spent some time with one of agents, Monique Sinclair, in a prison in France. Mrs Sinclair asked the woman to pass the handwritten message to her family in England should she ever be released from prison. It's been a few years but the message was finally given to us. to I don't know if it will be of any use but I thought we should pass it on.

Are we still on for golf on Sunday?

Yours, Sydney

Handwritten along the bottom was another message.

'**Passed to family and archived for records. Personal message from Monique Sinclair, code name Nanny, to her family. No use to the department. S.**'

Jayne's eyes widened, this was a message from her grandmother.
She pulled the file toward her and looked inside. A single sheet of crumpled paper lay at the bottom of the folder.
She took it out and unfolded it. At the top was a single line.

The following is a typewritten copy of a message from Monique Sinclair, NANNY. Original sent to family. Copy produced 20 April 1948 by Helen Mathers, secretary.

Dearest Martin.

The last rain day I saw your face, you were were sleeping. How time passes. Every time mummy thinks of you she remembers your smile. That is what kept me going. Ready to continue on even on the darkest days. And it's what keeps me going now in this prison. In the long minutes of the day and the longer hours of the night. The smiles you gave me as a baby. Or the way your cheeks puffed out like two melons. Remembering you is all I have. I know it's not much

consolation for you. So one day, when you read this. Do remember me, won't you? Even when you are old and grey, remember me. Remember my face and my eyes. In my heart, I miss you so much but I had to leave you. Crying my eyes out I left you. One day, we will be together I promise you. Until then, be a good boy and treat your aunt and uncle well. Remember me. That is all I ask you.

your Mummy.

ps Remember the first words of the bible, won't you?

Again, Jayne's eyes filled with tears. These were the last words of her grandmother to her son, Martin.

She read the message again, trying to understand how Monique felt when she was writing them in some cell after having been taken by the Germans.

Did she know she would never see him again?

For a moment, Jayne thought what her last words would be to her family. What would she say?

Her thoughts were disturbed by a light tap on her shoulder.

'I'm sorry we're closing the archive now.'

'But I haven't finished with this document…' Jayne tried to gain more time.

'I'm sorry, you'll have to come back tomorrow.'

The clerk smiled, turned her back and began to collect some of the documents from a nearby table.

Quickly, Jayne took out her phone and shot the last message of her grandmother to Martin. At least she could show her father this message, perhaps he had never seen it before.

It was some small consolation. Tomorrow she would have to tell him she had been through all the files in the National Archives and she couldn't discover the identity of the man who had betrayed his mother. The information may be here somewhere but it was like looking for a number in a telephone book when you only had the christian name.

A sense of failure accompanied her all the way back to her hotel in the tube. It was not a feeling she enjoyed.

Chapter Seventy-Four

Monday, January 05, 2018
Somewhere in the middle of Whitehall. London.

A slight tap on the door interrupted Penrose's thoughts. 'Enter,' he whispered.

Proctor slid into the room. 'Sir, our operative reports Mrs Sinclair has now left the National Archives.'

'Where's she going?'

Proctor appeared flustered. 'I don't know, sir, he never told me.'

'Well find out man. But before you do leave those on my table.'

Proctor placed copies of all the files Jayne had requested on the desk and fled the room.

Penrose sat there in silence, staring at the closed door. Had she worked it out? Had she discovered the secret that had lain hidden in the files for all these years?

Penrose had argued against the release of the SOE files in 2003, but the under-secretary, ever one for scenting the way the political wind was blowing, had countermanded him, pontificating, 'There is a new spirit of openness in the department, Penrose, you should flow with the times.'

'Balderdash,' he said out loud. They were the Secret Intelligence Service, their secrets should stay hidden not flaunted for every two-penny researcher to discover. He picked up the files and leafed through them. Mrs Sinclair had been thorough. She had requested virtually every relevant file on the SOE in the Archives.

The last file was particularly interesting. He hadn't looked at this since the death of David Strachan all those years ago. 'We made a mistake when we let this become public,' he said out loud to himself. Well if she had worked it out, he would have to clear up the mess again.

'Proctor,' he shouted.

The young man entered immediately, he had obviously been listening at the door. 'Yes, sir?'

'Have you found out yet?'

'She's on the tube, sir, seems to be heading back to her hotel.'

'Good. Arrange for two operatives to pay her a visit tomorrow morning.'

'Not now, sir?'

'Not now, I have a bridge game this evening. Mrs Sinclair will do nothing until tomorrow at the earliest.'

He handed Penrose a note. 'There is also this report from the prison, sir.'

Penrose glanced at the message and frowned 'This does put a whole new light on the matter, but it shouldn't change our decision.'

'We are not to inform Mrs Sinclair, sir?

'Not yet, Proctor. You have your orders, make sure they are carried out.',

Chapter Seventy-Five

Monday, January 05, 2018
The Premier Inn, Blackfriars, London.

That evening, Jayne stayed in her hotel room. She didn't bother eating, for some reason food didn't interest her at that moment.

On her way back to the hotel, she passed an off-licence, and thought about buying a bottle of Rioja to take back to the room, but decided against it. Drowning her sorrows in wine when she was feeling like this was not a good idea. Jayne has a simple mantra for alcohol; it was there to give pleasure not to deaden emotions.

She tried to book a visit to see her father, but the system seemed to be down. Never mind, tomorrow morning she would try again.

She wasn't looking forward to the visit. Having to explain to him she had not, could not, discover who betrayed his mother was going to be difficult. She had a feeling the only thing that had kept him alive all these years was the hope that, one day, somebody would discover the truth.

Tomorrow, she was going to destroy that hope.

She took off her bra and washed the make-up from her face. Looking at herself in the mirror, she could see the likeness to her father in the strength of her jaw and the colour of her eyes. How would he react to the news?

Not well, she thought.

She sat down at the her desk in the room. Should she go through her notes one last time?

Had she missed something?

She opened them, reading her precise handwriting. She had been though all the relevant SOE files catalogued in the National Archives. None of them gave a clue to any possible traitor.

There was always the possibility the files were still closed and not available to researchers but even then, a note would have been placed in the catalogue explaining such an absence.

She checked all her notes on Monique Sinclair. Leaving her son behind while she went off to war must have been difficult and there was no real explanation of why she had taken that course of action in any of the reports.

Jayne supposed many women would have been faced with the same dilemma during wartime. Family or Country? There must have been so much pressure, both external and internal, to take part in the war effort. 'Do your bit' as the posters of the day put it. The guilt at leaving a loved one behind with relatives must have been stifling.

What would she do in similar circumstances?

The truth was she didn't know, never having had any children, but it would have been a difficult choice, an impossible choice.

She read through all her notes one more time and nothing popped out. No clue to who had betrayed Monique.

She rubbed her eyes. An immense wave of tiredness swept through her body, the emotional discoveries of the day finally catching up on her.

One final job though before she went to sleep: Transcribe the last file she had discovered into her notes.

She opened her phone and found the picture of Monique's farewell message to her son, written when she was in prison in France, just three weeks before her death.

It was a sad note, full of strange syntax and sentence construction. One time, she even repeated a word as if her mind were wandering. Monique must have been in a terrible state when she wrote it; exhausted, fearful, missing her son and desperate that he should remember her.

Jayne stopped her transcription for a moment and put herself in Monique's place at the time she wrote the note. A sense of loneliness and despair overwhelmed her. She shivered as a wave of cold air drifted across her body. She felt totally alone as if she were the only person left alive in the world.

She looked up. Just a single dirty window gave light into the cell. A window that suggested there was a world out there, holding out the possibility of human warmth and succour but keeping it distant. Far away. Cold.

Jayne shook herself out of the feeling. She was back in her hotel room in London, the rain beating gently against her window and the sounds of water rushing through the pipes. Where she had just been was a dark place, not a feeling she would ever welcome again.

Poor Monique.

She returned to the note and finished transcribing the words written in it for her father. What a strange way to end a message to your son, she thought. '**Remember the first words of the bible, won't you**,' written as a PS.

Perhaps, Monique had become more devout after her arrest. Jayne remembered allusions to her Catholicism in the reports from the training schools. Had she rediscovered her belief in God during her incarceration?

Possibly.

What were the first words in the bible? Jayne went online to check. In the Old Testament, the first passage was from Genesis and it read, 'In the beginning God created the heaven and the earth.'

What a strange message to put on the end of final note to your five-year-old son. But perhaps indicative of Monique's state of mind.

Jayne rubbed her eyes again and yawned. There was nothing more to do except go to sleep.

Tomorrow, she would face her father and tell him she had failed. She didn't know who had betrayed his mother.

Nobody would ever know.

Chapter Seventy-Six

Monday, January 05, 2018
The Premier Inn, Blackfriars, London.

The answer came to her in the middle of the night in that strange way the brain has of working on a problem even when one is sleeping.

The doubled word. Wasn't that the security code for her radio messages?

She jumped out of bed and ran across to her desk. Her handwritten note of Monique's message to her son was still there.

She read through it once more.

Perhaps that is it. The answer was staring her in the face. How clever you were Monique. Even when you were in prison you were still thinking like an agent, leaving clues in your message and the last line.

Quickly, Jayne went through the message and marked it up.

"<u>T</u>he last rain day I saw your face, you were were sleeping. <u>H</u>ow time passes. <u>E</u>very time mummy thinks of you she remembers your smile. <u>T</u>hat is what kept me going. <u>R</u>eady to continue on even on the darkest days. <u>A</u>nd it's what keeps me going now in this prison. <u>I</u>n the long minutes of the day and the longer hours of the night. <u>T</u>he smiles you gave me as a baby. <u>O</u>r the way your cheeks puffed out like two melons. Remembering you is all I have. I know it's not much consolation for you. So one day, when you read this. Do remember me, won't you? Even when you are old and grey, remember me. Remember my face and my eyes. In my heart, I miss you so much but I had to leave you. Crying my eyes out I left you. One day, we will be together I promise you. Until then, be a good boy and treat your aunt and uncle well. Remember me. That is all I ask you.

She then wrote out the message spelt from the first letters:

The Traitor is Dericourt.

She sat back, admiring her grandmother's ingenuity. The problem was nobody was as clever as you. Nobody knew what you had hidden in a seemingly innocuous message to your son.

Well, Jayne now knew and soon her father would too.

Who was Dericourt? She remembered seeing the name in the files as one of the members of the Prosper network. She went back to her notes, going through all the references to a Henri Dericourt. Then she went online and discovered a biography and history of the man.

He worked for SOE as the co-ordinator of all agent arrivals and air drops from 1942 to 1944. Mysteriously, he was sent back to London before the D Day landings. He survived the war only to be arrested for smuggling precious metals at Croydon Airport in 1946. In 1948, he was put on trial by the French authorities as a wartime collaborator. But at the trial, he was supported by a former deputy head of the SOE and found not guilty. He then vanished from the records only to turn up in 1961 in Laos when he was reported as dying in an air crash. Was he working for the CIA, the French Security Services or the Corsican mafia then?

It didn't matter. From his history and character, this man was the one who had betrayed her grandmother, as he had betrayed many other agents, sending them callously to their deaths.

As the sun rose over a grey, bleak and wet London morning, Jayne knew she had the answer. This afternoon, she could tell her father and finally let him know the truth.

Did he still have the original message from his mother? Was this the final piece of the jigsaw he had hidden from her?

She would know this afternoon.

Jayne thought about going back to the National Archives and finding out even more about Dericourt from the records but decided against it, there wasn't time. And anyway, she had enough to tell her father now, she could find out more about Henri Dericourt later.

She stood up from her desk. Time for a shower and to put her notes in proper order, then she would have a good breakfast before booking a meeting with her father in HMP Belmarsh.

For the first time since she had started this investigation, Jayne felt content. She had solved the mystery. She knew who had betrayed her grandmother.

As she went into the bathroom, a loud knock came on her hotel room door.

She checked her watch. 8.30 a.m. Who could it be this early in the morning? She hadn't ordered room service or anything from the front desk.

Another knock, louder this time, followed by a male voice, 'Open the door please, Mrs Sinclair.'

Jayne slowly opened the door making sure the chain lock was still in place.

Two burly men stood in the corridor. The taller one spoke politely but firmly. 'We need you to come with us please, Mrs Sinclair.'

Chapter Seventy-Seven

Monday, January 05, 2018
The Premier Inn, Blackfriars, London.

The hackles rose on the back of Jayne's neck. 'Why? Who are you? What do you want?'

The taller of the two did all the speaking. 'If you will just come with us, ma'am, I'm sure we can sort they out quickly.'

'ID, now.'

They both looked at each other unused to being in a situation where they were receiving the orders. The taller one reached into his jacket pocket and pulled out a warrant card, handing it to Jayne through the gap in the door.

She checked it over. James Turner, a Secret Intelligence Service agent. But why were the spooks interested in her? 'I'll ask you again. What do you want?'

'I'm asking you to come with us. As a former serving police officer, I don't have to remind you that you are still bound by the provisions of the Official Secrets Act.'

How did they know she was an ex-copper? 'I don't have to go anywhere with you.'

The short one spoke for the first time. 'You're an ex-copper Mrs Sinclair, you know the drill. We've just been sent to ask you to accompany us.'

'You're not arresting me?'

The short one shook his head.

'So, I have no need to go anywhere with you.' Jayne moved to close the door.

'Please, Mrs Sinclair. We are taking you to see our boss, he would like a chat with you. We will be happy to wait while you change.' The man's voice had become polite, almost respectful.

Jayne nodded. Was this to do with her father and her visit to the National Archives yesterday? Had they been watching her? She had to find out what they wanted.

'It's just a chat, Mrs Sinclair. However, if you would like it to be made more formal, I'm sure we could arrest you for something. Disturbing the peace, perhaps? Or maybe something under the Prevention of Terrorism Act?'

Jayne knew from experience there was any number of charges that could be laid against her. None of them would stick of course, but they would allow them to arrest her. She loved the good cop, bad cop routine, having used it so many times herself in the past.

She thought for a moment. If she wanted to find out what they wanted, she would have to go with them. And much easier to go quietly than make a scene in the hotel.

'I won't be a minute.' She closed the door and quickly packed her computer and the notes from her research into a bag. She was going to take these with her just in case the friendly spooks decided to search her room in her absence.

She threw on a jumper and jeans, tying her hair back into a pony tail. She checked the bathroom mirror. No make-up, she almost felt naked with out it, but why bother? She was sure these men had seen far worse in their time.

She picked up her coat and glanced back at the room, opening the door as she did. 'Right, gentlemen, I'm ready.'

They were both still standing there, as if they hadn't moved. The taller one gestured politely. 'This way, ma'am.'

Chapter Seventy-Eight

Monday, January 05, 2018
SIS Headquarters, London

The man sitting opposite Jayne was old and monied. From his oiled grey hair through his cultured vowels, down to his Oxford brogues, he reeked wealth and privilege

His officers had taken her to a nondescript office near Vauxhall without saying a word. The taller one drove whilst the shorter sat in the back with her.

Jayne had tried to find out why they had asked her to go with them. 'Can you tell me what you want?'

Silence.

'Where are we going?'

A scratch of the nose and more silence.

'Who am I meeting?'

A slight shift in position but more silence.

After a while she had given up and just sat there, staring out of the rain-streaked windows of the car at a particularly depressing view of rush hour London.

They entered the building through the underground carpark. She was ushered up to the seventh floor in a designated lift and led to an elegantly appointed meeting room. A man was waiting for her inside.

'Good morning, Mrs Sinclair, I finally have the opportunity of meeting you.'

He rose from his chair and gestured for her to sit opposite him. The men who brought her exited the room, closing the door behind them.

Jayne sat down, followed by the man. He steepled his fingers in front of his face and said nothing.

Two can play at this bloody game, she thought. She just sat there looking at him.

Finally, he spoke. 'I'm afraid I have some bad news, Mrs Sinclair. Your father passed away last night.'

Jayne's mouth opened. 'What?'

'Your father died yesterday evening around 6.35.'

'But I...I was going to meet him today.'

'We don't know how he died, we presume it was a heart attack. But rest assured, as he died while in the custody of the crown, there will be a post mortem and a coroner's inquiry.'

Jayne closed her eyes. Her father was dead? But she had only just met him again. And then it struck her, she hadn't told him about her discovery. He never found out the identity of the man who betrayed his mother.

'Would you like some water or something stronger? A brandy?'

She shook her head. She must hold it all together. What did this man want? 'You could have told me this news at the hotel, why did you bring me here?' And what is your name?'

He smiled, briefly. 'Yes, I am sorry about that, my men can be a little abrupt. They are used to much more...physical methods of solving problems.'

'I am a problem?'

His mouth made a small moue of distaste. 'Not really. A potential hiccup, but not really a problem.

'You still haven't answered my question.'

The beautifully manicured hands steepled in front of his face again. Jayne could see the liver spots on the skin, the perfect crescent moons at the bottom of the nails, a gold band on the right hand and another ring next to it with a large crest in the centre.

'My name is Penrose and I...'

There was a slight tap on the door and a young man entered, passing a beige folder to Penrose. The older man opened it, scanned the contents and nodded. 'Thank you, Proctor.' He switched back to Mrs Sinclair. 'Are you sure you wouldn't like something, the news of your father's death must have been upsetting.'

Jayne shook her head.

'As I was saying, my name is Penrose and I am in charge of Department Eight of the Intelligence Service. My remit, if you would call it that, is the reputation of the service and its operations.'

The penny was beginning to click for Jayne. This was about her research.

'You have been busy lately. I presume you cracked the code.'

Jayne nodded. 'It was the first letters of each sentence. It set out the letters of the name of the traitor. Henri Dericourt.'

'If I be so bold as to ask, what led to that conclusion?'

Jayne shrugged her shoulders. Why shouldn't he know? 'It was the use of 'rain' and the repetition of the tenth word in the message. I remembered reading this was part of security code for her messages. And of course, the biblical reference in the last line led to the answer.'

'Well done, Mrs Sinclair. It took us until 1972 to crack it and by then it didn't matter very much anyway, Dericourt was already dead.'

'But that was before my father killed David Strachan...'

'Exactly. David was one of our better officers in SOE during the war. Of course, there were investigations into the identity of the traitor but nothing could be proven conclusively even when Dericourt's name came up in German SD files. You see, the leaders of SOE at that time could not bring themselves to accept the man they had trusted so much could be a traitor. A wilful blindness, I believe, but it is always difficult to understand the pressures the men were going through at that time, is it not?'

'I was going to tell my father this afternoon. He spent his life trying to find the traitor and now he will never know.'

'Neither must the rest of the world, Mrs Sinclair.'

Jayne frowned, 'I don't understand.'

'We would like you to keep the results of your investigations a secret.'

'Why?'

The man sat upright. Jayne could see a keen intelligence behind the green eyes. 'For two reasons. The first is re-opening the old wounds of a war long forgotten would save no purpose. The brave men and women who died would not thank you for besmirching the name and reputation of the organisation they served. Yes, they should have found the traitor during the war. But given the uncertainties of the time, it is no surprise he evaded discovery.

'As did others…'

'You are so right. The Cambridge Five worked for over twenty years before their treachery was brought into the light of day. The Intelligence Services and the world have changed immensely since those dark days.'

'You said there was two reasons…'

'The second is far more personal, Mrs Sinclair. Why would you resurrect publicity for your father's crime once again? In order to publicise Dericourt's treachery, it would also be necessary to revisit your father's murder of David Strachan. He shot an innocent man, a good man, dead.'

'My father became obsessed with the death of his mother, Mr Penrose.'

'An obsession that led to murder and one that does not seem to have been lessened by the passage of time. I would ask you to consider your next course of action, Mrs Sinclair. Nothing would be achieved from resurrecting the mistakes and crimes of the past.'

Penrose stood up. 'And now, I will ask my men to return you to your hotel. I have arranged with the prison authorities for you to see your father's body if you so desire.'

'Is that it? I am free to go?'

'Of course, what did you think, Mrs Sinclair, we would drug and torture you?'

Jayne remained silent.

'I'm afraid you have been reading far too many James Bond novels, Mrs Sinclair. My job today was to point out to you the viewpoint of the department and to request you leave the secrets of the past alone and undisturbed.'

'So I can still publish my research if I want?'

'It is a free country, Mrs Sinclair, you can do what you want. However, the department, my department would prefer you didn't. We simply don't think any good can come from it. For either your father, yourself or the Security Services.'

He reached out his hand. Jayne shook it. 'I will think about what you said. Mr Penrose.'

He smiled. 'Actually, it's just Penrose.'

'How can I get in touch with you again?'

'You don't, Mrs Sinclair. I'm afraid my department flies beneath the radar, to use a horribly modern phrase. Proctor will escort you to your car and take you back to the hotel.'

The young man was waiting at the door. He had entered without knocking.

'Goodbye, Mrs Sinclair. I do hope we don't meet again.'

'So do I, Penrose, so do I.'

Chapter Seventy-Nine

Wednesday, January 28, 2018
Buxton Residential Home, England

There were only three mourners at her father's cremation. Jayne, Robert and Vera. A local vicar said a few words about a man he didn't know and a button was pressed, curtains opened and her father's coffin was swallowed up into the interior of the crematorium.

The coroner had released the body after the pathologist had certified the cause of death was a massive coronary thrombosis.

Her father had died quickly, collapsing in his cell and being discovered not long after by a prison officer on a routine patrol. The pathologist had stated in his report that her father didn't have long to live anyway. The cancer had already spread to the lymph nodes and the liver.

After the cremation, they went back to the Home.

'What are you going to do now?' Robert asked.

Jayne ran her fingers through her hair. 'I've thought long and hard about it, and Penrose is right. Nothing would be served by publicising the information I discovered.'

'But wouldn't people like to know the truth?' asked Vera, 'don't they deserve to know?'

'Perhaps. But it would bring to the surface my father's crime once more. I think it's time to forget about it all and move on with our lives.' She was silent for a moment as she stared into mid-air, finally reaching for Robert's wrinkled hand. 'I met him and I'm glad I did. But this man has always been my father and always will be.'

'Thank you, lass. I tried to be a good father to you.'

'And you were the best. Nobody could have asked for a better dad.'

'He's a good man, isn't he?' Vera took her dad's other hand.

'I don't think I can survive this from you both, smothering me with kindness. I should go back to the bloody hospital,' he said blushing.

Vera kissed him on the cheek. 'Ever the northern man, uncomfortable with a bit of tenderness.'

They both laughed and Robert reddened even more.

Jayne stopped smiling. 'There's one thing that came out of this which I will never forget.'

'What's that?'

'I learnt that my grandmother was an incredibly brave and devoted woman. Somebody I will remember for the rest of my life.'

'And you still have her side of the family to research. Who were your French relations? What's their history?'

Jayne held up her bag. 'And there's still the history of the Sinclair's from Alnwick and the Harrisons from Ireland. But I think I'll have a break from family history for a while. Go for a holiday, somewhere warm where I can read and relax and just concentrate on perfecting my tan.'

'Sounds perfect,' said Vera.

'Why don't you both come with me? It would be great for Robert to go somewhere warm to help clear up his chest and I'm sure you could do with a break, Vera.'

'What about a cruise to the Caribbean? I've got some brochures in the room.'

As Vera rushed off to get the brochures, Robert looked across at his step-daughter. 'You sure you're ok, lass?'

'Honestly?'

He nodded.

'I didn't know it would be such an emotional journey for me, Robert. I discovered so much about my family and about myself, I just need time to absorb it, to work it all out.'

'Family history is like that. It's often an emotional journey, not merely dredging through some old documents. We discover things about our ancestors and about ourselves that, sometimes, we would prefer to avoid. He reached over and touched her face. 'I'm here if you need me, lass.'

She smiled at him. 'You've always been there for me. The strange thing is I now have another friend in case I ever need help.'

'Who's that?'

'My grandmother, Monique. I know the memory of her strength will be there if I need it.'

'That's the point, isn't it? Those family members are always with us when we need them. Their strength, their resolve, the things they endured.'

'My grandmother was an amazing woman, I'm so proud of her.'

'Don't forget your father, lass.'

Jayne stared into mid-air. 'Brought up with such a weight on his shoulders, I wonder what went wrong…'

'I knew him, lass. He was never a happy man. He became possessed by an obsession and nothing good ever comes from that.'

Listening to Robert, her real father, Jayne felt an immense weight being lifted from her shoulders; the weight of the past.

At that moment, Vera came back. 'I've found it. A two week Caribbean cruise calling at Montserrat, St Lucia, Barbados, St Kitts and Antigua, sailing from New York in February.'

'Sounds perfect, shall we book it?' said Jayne.

'Why not?' replied Vera.

'You can still fit another case in before we go, Jayne.'

'As long as it has nothing to do with my family, I don't think I can handle any more emotional trauma for a long time.'

Robert smiled. 'Your mother did tell me a little about the Harrison's though a long time ago.' He closed his eyes trying to remember, 'Something about Ireland and America, now what was it…'

The End.
(Or is it just the beginning of another adventure?).

Historical Note

This story is based on the early days of the war, the defeat in France in 1940 and the subsequent formation of the Special Operations Executive.

The SOE and its undercover work in World War Two has been well documented in films, books and documentaries. Less well documented is the immense courage shown by the RAF in the early days of 1940.

A courage that has been overshadowed by the later Battle of Britain. But it was these airmen, often massively outclassed and outnumbered, who attacked the bridges near Sedan, against overwhelming odds.

At the time, they were accused of being absent from the skies by the retreating squaddies but the truth was they were flying old, often outdated bombers which were easy prey for the new Messerschmitt 109s and 110s. The Hurricanes fought bravely but were often overwhelmed by sheer weight of numbers.

John Sinclair's story deserved to be told, as the bravery of men like him has been long forgotten.

Jayne's grandmother, Monique Sinclair, nee Massat, is a fictional creation based on a composite of some of the stories of the incredibly brave women who were dropped into occupied France to work with the resistance. The stories of Noor Inayat Khan, Nancy Wake, Yolande Beekman, Andrée Borrel,

Yvonne Cormeau, Virginia Hall, Vera Leigh, Sonia Olschanezky, Diana Rowden, Yvonne Rudellat, and Violette Szabo have all helped form the basis of the character of Monique Sinclair.

The training these women underwent is as described in the now-published SOE Manual. Other sources include personnel files held at the National Archives, memoirs, and biographies of the SOE agents, including those of Szabo, Leigh and Khan.

The events that she witnesses, the German infiltration and destruction of the Prosper network in Paris in 1943 and 1944, are as accurate as I can piece them together from the records in the National Archives. It seems Henri Dericourt betrayed his comrades to the Germans.

The mistakes of the leadership of the French section of SOE were numerous, even down to telling a captured wireless operator that they had forgotten their second security key, as detailed in the novel.

Unfortunately, in my opinion, F Section was still an amateur operation run almost as a exclusive public-school club by Buckmaster and Bodington. Exactly the same failings bedevilled the British attitude to the war in its early years, leading to the defeats in France, Norway and Singapore.

It is fascinating reading the records from 1944 to 1946 and seeing how confused the leaders of the SOE, Buckmaster and Bodington, were by the machinations of the SD, the Abwehr and, to a lesser extent, the Gestapo.

Even after the war, when captured SD files indicating that Henri Dericourt was a double agent working for the Germans, were found, the SOE still could not believe they had been duped.

Not merely that, Hugo Bleicher, a senior Abwehr non-commissioned officer charged with working against the Resistance, admitted the truth in a sworn testimony in June 1945.

But even then, SOE developed multiple excuses as to why Dericourt was not a double agent. Admitting that he was, would also be accepting they were incompetent and had been played by the German's. Something they could not admit to themselves, never mind to the British public.

Since then, even murkier stories have emerged. Robert Marshall in his book, All the King's Men, accuses Dericourt of being a triple agent working for MI6, betraying the secrets of the SOE in order to keep the date of D Day secret! I can find no evidence for this accusation in the National Archives (but many of Mi6's files on the period are still closed).

Dericourt is a fascinating character in his own right. He survived the war, was arrested at Gatwick for smuggling bullion out of England in 1946, was extradited to France, stood trial as a traitor and was acquitted when Bodington, the second-in-command of the SOE, stated from the witness box that he ordered Dericourt to make contact with the Germans.

The man spent the next ten years on the fringes of the various secret groups operating in Europe after the war. He supposedly died in a plane crash in Laos in 1962, while transporting gold and heroin for the Sicilian Mafia (the famous French Connection) but anybody who has read Dericourt's history may have doubts that this actually happened. His body was never found.

However, this is not to take anything away from the immense bravery and self-sacrifice of the men and women of the SOE, 117 of whom were executed by the Germans in concentration camps, firefights, prisons and in attempting to escape.

They were the bravest of the brave.

I have tried to tell their story through Monique. They should be remembered for ever.

Their epitaph is perhaps best expressed on the SOE monument near Lambeth Palace in London.

"In the pages of history, their names are carved with pride."

If you enjoyed reading this Jayne Sinclair genealogical mystery, please consider leaving a short review on Amazon. It will help other readers know how much you enjoyed the book.

Other books in the Jayne Sinclair Series

The Irish Inheritance

When an adopted American businessman dying with cancer asks her to investigate his background, it opens up a world of intrigue and forgotten secrets for Jayne Sinclair, genealogical investigator.

She only has two clues: a book and an old photograph. Can she find out the truth before he dies?

The Somme Legacy

Who is the real heir to the Lappiter millions? This is the problem facing genealogical investigator, Jayne Sinclair.

Her quest leads to a secret buried in the trenches of World War One for over 100 years. And a race against time to discover the truth of the Somme Legacy.

The American Candidate

Jayne Sinclair, genealogical investigator, is tasked to research the family history of a potential candidate for the Presidency of the United States of America. A man whose grandfather had emigrated to the country seventy years before.

When the politician who commissioned the genealogical research is shot dead in front of her, Jayne is forced to flee for her life. Why was he killed? And who is trying to stop the details of the American Candidate's family past from being revealed?

In her most dangerous case yet, Jayne Sinclair is caught in a deadly race against time to discover the truth, armed only with her own wits and ability to uncover secrets hidden in the past.

The Vanished Child

What would you do if you discovered you had a brother you never knew existed?

On her deathbed, Freda Duckworth confesses to giving birth to an illegitimate child in 1944 and placing him in a children's home. Seven years later she returned for him, but he had vanished. What happened to the child? Why did he disappear? Where did he go?

Jayne Sinclair, genealogical investigator, is faced with lies, secrets and one of the most shameful episodes in recent history as she attempts to uncover the truth.

Can she find the vanished child?

The Silent Christmas

In a time of war, they discovered peace.

When David Wright finds a label, a silver button and a lump of old leather in a chest in the attic, it opens up a window onto the true of joy of Christmas.

Jayne Sinclair, genealogical investigator, has just a few days to unravel the mystery and discover the truth of what happened on December 25, 1914.

Why did her client's great grandfather keep these objects hidden for so long? What did they mean to him? And will they help bring the joy of Christmas to a young boy stuck in hospital?

Printed in Great Britain
by Amazon